Dark Muse

A Novel

David C. Smith

Pulp Hero Press
The Most Dangerous Books on Earth
www.PulpHeroPress.com

Pulp Hero Press publishes its books in a variety of print and electronic formats. Some content that appears in one format may not appear in another.

Editor: Bob McLain
Layout: Artisanal Text

ISBN 978-1-68390-198-3
Printed in the United States of America

Pulp Hero Press | www.PulpHeroPress.com
Address queries to bob@pulpheropress.com

For Mike James,
in thanks for untold hours
of splendid conversation.

How is it that an intellectual, poet and psychiatrist like Karadzic could do such a thing? It took me time to understand that this is the wrong question. It is wrong because it takes for granted that people like this—the educated ones, the sophisticated ones, the artists, for God's sake—should know better. Don't they have higher moral standards than ordinary people? The answer is no.

—Slavenka Drakulic
"Radovan Karadzic Captured After 12 Years on the Run"
The Nation, July 22, 2008

*I was the world in which I walked, and what I saw
or heard or felt came not but from myself;
and there I found myself more truly and more strange.*

—Wallace Stevens
"tea at the palaz of hoon"

CHAPTER ONE

The man in the well was yelling again.

Cordell, finishing his coffee in the kitchen, heard him in the cellar. The sounds of him were muffled, but he was loudly demanding to know why he was here and where he was and who was responsible for this.

Cordell would not allow himself to be rushed. Night was coming. The light was going, but the stars were not yet out. The last of the day, between here and there, darkness soon but darkness incomplete. He was partial to darkness.

The big maple just outside the kitchen window caught a breeze, and the branches, alive, fingered the glass. Cordell watched the beautiful leaves, golden and red and orange, themselves halfway between here and there, summer going, winter coming.

Why am I here and who are you and why are you doing this?

Cordell sighed, stood, and carried his coffee cup and his plate and dinnerware to the sink, rinsed them off, and set them carefully in the rack on the left-hand side of the sink. Carefully. These were his parents' dishes, the set his mother had bought umpteen years ago when she and his dad had gotten married. Bought them on time, a dollar a week, at Marshall Field's downtown. Not one plate had been broken in all that time, not one fork lost, not one cup cracked. When you take care of things, they last. Mind what you are doing, take care of things, and they will last.

Cordell sat at the kitchen table again and took a cigarette from the pack of Chesterfields he kept by the sugar bowl in the center of the table. He lit the cigarette with a wooden kitchen match. Bad habit, but he and his father used to sit of an evening on the porch and watch the back yard and smoke. It was relaxing. He'd kept the habit even after his parents were gone, after he and Bobbie had gotten married and moved in here, and since her death. Everyone was gone, but he could still relax and have a cigarette after dinner and watch the day go.

As the last of the sun fell behind the maple, Cordell stamped out the cigarette in the heavy old glass ashtray beside the sugar bowl and stood again and went to the cellar door.

As soon as he opened it and started down the steps into the cellar, the man in the well shouted very loudly.

"Who are you? Tell me! Where am I?"

He loved the smell of going into the cellar. The farmhouse was a hundred years old, and when Cordell was a boy and growing up, this big cellar was a world unto itself for him. It stretched the length of the farmhouse and held seven rooms separated by brick walls, timber, stones, whatever had been handy. The laundry area was the most modern. His father and grandfather had mixed concrete down there for the floor and run extra electric lines, so the laundry room was well lit with fluorescent lights and power to run the washer and dryer and the sump pump.

The corner where Cordell did his writing was clean, as well, and lit with hanging fluorescent lights. It sat directly across from the bottom of the stairs. He had demarcated his writing area by building a platform, a raised dais that sat six inches off the earthen floor, and here were his desk and computer and swivel chair, his file cabinet. He could sit on the dais and survey the old cold brick-walled and earthen rooms of his childhood, and then turn his attention to his computer screen, type, write, then sit back and look into the old rooms again, the darkness at the back of each of the rooms all around him.

Canned goods on the shelves. The ancient small coal cellar from when they'd once burned coal to heat the place, and the big oil drum on its metal stand from when the house had been kept warm with heating oil. Boxes of old magazines and newspapers. His grandfather had kept every copy of every *National Geographic* he'd ever received from 1917 on. Cordell remembered being thrilled when he'd discovered that one of the *National Geographics* from the mid-1920s with its heavy slick clay paper had contained the original article written by Howard Carter about finding King Tut's tomb. It was like having an old movie come to life, reading Carter's first words about breaking into the royal tomb. Today everyone thinks that King Tut was a myth. No one knows history anymore or cares about anything, but here was the first story ever in print about the great romance itself, Howard Carter peeking through the little hole he had made in the door of the tomb of the boy king, and Lord Carnarvon whispering to him, "Can you see anything?" and Howard Carter answering him with the famous words, "Yes, wonderful things."

Cordell, when you look into the darkness, can you see anything?

Yes, wonderful things.

"Let me out of here!"

The well was in the center of the cellar, the big room off which the others led, catty corner to Cordell's writing area. The well was deep, something like fifteen feet down, and wide, four feet in diameter. What purpose it had originally served, Cordell did not know. It hadn't always been so deep. Cordell himself had laboriously emptied out the last four or five feet of it to make sure that it would be inescapable. Still, a strong person, having fallen in, could have managed to get back out by stretching his or her legs and arms and climbing up that way. Difficult, but possible, especially because the walls had been lined with brick and so provided toe holds and finger holds. Cordell therefore had screwed sheet metal plates into the brick all the way around, so that the sides were now smooth, and then he'd coated the metal with motor oil, so that the walls of the well were thoroughly slick. Anybody in the bottom of that well was staying down there.

Cordell walked to the edge of the well and looked down.

"You son of a bitch," the man down there said. "Get me out of here."

He was about thirty years of age and plump. He was very modern, with short hair and something like a goatee on his chin, which he had grown until it was about a foot long. Maybe he thought he himself was King Tut. Maybe it was supposed to be clever, hair growing like that, but it looked stupid as far as Cordell was concerned. The young man was big enough that it had been a job for Cordell to get him into the back of his pickup truck and drag him into the house and drop him into the well. He'd spotted him in a grocery store on Dundee Road in Palatine, out by Route 53, and had followed him into the parking lot when he left and then to one of the forest preserves, where the young man had taken out a paperback book and sat at a picnic table to read while eating the salad he had bought at the grocery store.

Public areas are funny. Sometimes they're as crowded as downtown at lunchtime and other times, you might as well be by yourself out somewhere desolate. This afternoon for a few minutes, Cordell and the plump young man had been left to themselves. Cordell had parked his truck next to the man's red Camry and then lifted the hood on his truck and taken his jumper cables out of the back. Called over to the young man and asked him, Hey, could you give me a hand?

The young man acted irritated but had walked over, opened the hood of his Toyota, and as he was leaning over, Cordell hit him on the back of the head with a brick he kept under the front seat of his truck. The man had grunted and gone forward, but Cordell thought it prudent to hit him again. Once he'd done so, the young man relaxed and dropped to his knees, and Cordell quickly secured him with some rubber tie-downs, arms behind him and more of the straps around the ankles.

As he was lifting him into the bed of his pickup, Cordell saw an elderly couple looking at him. They were on a path that took them through the trees and past the parking area, and they were watching him as he loaded the plump young man into his truck.

"I know!" Cordell had laughed at them. "But he comes out here to get high, and this is what I have to do!"

The elderly couple had watched for another few moments, then gone on their way.

This is how the world is, Cordell thought. Whatever you do, it doesn't matter because people will consider it to be normal for you, so tell them right up front, Here is what I am doing, and they'll shrug and go on their way. Constrain a guy with rubber tie-downs and then roll him into the bed of your truck in a public area?

I know! But this is what I have to do!

Well, why not? people will say. Probably they are lovers. This is what the world has become.

"What are you doing to me?" the young man now asked Cordell.

He was looking straight up at him, and Cordell could see him plainly, as far down as he was, because of the lights overhead, while he himself was no more than a shadow, he knew, a silhouette backlit by the brightness.

"Well?" the young man asked. "*Well?*"

His hands were still caught behind him with the tie-downs, and his feet still bound, too. But he was standing. Cordell had dropped him feet first into the well.

Cordell told him, "We're going to do something together."

"Are you going to get me out of here and untie me, or do I call the police?"

"I took your cell phone. And your wallet."

"Why are you doing this?" the young man demanded. "Just tell me. What did I do? My head *hurts*, you fucker! Just tell me. I don't care, but I'm scared. You want me to be scared? You got me scared. I am good and scared."

Cordell had noticed that people he put into the well, when they bargained with him, went through a pattern similar to that of dying people when told that they didn't have much longer to live. How did that go? Denial, first. Am I in a dream? Who are you? Are you going to wake me up now? Then anger, like this young man, and then bargaining or negotiating. Look, we'll forget this ever happened, just let me go, I'll be on my way, I promise I won't tell anyone.

For anyone who'd been given a bad diagnosis by a doctor, depression was next, and then acceptance. But people in the well never got that far. Usually they became angry, then they tried to bargain, then they'd get angry again, and threatening, and then maybe bargain some more.

"*Tell me what you want from me!*" the young man demanded.

Cordell said to him, "You remember the Oakland earthquake in 1989?"

"No, I don't. Come on, I was a kid."

"Quite a few people died. Part of an overpass collapsed. Part of the highway was in two tiers. The top goes one way, lower part goes the other way, and the earthquake shook it apart, so now the upper tier falls onto the lower part of the bridge. Killed whoever was underneath it. Crushed them. I remember hearing about it on the radio. They were interviewing some of the rescue personnel. You know, they have to clear away the concrete and steel and whatever holds up these roads, and then they have to deal with whatever's left of the people who were crushed to death. Here's this, you have this concrete highway that's however high up in the air, and it comes down on top of people sitting in their cars, and what does that lead to, what's the result of that? Can you imagine what they felt, looking at what was left of people who had an entire road fall onto them? What happens when a person is trapped inside a tin can and a slab of concrete as big as a skyscraper falls on him?"

The young man in the well said, "I don't know. I don't have an answer. Why are you talking about this?"

"I've never forgotten that feeling. I couldn't get rid of the image, it stuck with me for days, because what's left doesn't seem human after something like that happens. It's garbage, basically. We only know what to do when something has this human quotient to it. It really did something to me. It was an accident, but why would that happen? Did those people deserve to have something like that happen to them? It just happened. And I started thinking about it, and things happen for no reason, but we need to find reasons. It became very philosophical for me. I was married at the time, I was about your age. What are you, thirty?"

"Thirty-two. Please. Listen, please don't—"

"And my wife died. Same thing. Boom, comes out of the sky, accidents happen, she's here and she's gone. Crazy driver. Drunk and in one of these big SUVs. Why did it happen? Why did he buy that particular car? Why was that guy at that intersection at exactly the same time as my wife? What if he'd left his house a few seconds later? What if my wife had been born a day earlier or a day later? Would the same thing have happened? You have to wonder."

Silence. The young man had nothing to offer, until he said, "You want me to feel sorry for you? I don't know what to tell you! Let me out of here! Come on, dude! *Please!*"

"I know," Cordell told him sympathetically. "I know. But this is what happens. People don't last. People die. Stories last." He stepped away from the well.

"Hey!" the young man yelled. "Where are you going?"

Cordell returned in a moment with a gasoline can, an old round one, red metal. It was about halfway full, and he tilted it so that all of the gasoline poured into the well and all over the young man.

"Stop it! Stop it, *stop it, don't do this!*"

Cordell had constructed a cover for the well, a large square about five feet by five feet, made of two-by-fours and planking, and then had covered all of it with sheet metal. It would get hot, but it wouldn't burn.

Cordell heaved up the covering and balanced it with his left arm, leaning into it, as he pulled a small box of wooden matches from the right-hand pocket of his jeans. He held the box in his left hand and struck the match against the rough strip on the edge of it.

"*Buddy, don't do it!*"

He dropped the burning match into the well and immediately backed away to let the cover fall into place. Still, as the powerful *whoosh* came, flames and heat slipped out from beneath the cover as it slammed onto the earthen floor.

The young man's screams were extremely loud, despite being muffled, and continued for nearly a minute.

The stench of him came almost immediately.

Cordell kept a number of indoor fans standing behind the stairs. He brought these out and faced them toward the well so that, when he turned them on, they pushed all of the bad air into the farther rooms of the cellar.

The whirring sound of them did not disturb him as he sat at his desk, turned on his computer, and began typing. Tears moved heavily down his face, and he wrote well.

CHAPTER TWO

Emmett said, "Your theory is true only up to a point."

"Not so," Jack told him. "It's not a switch you can turn on and off where you're either nuts or not. It's a continuum. It's a range."

Emmett leaned forward and took a piece of candy from the bowl on Jack's desk. "So somebody is partially nuts, or more or less nuts, but not completely nuts? Jack, *that* is nuts." He unwrapped the candy and popped it into his mouth.

"You're not following me. Take...Franz Kafka."

"You take him. Take him to dinner. I never cared for Kafka."

"Franz Kafka," Jack insisted. "He was functional. But he was eccentric, he was more than *eccentric*—"

"You're confusing eccentric with being completely nuts. Kafka was clinical. Wallace Stevens was more normal than you and I put together, and he ran an insurance company. Jack, how old is this candy?" Emmett took it out of his mouth and wrapped it in a Kleenex from the box on Jack's desk and pitched it across the room. Basket.

"It's a *continuum*!" Jack insisted, and shook his head.

He turned in his chair and indicated the view outside his office window. The publisher he worked for, Everson, was on the thirtieth floor of the United Building on West Wacker, so he had a heroic view of the North Loop, the famous Marina City corn cob towers on the other side of the Chicago River, the Trump Tower, the Dearborn Street Bridge, State Street and Michigan Avenue, and everything that filled the sky to the lake.

Jack said to Emmett, "Think how many people out there are writers, and then ask yourself, how many of them are going to give us stuff that really lasts?"

"Who cares if it lasts? Give the people what they want."

"Some of it will remain meaningful."

"And who decides that? I know. We'll let Jack decide. You tell me who won the Nobel Prize for great writing in 1917. There's a great writer who's lasted."

"I have no idea," Jack admitted.

"Exactly my point. I think I lost a tooth on your candy."

"But that's my point, too," Jack countered. "You know who was a completely forgotten writer in 1917?"

"You tell me. I know you're going to tell me."

"Herman Melville. *Moby-Dick*?"

"Really?" Emmett waggled a finger around in his mouth and decided the tooth was okay.

"Really. He wasn't rediscovered until the twenties."

"But was he truly eccentric enough to be discovered?"

"Yes!" Jack laughed. "Emmett, all I'm saying is, my point is, is that we don't know who's doing really good stuff that will mean something to people in the future, but the best guess we can make is that they're eccentric or nuts. And I accept that. I just want to find out about as much really great art as I can, and my point is that most great work comes from people who are nuts, and I accept that. You get a writer who's nuts but he gives us great art, to me, it's worth the tradeoff."

"Like Lewis Carroll was a child molester, only he gave us *Alice in Wonderland*, so that's okay with you."

"We don't know he was a child molester."

"What if he was? Would that be okay with you since he gave us *Alice in Wonderland*?"

"It would have to depend on whether we agree that *Alice in Wonderland* is a great work of art."

"You're a hypocrite, Jack!"

"I am not a hypocrite."

"You can't pick and choose."

"All I'm saying is that, *theoretically*, we can't—"

"*Theoretically*, your theory is that if a person is nuts enough to create great art, then being that nuts is forgivable."

Jack grinned. "That's exactly what I'm saying. Thank you."

"Then, case closed," Emmett told him, "because I'd rather have less art if it means fewer criminals and crazy people."

"I think we have to keep the big picture in mind."

"You keep the big picture in mind. I'm willing to live without *Alice in Wonderland* if it means the guy who wrote it was hurting little kids. End of story. Give me something old fashioned and straightforward and morally uplifting. Conan the Barbarian."

"Another eccentric!"

"Really?"

"Emmett, yes. The higher up the ladder we go, the better the writer, the more insightful or whatever you want to call it, the vision of the writer... the higher up the ladder you go, the weirder the writer."

"Conan the Barbarian is my limit."

Sam, the young Hispanic guy in the mailroom, came in with the mail cart and dumped half a dozen manila envelopes onto Jack's desk, along with some white business envelopes.

Jack reached for a rough envelope of brown paper that he apparently recognized. He said to Emmett, "Here. This guy is so good, he's got to be nuts."

"Or not. You can tell who it is from the envelope?"

Jack slit one end of it open with his letter opener. "He makes his own envelopes. He wraps his manuscripts in butcher paper or this brown paper of his and tapes it all together. I've got a whole big box of stuff from this guy. Here we go again." He set the thirty or so pages on top of the large desk calendar that filled most of his working space.

Emmett asked him, "You know it's a he?"

"You can tell. The voice. The guy is brilliant. He writes so well, and the stuff is great, but here's the thing. If you find out who he is, tell me, because I have no idea."

"Oh, *this* is the guy."

"This is the guy. He's overdue. I usually get something from him every couple of weeks. He must have gone on vacation."

"What's he write?"

"Short stories."

"And you don't know who he is? How's that possible?"

Jack pointed his thumb over his shoulder, indicating everything outside the thirtieth-floor window. "Look out there and tell me if you see him. Somebody down there must be him. But if he walked in here at this moment, I wouldn't know him from the air conditioner guy. Where's this one from? Elk Grove Village. I've gotten them postmarked from Edison Park, Wilmette, Barrington, East Chicago—everywhere."

"Montana."

"I wouldn't be surprised to get one postmarked from Montana." Jack started surveying the manuscript, scanning the lines quickly, until he'd gotten a few pages into it.

"How can we publish a guy when we don't know who he is? Who's his agent? Doesn't he have an agent?"

"He doesn't have a *name*."

"Does he know we can't do anything with it?"

Jack looked up. "I don't know. Or he doesn't care."

"Well, why's he sending this stuff to *you*?" Emmett asked.

"I don't know."

"Don't you wonder?"

"Of course."

"When did this start?'

Jack looked somewhat exasperated. "I don't know. A year ago. Not quite a year ago."

"They come from out of the blue."

"Yes."

"Addressed to you?"

"*Yes*." Jack showed him the front of the homemade envelope. On it was an ordinary Avery self-sticking address label with the address done by an ordinary desktop printer:

Everson Publishing Co.
Attn: Mr. Jack Mathis
77 West Wacker Dr.
Chicago, Illinois 60601

"Well, you have a mystery."

"I know. And I don't know what to do about it because I have no idea if he's sending these just to me or to everybody else around the country. But at least I get to read his stuff."

Emmett stood. "Only you," he said. "I think it's somebody who works downtown, probably at the deli, and they're too shy to admit it, but they want to write."

"They already know how to write. That's why this is so weird."

Emmett walked to the door. "I'll leave you to it," he said, and then, before going out, he told Jack, very sincerely, "I envy you. I do."

Jack smirked. "This is new. Where's this coming from?"

"I mean it. You're still a kid."

"I'm thirty-three. I'm not a kid."

"But you are. And I think it's wonderful. You still have this fire going for great art and great writing. Everything's still possible for you."

"Don't patronize me, Emmett, please."

"I'm not patronizing you."

"This guy is a superlative writer. Don't you want to be associated with excellence?"

Emmett told him, "But this is why I admire you. You don't have any doubts, do you?"

"About what?"

"Excellence. Great writing."

"I don't think I know everything. I'm not a snob."

"I know you're not. You're sincere, and that's wonderful. You almost make me feel young again myself. I'm old enough to remember when paperbacks cost a quarter and publishing was still publishing."

"You're not that old."

"I bought my first book when I was a kid and it cost fifty cents. Fifty cents is a while ago."

"What was it? Do you even remember?"

"*Frankenstein*."

"Really?"

"The Airmont paperback. I still have it. I'd seen the movie and wanted to read the book, but I was disappointed. No Boris Karloff."

"But a lot of philosophy."

"A lot of philosophy for a kid, that's for sure. Let me read that when you're done with it."

"Seriously?"

"If this guy is such a great writer, I want to feel that sense of hope again."

Emmett went out, and Jack leaned back in his chair.

What was it about this writer that affected him so powerfully?

He'd decided, after reading the seventh or eighth manuscript that had shown up, that it was—no better word for it—sincerity. Sincerity combined with an almost supernatural sense of rightness in the way he wrote, his word choices, the way he paced his sentences, right down to the syllables.

The mysterious man was the farthest thing possible from the formal or mannered writers esteemed by literary purists. Certainly academic writers were sincere, and they had skill, but the machinery was always showing in what they did, the gears. It was like listening to a technically perfect musician. Everything was right where it should be and was note-perfect but without a soul, without a connection, at least for Jack. Like watching a self-aware actor watching himself while the audience watches, too. There are layers of pretense in the arts, conventions that must be accepted, and how far you're willing to go to suspend your disbelief has a lot to do with how far you're willing to go to accept what the artist is doing. If an artist is more performer than craftsperson, is just showing off...well, some critics and readers esteem that sort of posturing. It allows them to be current and trendy.

But the only convention Jack's mysterious writer seemed to adhere to was to have the words on paper read as easily as water flowed downhill. He wrote as someone wholly free of pretense. There was no machinery showing, no subterfuge, no tricks or footnotes, just words put together perfectly. Jack thought of him as being nothing more or less than akin to a great blues musician from the 1920s, a sincere man with talent enough to frighten anyone else in the vicinity, with that absolute simple directness and plainness of greatness expressing itself as easily as the wind blowing or the grass growing. A great blues artist, or Homer reciting the tale of Troy, or Emily Dickinson writing verse.

One of the mystery man's stories was about how scientists discover the secret of longevity so that human beings live to be hundreds of years old. What no one anticipated was that, by extending human life to such a degree, something genetic kicks in, and all of us turn into animals, into wolves and dogs and birds and apes. It was as though, because we pushed Nature to her limits, Nature made sure that she took us back to the animals we truly are. Now we have to try to act as the human beings we want to be even though our true, ultimate natures have been exposed.

Then there was the story about the psychic man who, while asleep, overhears the conversations of dead people, the ghosts and the spirits who have conversations among themselves while they pass the time before they return to earth. Finally the sleeper realizes that the dead are not those who have survived the life after this one but are, in fact, his own living neighbors and family. We are the dead. We are the ones passing the time until we can move on to our actual lives, which occur after what we call death has taken place. But what we call death isn't death at all. It's birth, or rebirth. The land of the dead is the world all around us. The insanity and foolishness that we cause and that humanity represents is a by-product of the fact that we bump through our existence on earth randomly and without much sense because we are actually in a dress rehearsal for the lives that really matter, the lives that occur after we die, our real lives.

And now, this one, another story. Jack couldn't resist beginning it. Usually he would take these manuscripts home, but he was in the mood now to see what his mysterious scribe had come up with after taking so long to get this to him.

He hadn't even given it a title. Most of his stories had no titles at all.

Here, the protagonist discovers that each one of us contains a small spark of the meaning of life, the essential mystery of creation. If someone could access a sufficient number of individual souls, the Truth would be discovered. So the protagonist learns black magic in order to put his soul inside the bodies of others at the moment each of them dies. He proceeds to track down and murder people randomly, or apparently randomly. The authorities think he is a serial killer, and technically, no doubt he is, but in a larger sense, he's killing part of himself each time he shoots someone or runs him over with his truck or decapitates her or burns him alive, and he's doing it for the greater good of humanity, to establish the Truth.

Jack found the story to be unnerving. It was different from what his writer had done previously. It was perfect, of course, but it was the darkest thing he'd done yet. And there was something else.

The sheets of paper smelled of gasoline.

What had Mystery Man done, printed these out in a garage while he got his oil changed?

Well, the guy was eccentric, no doubt about that. Let him write in the back room of a service station if he wanted to. Maybe that's what he did for a living and scribbled on the side, his genius incognito and unrecognized by the grease monkeys around him.

But the last page of the manuscript upset Jack the most.

It was a note, and undoubtedly addressed to him.

He had never before had any communication from Mystery Man, not a pencil jotting, not a word, nothing, just the stories that had begun showing up in the mail. Obviously there was nothing that Jack had in common with this guy. There was nothing between them, and Jack accepted that. The oddness of the situation perhaps made Jack feel special and important, but he'd accepted it for what it was, like getting money from a strange benefactor or a note from a secret admirer. That's what this was.

But now, after nearly a year of this, here comes this story, beautifully written, compelling, dark, and then a few words that seemed to make Jack himself complicit in the creation of it, Writer Unknown intruding where Jack had never invited him. Jack didn't know what the note was referring to, but there it was, the Mystery Man's personal voice written in blue ink, as honest and naked and plain and genuine as anything else the guy had written:

*You probably don't remember me,
but thank you for inspiring me.*

CHAPTER THREE

Following the death of his wife, Cordell had not done much with himself. Nearly forty years of age at the time, he had found himself alone in the most essential ways.

Friends of his and Bobbie's had come to the funeral, of course, as well as her parents from out of state. But he had never been close to her parents or to her two brothers. They were from Michigan. Bobbie had been raised outside Detroit. Cordell understood that where you're from is who you are. It makes all the difference, the air you breathed while you were growing up, the soil in which you were raised. So it meant little to him that, during the first year following Bobbie's death, he communicated less and less frequently with her family, and then not at all. There were no ties to keep them in contact, no children. Falling leaves scatter.

It was the same with their mutual friends, the few they had had. Cordell had grown up on this farm with his parents and no other family, and the handful of people he had been close to during high school had moved away. Any friends he had known for the two years he went to college, never getting his undergraduate degree, also were in the past. He liked some of the people with whom he worked at the plumbing supply warehouse, but the acquaintances he and Bobbie had had were largely people she knew, people she worked with downtown. There was a wide stretch there that no one was quite comfortable crossing, Bobbie the college-educated, artistic design major and her funny husband, who worked a blue-collar job but had spent all of his spare time poking around in intellectual pursuits. How was it possible that an odd duck like Cordell was who he was? Maybe Bobbie was right, her friends finally decided, and he was brilliant, a prodigy, but by an accident of birth, unable to fit in comfortably anywhere.

Cordell was not self-conscious about it. He had accepted Bobbie for who she was and her friends for who they were, but when the time came that she was not there anymore, then they were just as relieved to return to their parties without him, and he was just as happy to sit on the back porch and smoke and follow the wind through the trees, or listen to the Borodin string quartets while refinishing the downstairs bathroom, or jot down notes while he took long walks late at night in the fields and woods around the farmhouse.

He owned nearly a square mile of woodland and pasture, having inherited it from his parents upon their deaths. And after the accident that killed Bobbie, he received a small fortune from the other driver's insurance company.

But Cordell didn't need a small fortune. He didn't need or want a great deal of money. He had never been sure what he wanted in life except that he liked to walk and read and think and, perhaps, write. As a boy, he had liked going to the library in town. Now he could afford to order books through the mail. He did so, and he bought a new computer.

He had taken time off from his job to stay home for a while, following Bobbie's death, but then returned to the warehouse. However, he felt that he was not welcomed back as the same person he had been. Or perhaps it was he himself who had changed, not his coworkers. After a long week of working on the loading dock and driving the forklift, he decided to stay away for good.

So he'd quit his job and gone off for days at a time, driven his truck all day long with no destination in mind, stopped at random motels, slept in lonesome beds in small rented rooms, and began keeping notebooks of his thoughts.

He wrote.

He wrote and wrote and wrote.

Some hours in the late morning or early afternoon he would spend at the cemetery where Bobbie was buried, she and his parents, but very soon this became a pointless exercise. The dead are dead, and he wasn't going to bring her back. Some things do indeed seem to happen for a reason, while other things do not. Falling leaves do indeed scatter, and the cemeteries are full of these leaves. As are battle-fields. Ditches. All of the lost and lonesome places of the earth where the dead go to be dead together.

He meditated on these matters in his notebooks and on his new computer. As a boy, Cordell had enjoyed reading mysteries. Now he came to understand that these fictional mysteries are simply echoes of the fundamental mysteries of life, the great mysteries into which we are born.

He had said something like this to Bobbie once, and she had complimented him. "You connect things in the most unusual ways," she'd said to him.

"What do I do?"

They were walking along one of the country roads by his parents' house. His parents by then were dead, and the sun was setting.

"I don't know how, but I love it. It's like you think about things that never occurred to me. The same way you read people."

"I don't *read* them."

"Cord, you do. You were seeing things in Uncle Mark none of the rest of us did. Him and the war. You got him to really talk about it. He never talks about it."

She was referring to a picnic with her side of the family that they'd attended.

"I just think you have a knack for understanding people," she'd said to him. "You read them. You do."

People, he had told her, aren't that hard to understand. All they want is to be flattered or paid attention to, or told something that sounds halfway reasonable when they're depressed or in doubt. However, it should be rather out-landish, what you tell people. Most of us would rather believe something fantastic than the simple truth. It flat-ters us. That's all we want, to be at the center of something impossible or fantastic.

And then she had died, been killed, was no more, was silent, had gone where the dead go.

He continued to write stories and began sending them to publishers and editors. None was bought, although he quickly began receiving praise for how well he wrote. He also made the effort to join a writers' group, which held meetings at a library, and he began to take a seat regularly, a few times a week, at a coffee shop where other creative people met.

Yet he had little in common with these other bright people. What he was trying to convey—the depth of what he was going after...Cordell was looking for clear light. He wanted to hear pure, uninterrupted sound. He wanted to be the first person to breathe a certain kind of air that he himself had just discovered or invented. He wanted to paint with colors that no one had seen before.

Still, nothing he did was satisfying until he heard Jack Mathis speak at the writers' group one rainy spring afternoon at the library.

The library had invited a number of writers and editors to talk about their experiences as editors, authors, and poets. What the young man at the far left said impressed Cordell the most. Jack, as enthusiastic as ever about what can be done with fiction, had paraphrased the apocryphal advice that Alfred Adler, the famous early psychologist, had allegedly given to neurotic patients unable to advance in life. What would you do if you could? Adler supposedly had asked his patients, and then, when they had told him: Well, go out and do it!

And then Jack had said something even more interesting, said it at the end of the library session when the large audience had already begun to break up. People were chattering in knots of twos and threes, others were at the vendor tables where the local poets and novelists had brought copies of their books to sell and inscribe, and Cordell remained seated in the back, a rather large, middle-aged man appearing not particularly out of place, although one person originally seated near him had moved, frowning back at Cordell and holding her nose as she did, as though to question when the last time was that he had bathed. A woman in the front had asked Jack a question that Cordell had not heard, and Jack, answering her, had told her, Well, the really great artists *are* a little peculiar, aren't they? Some of them are from another planet! I wonder sometimes, we hold some of what these people do in very high esteem, and a lot of them were not people you'd want to know, but they gave us such great works of art. I don't think that that's an accident. Wherever that inner voice led them, some of these writers followed it, and they left us some great work, but it was definitely a tradeoff for them, they had to go where no one had gone before. And the woman had asked him, Do you recommend doing that? And Jack had laughed and said, I recommend doing anything that gets you writing. Sit down and write. But it's whatever comes from inside, it's your own voice. See where it leads you, and you might give us something really great.

The woman had smiled and nodded politely, Jack had turned to talk to some other people standing beside him, and Cordell had left the library as quickly as he could, gotten outside into the rainy air as soon as possible so that he could stand under an overhang, smoke a cigarette, look at the wet asphalt of the parking lot, and try to calm himself, for what Jack was talking about was what we bring to life, what we neglect and never bring to life, and what is gone and will never have life again.

Cordell knew then what it was that he had to do.

Most people lead small lives, lives of sameness, lives like those leaves falling, unchallenged, remote as they drift, these lives. Cordell himself might have lived such a life, at home among the small and immediate tokens of the day, within an envelope of time going slowly, among the many others who do not find flesh on bones remarkable, who are not astonished at the colors in sunlight. There is no sense of loss for these people because there has been no aspiration for gain. There is no uncertainty because in sameness there is certitude. There is no hurt of abandonment because there has never been separation from routine. Therefore, these lives are small and are done alone with eyes closed, lives lived in a colorless Now.

Cordell considered these elements of living small as he cleaned out the well and imagined the small life of the man who had been in the well.

The only way to clean out the well, as he knew from experience, was to use water to cool anything hot that remained down there, then with a long ladder move into the well and load into plastic bags whatever had not been consumed, bones and teeth and even some of the meat, all carbonized. He turned on his standing fans and wore a mask tight over his nose and mouth as he moved up and down the ladder with his plastic bags, tying their tops and setting them by the steps so that he could take them outside.

By killing this young man and carbonizing him, Cordell had heard the screams and felt the heat and had touched something so profoundly spiritual that it went beyond words and language and waited in the moment. So he had put down words to express this sublime insight, and by doing so, he had been taken into the air, lifted high. He had passed through clouds, he had seen the colors in sunlight, he had heard the voices of the things that live invisibly elsewhere, he had seen the young man's spirit pass into a realm of silence and clarity, where his spirit was welcomed by others who had suffered and who had been there longer than could be told. Cordell had written this, and he had succeeded. And the air had written it, a cadaver had written it, the young man's escaping spirit had written it to share with the world.

In the woods beyond the house, in a small clearing where Cordell had placed the remains of others into the earth, others who had assisted him, he sat, sweating in the early afternoon, having a smoke, taking a break, and looking at the circular patch of dirt under which was the carbonized young man.

Off to his left was where he had placed a middle-aged woman the age that Bobbie might have been by now. Past her was a man he used to work with at the warehouse, and beyond him, a screaming boy, and farther on, another man, this one in his thirties. Cordell no longer remembered much about the man in his thirties other than that he had become the story about an energetic person who moves so fast in life that he finally grows wings and flies above everyone else in the city. *I have wings! I've grown wings, wings!*

His first victim was buried over there, off to the north-west, deeper into the trees. Slender man, dark-haired, who had driven a sports car. A smart aleck. Cordell had surprised himself when he took this man's life because the act had not been anticipated. It occurred a month after Bobbie's death. Late one evening, while driving in his truck down a wavy country road flanked on both sides by thin woods, Cordell had managed to tick off the guy in the sports car by driving slowly and taking the turns on the gravel road carefully. The speed demon had honked his horn, flashed his brights, and flipped Cordell the bird several times before managing to get around him. He then continued to aggravate Cordell by slowing down several times, nearly causing Cordell to rear-end him, then accelerating and shooting gravel onto the truck's windshield. The third or fourth time this occurred, Cordell did not brake but instead ran into the sports car, knocking it diagonally to the side of the road. When the smart aleck stopped, got out, and walked toward Cordell to complain, Cordell ran him over. Bumpety-bump, under the truck he went.

There was no one around to see what had happened, so Cordell had wrapped the body in blue plastic tarp and deposited it into the back of the truck, then driven the sports car several hundred yards into the woods. He'd buried the body, then waited for a week, now very frightened, certain that someone would come looking for the smart aleck, establish what had occurred, and arrest him.

It never happened.

The sports car driver might have fallen off the edge of the earth. Whoever he was, whatever he had been doing, whatever the reason for his being in such a hurry that Thursday night, he'd pushed his life as far as it was meant to go.

Cordell wondered why he had killed the man. Was he so despondent over Bobbie's death that he no longer cared whether he himself lived or died? Is that why he had killed, so that he could be found out?

But that couldn't have been true. He didn't want to be found out. And if he wanted to join Bobbie, he could easily do himself in by any of several means right at hand.

He had been depressed and angry. Despondent over Bobbie's death, yes, but also unable to write, and drinking. Was any reason greater? I'm drunk and in an angry mood, Cordell thought to himself, and a man pisses me off, so he suffers the consequences. Why does it need to be deeper than that?

It needn't be.

It was simply an intertwining of lives, occurring sometimes for a reason, sometimes for no reason. Cordell himself might have been a collapsing bridge as far as the smart aleck sports car driver was concerned. I'm now falling on you, bumpety-bump.

During that week of waiting, as he worried about being found out, Cordell wrote as he had never written before. Astonishingly well. He called off sick from work, lived in his cellar, and typed quickly and steadily. And what he wrote was good, very good.

This was his life now. Each time he killed, he felt as though a great gift had been renewed, and he accepted that. Of course, he had been careful to stagger his taking of lives, spacing them as wide apart as he dared, traveling over as wide a distance as possible, and varying his method. He had driven as far south as Kansas City. He had taken a flight to Florida once for a week's vacation. He had hiked in Colorado, and visited Old Santa Fe. Every trip had been productive. And he had experimented, getting into the minds and personalities and souls of many different sorts of human being. Take an old man, then a young woman, then a strong young man. What would come to him after each of these takings? How would he write each time? Perhaps that was why no alarm had been raised. Kill an old man in Lake Geneva, Wisconsin—what did that have to do with beheading a woman in Akron, Ohio?

Cordell returned to the house and took a shower, made himself a lunch of soup and a sandwich, turned on the radio and listened to the news, and decided that it would be good to begin another story.

CHAPTER FOUR

On the Metra train going home, Jack noticed a man at the far end of the coach facing him and watching him intently.

Was he really staring at Jack?

Jack looked away. Glanced back. Looked away again, and then back once more.

What was this guy, poorly schooled in the etiquette of riding commuter trains? You don't sit there like a dead fish staring at someone like you're trying to use your x-ray vision.

It occurred to Jack that this man, this odd man, might be his mysterious writer.

That made it all different. Was it possible? Really?

It would make sense. Mystery Man knew who he was, so why shouldn't he get on the same train as Jack and keep an eye on him? Maybe he'd been following Jack around for nearly a year, just out of curiosity.

If the guy could write stories as brilliant as the ones he'd sent Jack, why couldn't he sit mutely at the other end of the train coach and just...watch?

Watch Jack.

You probably don't remember me, but thank you for inspiring me.

Finally the man looked away without ever acknowledging that he'd been staring. Jack settled back in his seat, crossed his arms over his chest, and closed his eyes. He considered becoming the writer *himself* this time and developing a story about a strange individual who stares at people on the commuter train.

In fact, Jack actually was a good writer—even, he had been told, a very good writer. He'd had four paperback novels published only a few years ago. But many very good paperback novels are published each year, and it wasn't merely to be published that Jack sought. He wanted something much rarer—real talent, real artistic excellence, great writing. He knew that his critics had been correct when they had given his own books moderate reviews. He had not lived sufficiently or experienced enough or written enough to achieve anything exceptional. Perhaps, his critics had told him, if Jack were to spend years in solitude, or if he were to be shocked or tricked by life—perhaps then he might achieve such a level of sublime excellence that his work would become transcendent.

Instead, Jack had changed his focus, given up writing and become an editor, and now looked for talent rarer than his own. This was the quest he had given himself since starting at Everson Publishing.

He was, of course, disappointed with nearly all of the material that came to his desk. The most commercially successful manuscripts are usually the most poorly written. He had had to make his peace with that fact. Most of the writers who are rewarded commercially perform habitual rituals for their readers, some with fine language and literary conceits, some with unpretentious plots and characterizations or with erotic or adventurous generic tropes. Jack wanted more. He wanted to be surprised by something so deep and heartfelt that it had barely gone through the writer's alert consciousness. He wanted an artist who understood the craft so well that the craft was left behind. He wanted jazz. He wanted medieval cathedrals. He wanted beauty and honesty. And he wanted it done perfectly, wanted stories that contained the world within themselves, stories and writing that startled in many ways at once, stories vulgar and angelic at the same time, stories with characters full of fear at being alive but still—still—filled with wonder despite the fear.

A few writers had done it.

Jack wanted to find the next writer to do it.

For this reason, he now told himself each morning as he looked at his reflection in the bathroom mirror, "Today's the day." Today's the day I find the next great writer. Today's the day the manuscript comes in from someone so daring and new and full of voice and heart that the genius of the work is self-evident. Today is the day I find that writer.

That day, in fact, had come a year ago, and the irony was that Jack had no idea who his brilliant writer was, or where he was, or anything about him other than he could put words on paper like the devil's own angel.

That, and the fact that he was now thanking Jack for inspiring him.

Which meant—what?

Cordell drove east in his pickup truck to the Springhill Mall outside Elgin. Here he went to a bookstore and a music store, bought nothing, sat on a bench, looked at passers-by, and waited.

He saw a bearded young man who resembled somewhat the person he had recently sacrificed, whose story he was particularly proud of, but he did not get up from the bench to follow him.

He noticed one woman in particular who intrigued him, and nearly rose to follow her, but then thought better of it. He needed to be sure.

He continued to watch.

Perhaps that one, or her over there.

Or, wait—No, no...

Finally, when he settled on her, Cordell at first thought that she was too broad in the hips and too tall by a couple of inches, but as he looked at her face, he decided, yes, that she resembled Bobbie sufficiently that now it was time, now he was ready to deal with Bobbie's death.

He followed her home from the mall, driving in his truck and keeping some distance behind her, letting cars come and go between them until, as she at last pulled into a driveway, Cordell continued driving beyond her house, went around the block twice, then pulled into her driveway, too, parking his big truck behind her little Mazda. Taking his roll of duct tape with him, he stepped out and walked onto the back porch.

It was a slab of concrete with slender metal posts in it and a metal awning or roof, not much else. An old wooden bench was there, part of a picnic table on which she had set out half a dozen pots with flowers in them, some of the flowers dead, some of them still flourishing.

He knocked on the door, holding his hands behind his back so that if she looked out the window at him before opening the door, she would see a middle-aged man with his hands behind his back, smiling at her, and wonder what on earth could someone so simple have to do with her?

The inside door opened, the back door, and the woman who looked sufficiently like Bobbie leaned to one side and said to Cordell through the screen door, "Yes?"

"Your purse."

"What about my purse?"

"I found it."

"You found it?"

Cordell rested his left hand on the metal handle of the screen door and pressed down. The door opened. Still holding the roll of duct tape behind him in his right hand, he pulled the screen door open and tentatively poked his head around the side of it. He explained, "I don't know what it was doing there. It was in the driveway."

Predictably puzzled, she looked behind her as though expecting to see her purse right there and said, "I was sure that I'd—"

Cordell pulled open the screen door and stepped quickly into the kitchen. He looked the woman in the eyes as she stood in front of him with a What? expression. He brought his head down quickly, butting her in the forehead so hard that the crack of it sounded like two rocks being struck together.

She staggered. Cordell reached for her, assisting her onto her knees and then to the floor, where he took a handful of her hair and, by holding onto it, slammed the side of her head onto the tiled kitchen floor one two three times until the air went out of her and she relaxed. Then he wrapped duct tape around her mouth several times, leaving her nose clear so that she could breathe, and unrolled more tape to catch her around her wrists and ankles.

When he straightened and looked down at her, Cordell was sweating a little on the back of his neck, and he felt sweat damp around his ankles, under his socks. But he was looking at Bobbie down there, Bobbie Bobbie Bobbie, and it was time, yes, for him to deal with Bobbie's death.

When he got her home, he carried her down into the cellar and propped her in a corner on the floor. He'd put a blanket down first, though, because the cement of the floor was cool. Then he looked at her while having a cigarette as he sat in a lawn chair he had down there. When he finished the cigarette, Cordell went upstairs and in a corner of his bedroom where he'd put some of Bobbie's things, he found her old makeup case. He took this with him back down to the cellar.

The woman moaned, coming awake, as Cordell did his best in applying some of Bobbie's makeup to her face. He'd never used makeup in his life. He had no idea what the difference between eyeliner and lip liner was, let alone how to apply such things as eye shadow or lip gloss. But he went by colors, and so he was able to darken the woman's eyes somewhat and add some color to her cheeks and to her lips.

When he'd finished, she resembled a circus clown, but Cordell didn't mind. She still looked enough like Bobbie and was wearing some of his wife's makeup, and that was what mattered.

He sat in the lawn chair and watched her as she opened her eyes, moved a bit, moved more strongly, and finally became aware of her circumstances. She made sounds in her throat, and Cordell could tell by them that she was asking questions.

The questions were in her eyes, too, of course.

He cleared his throat, leaned forward casually in the lawn chair, and explained to her, "I can't tell you where you are or who I am. That's self-evident, I'm sure."

She made more sounds.

"I put that makeup on you. It was my wife's makeup. You look an awful lot like her. You have to understand there's no easy way to deal with this. You're not in a good situation."

She made further sounds and tried to sit up or rearrange herself, but her position was too awkward.

"I miss my wife. She died in a terrible car accident some years ago. That's why you're here. I'm not going to bore you with everything I've done since then, but I've spent a lot of time trying to make sense of it, and it really comes down to trying to make sense of life. That's not easy. I've wrestled with a lot of big questions. What it comes down to is this, quite frankly. None of us gets out of this alive. We all die. I know that's not exactly a newspaper headline, but it hurts when you face it, when it's right there. It really, deeply hurts. What?"

She was making sounds again. Cordell saw that she had tears in her eyes.

"I know," he told her. "I know. I do understand. I'll make this quick. It's about stories. It sounds ridiculous, but you know what it is about stories? They're almost more human than we are. I've had to realize that stories really do live. It's like they become living things. They're more than we could ever hope to be. When I write stories, so much becomes clear."

He stood and continued to look at her.

"My wife died in a car crash. Character comes out of nowhere, and that's what happened. And he got away with it. Kept driving, and he's never been found. I have no idea who he is. Fortunately for my wife, her name was Bobbie, Roberta, we called her Bobbie, the impact broke her neck immediately. They told me that, and even if they were trying to be kind, I can believe it. Her neck was broken, but her body was hanging half out of the car. The door flew off and she was tangled in the seat belt and the car kept spinning around. They found pieces of her all over the place. She broke apart like a doll. Just came apart as the car spun around."

Now the woman was sobbing and making very deep sounds in her throat. She tried to sit upright or get herself into a position whereby she might exert control, fight back. But that was not realistic.

"We used to talk about the overpass that collapsed in San Francisco in 1989. They had an earthquake, and the overpass collapsed, and the people who were in their cars were crushed. I used to tell Bobbie that it bothered me to contemplate that, and she'd say, 'Well, what can you do? Those things happen in life.' And then it happened to her. She was turned into garbage. And that's when I told myself, Stories aren't garbage. Stories are better than us. They're transcendent. So I've worked at that. And it helps me. God, you really do look like her."

She squirmed and made more sounds.

Cordell walked away, going into one of the dark rooms behind him, and made some noise, turned on a fluorescent light, turned it off, and came back with a rip saw and a hammer and chisels.

"Like the blind man," Cordell said to her, smiling. "I reached for my hammer and saw."

The woman moaned and tried to shriek. The noises she made were contained within her throat, although she did her best to let them out. She kicked, or tried to, but her legs were held tightly together with the duct tape.

Cordell set the tools on the floor, walked to her, and stood behind her. He placed his hands on either side of the woman's head.

She tried to fight him.

Cordell leaned forward, pushed quickly, and broke her neck.

"I want to do this," Jack told Corinne as they sat at the round kitchen table in their little condo.

"I know that. Only when?" she asked him.

"Soon."

"How soon, Jack?"

He looked at her. His wife was pretty, slender, with light brown hair and hazel eyes that shined, really shined. She was all Jack wanted. Had been all along. And he knew that *she* wanted a family, which he did, too, only...when?

"Really soon," he told Corinne. "I know how important this is for both of us."

"I'm not hearing a lot of sincerity in that."

"I mean it. It's tough for me to envision it, that's all."

"What if we planned for next spring?"

"Corinne, unless you're not telling me something, we need to plan on starting to try in the spring, right? What works for me is when there aren't any surprises, just, I just need to know, here's the decision, we've decided, this is it, plan on it. As long as I can plan on it, I'm fine."

"Next spring, then."

"Then we'd better—" Her tone had changed, and she'd started to smile. He asked her, "Really?"

"Really, Jack."

"This is not—You're serious."

"Sweetie, I am very serious."

"Boy or girl? Do you know, do we know?"

"No, we don't know yet!" she grinned.

He got up and came around the table and stood looking down at her, feeling very awkward.

Corinne was smiling up at him, utterly smiling, because Jack had no idea what to do.

"Give me a minute."

"You have your minute."

He hugged her self-consciously and held her very tightly, more tightly than he'd ever gripped her before, and with some fear in his arms, or something close to fear. Anticipation. What?

Then he sat on the floor cross-legged and turned his face up at her. "This is going to be different."

"Very different." Corinne got down on the kitchen floor, too, still grinning at him.

"Don't be—" He searched for words. "I'm not saying there's anything wrong, although I'm surprised, and we talked about trying, but I thought we were going to wait a while and we were going to try to keep being safe."

"We were. Except for a couple of times."

"Yeah." He looked Corinne in the eyes. "I am stunned."

"I can tell."

"I'm happy, but I'm not showing it."

"It's okay. I'm surprised, too. I know it's sudden."

"It is," he said.

"I wasn't expecting it this soon, either, but I don't feel bad about it."

"Neither do I. Just...stunned. Do I look stunned?"

"Very." She reached over and tapped the tip of his nose with an index finger. "Love you."

They'd done this for years. Jack tapped her nose. "Love *you*. What'd you do, go to the drugstore and get one of those kits they test you with?"

"I missed my period, and I thought I'd better see, and it came out positive. Last week. But I thought I'd better be sure, so I did it again today."

"Wow."

"I made an appointment to see the doctor next week."

"What else do we have to do?"

"Not much. Just everything. We'll be okay here for a while, but we're going to have to decide if we want to stay here."

"Do we have to have a bedroom for her? Or him? The baby?"

"We should plan on that."

"God, God," Jack said, and then laughed. "It was that *easy*? We didn't do anything special, we just did what we always do. Wow."

"Pretty easy." Corinne stretched out on the kitchen floor with her head in Jack's lap and looked up at him. She took one of his hands and held it in hers. "This is a good thing," she said. "It's big, I know, and we planned on it, only not for now, but we'll be fine. I have to say one thing."

"What?"

"I know how much you love your job. And I want you to get back to your writing. I do. You're that good."

"*But.*"

"*But*...we both have to refocus here. I know how you can get, and you put all of your energy into that, but we really have to be a team here, now."

"I know. You're right. It'll be fine."

This really was good, Jack told himself. Really. He'd spent all this time trying to find the best new writer in the world, but what did that matter now, really? Writers can take care of themselves. This was better.

Corinne grinned at him. "Love you," she said again.

Jack smiled at her. "Love you." He meant it.

CHAPTER FIVE

"It's the most incredible thing I've ever felt," Jack told Emmett.

"I know what you mean. It's a big step. How's Corinne?"

"Glowing."

"Lucky you. I miss having my boys be boys. You're going to love it."

"I love it already. My life has a *purpose*!" he smiled.

They were in Jack's office. Emmett was in the chair opposite Jack's desk, looking at some papers. He stood as Amy Garcia, one of the proofreaders, walked in.

She was slender and dark haired, and Jack liked her because she was perennially upbeat, although he claimed that that annoyed him. "Don't you ever say anything *negative*?" he'd asked Amy one time, and she'd looked him straight in the eye and said, "No." It had taken him a second. Then, "Ah ha!" Jack had smiled, pointing a finger at her, and Amy had said, "Ah ha!" and waved him away.

Now she dropped a package on Jack's desk, a dark brown envelope. "For you. Some guy dropped it off."

"What guy?"

Amy was already on her way out. "Carl gave it to me. The security guard accepted it."

Carl was a new associate editor—young guy, blond, athletic, very personable and likable.

Emmett watched Amy leave, then dropped the manuscript pages he'd been reading onto Jack's desk. "Just do the least possible with this thing," he said. "I know he's terrible, but he could write upside-down and backwards and we'd still sell a hundred thousand— What?" He noticed that Jack was not paying attention to him.

"Another one," Jack told him, and reached for his letter opener.

"Your genius?"

"Yup."

"When do *I* get to read his stuff?"

"Whenever you want. Let me know."

"You treat him like he's your big secret."

The phone rang, and Jack picked it up.

Corinne. He listened for a second, and then said to her, "I know. Sweetheart, I know. No, it's fine. On my way home. Tonight. Really, it's fine." He rolled his eyes at Emmett. "No, no one's here. Emmett."

"Now I'm no one?" Emmett asked him.

Jack told him, "Corinne says hi."

Emmett said loudly, "Hello, Corinne!"

"That I can do," Jack said into the phone. "I will. Tonight. You, too. Oh, Emmett doesn't care. You, too. Bye."

Emmett told him, "You can coo to your wife while I'm in the room. I promise to take absolutely no notice."

"I know that."

"Look, this is why I'm here. Peterson is unreadable. I know that. But he sells a hundred thousand copies, and he'll do it with this one, so do the minimum. No one cares."

"He fries my brain."

"Mine, too. But he's doing his job. He's safe. You read him, you're entertained, you're done, in and out. Now what about your genius?"

Jack slid the end of the letter opener into the package and sawed back and forth with it. "Jeff Peterson wishes he wrote as well as this guy," he said.

The phone rang again. Jack set aside the letter opener. "Watch," he said to Emmett as he reached for the handset. "This is what she's doing now. She forgets things because she already has Mommy Brain."

"That's a real syndrome, you know."

"I know," Jack said, and, into the phone, "Corinne?"

The male voice on the other end asked him, "Jack, do you know who this is?"

His heart stopped. Jack felt the weight of it in his chest. Very carefully, he replied, "No. I'm sorry, no. I don't recognize who this is." He gestured to Emmett, pointing his index finger at the brown homemade envelope, then to the phone, back and forth.

Emmett made a face. Really?

"I think you do know who this is, Jack."

"I don't— I do think I know. Let me ask you, because I want to be sure, but are you the—do you write, are you a writer?"

"Yes."

"Really. Really? I'm very glad to talk with you."

"You've read the stories?"

"They're brilliant. You have to give me your name and give me some information because I think these should be published. You say we met somewhere? I inspired you?"

Coughing, then, and the line went dead.

Jack looked at Emmett.

"What?" Emmett asked him.

"He hung up." Jack put the handset back in its cradle.

"Who is he? Did he tell you?"

"No."

"What did he—?"

The phone rang again.

Jack picked it up and listened carefully.

"Jack, I'm back."

"Did we get cut off? Because if we did, I apologize."

"Jack, what I wanted to know is if I could trust you with my stories. Trust my stories to you."

"Of course you can. Absolutely. Trust me for what?"

"I just wanted to know if you liked the stories."

"Listen, the stories are great. Is there a reason for you to remain anonymous? Because I'd prefer to—"

"For the time being. Although I think we should meet."

"I'd like to publish you. I want to be clear about that."

"I'd like that. I really would."

"Let me ask you, what have you had published so far?"

"Nothing."

"That's remarkable. You're really quite—"

"You really did get me started, Jack. You inspired me."

"That's very flattering. Thank you. What I want to know is, would you like to talk about the possibility of being published? Do you want me to look into that for you?"

"I think we should meet."

"Well, all right, that's fine, we can start there. Where?" He reached for a pencil.

"Did you read the new story?"

"No. The one that just arrived? I have one that just got delivered. Is that it?"

"That would be it."

"Where can we meet?"

"Let's do it tomorrow night."

"That's fine. Where? Do you like any place in particular?" Silence.

Had he hung up again?

Jack said into the phone, "Was there, is there any place in particular? To meet? What works for you?"

The voice said, "Let's meet in a bookstore I know. In the coffee area, where they sell the coffee. Is that all right?"

"Yes, absolutely."

"I want to remain anonymous for the time being."

"That's fine. Which bookstore?"

The man on the phone said, "Let's meet at eight o'clock tomorrow night. Eight o'clock."

"Where?"

He gave Jack the address of a chain bookstore outside the city, west of the collar suburbs and west of Arlington Heights, in fact.

"How will I know you?" Jack asked.

"I know you, Jack. From when you gave your talk. I'll bring another story for you."

"Okay."

"Tomorrow night, then."

"Good, fine."

"You can tell me what you think of the story you just received," the man said.

"I will. I'm looking forward to this."

"Me, too. Good-bye, Jack."

"Good—"

But he'd already hung up.

Jack looked at Emmett. "Wow."

"Strange, huh?"

"Just a little. Jesus! I finally get to *meet* this guy. This is *great*."

"Give me some stories. If we're going to publish him, I'd better get started."

Jack opened a bottom file drawer in his desk and pulled out two file folders thick with paper. He handed them to Emmett.

Emmett riffled through the paper in the top folder. "These are photocopies."

"The stuff he sent me is at home," Jack explained. "I'm taking no chances."

"I wouldn't, either. I'm actually looking forward to reading this."

"You will absolutely thank me. *Jesus!*" Jack said again. "I don't care how strange the guy is. Emmett, Emmett, I have a feeling, I know it...I've found the guy. I've been looking for him, and...he's here." He put his right hand on the package in front of him.

"Only you," Emmett told me. "I don't know how you find them."

"Hey, I don't know how they find *me!*"

Emmett had a meeting but made Jack promise that they'd go across the street in an hour for lunch. Jack agreed, then sat for a few long minutes looking at the manuscript, just looking at it, then glanced at his phone as though it were some magical device that had mysteriously brought him this wonderful gift, this strange writer of such incredible talent.

"You really did get me started, Jack. You really have inspired me."

Whatever that meant, Jack was more than willing to take credit for it. Strange guy? What had Dryden said four hundred years ago? "Great wits are sure to madness near allied," went the poem. "And thin partitions do their bounds divide."

Fine, Jack thought. So long as no thin partitions divide you and me until we get your name on a book.

He set the Peterson thriller aside—there was no way on earth he was going to be able to concentrate on that pile of words now—and started in on the story. The title, typical for this guy, was just the first couple of words of the first sentence, as if it were a poem. "Coming Apart."

Five thousand words, which was the man's usual length, although sometimes he wrote much longer pieces. And beautifully written, of course. But darker than the other stories Jack had gotten so far. Much darker, in fact:

> In a remote country long ago, a grieving man mourns for his dead wife. She was killed horribly, with parts of her body scattered in every direction across a wide area. The man had searched for the missing parts but could not locate all of them, so he sets out to kill other people to replace the parts of his wife that he can't account for. Finally he has everything except a foot. He cuts off his own foot. Now his wife is whole and able to move on into the next world. She does so, abandoning the man who loved her. The spirits of the other people he killed now return to him and take what they need from him—his other foot, his eyes, his jawbone—so that they, too, can move on. The sufferer is left a wreck, a piece of garbage, but he has touched infinity by dealing with these ghosts, and he knows how joyous the afterlife is. However, he can't die until someone finds him and kills him, does the same thing for him that he did for his wife. So he wanders everywhere, begging for understanding and help, but he causes only fear and horror. How can I become whole? he screams. No one has an answer for him. Kill me! he commands. I'm still a person! But everyone avoids him. Who will save him from himself?

Jack gave himself a moment when he'd finished. Sat there. Let the story stay with him for a long minute. The writing was perfect and the pain evoked, intense. He tried to shake it off.

Emmett knocked on his door and stuck his head in. "Lunch? Hey, you feeling okay?"

"He's outdone himself."

"Really?"

"This fucker just keeps getting better, Emmett." Jack stood and reached for his jacket. "I have no idea how he does it, but I'm going to find out."

Corinne was glad for Jack that evening and happy that he was finally going to meet this writer he'd been bragging about for the past year, but her own concerns were much more domestic. Jack helped her in the kitchen as they put pasta and salad and rolls on the table, but when he told her he'd agreed to meet this person tomorrow evening, Corinne became unhappy, no hiding it.

"Tomorrow?"

"Yeah."

"Tomorrow I wanted to go look at paint."

"For the baby?"

"They have a sale starting tomorrow."

"We'll go Thursday. Corinne, I have to do my *job*."

"I'm not asking you not to do your job. But we have to paint the room, and I need—"

"Tell me what color." Jack reached for a roll.

"A soft green. Sage, maybe."

He considered it. "That's very practical. Actually, that's pretty smart."

"Actually, it is. I want to stay away from this pink and blue and do something restful."

"And this is the office?"

Corinne wasn't sure how to take his tone of voice. "Please don't throw a fit. I can't think of anything else to do, and I've been trying."

"No, it's fine. It's logical." Jack was apologetic. "Give the baby my office."

"We'll do something else for you. You still get your office. We can rearrange the living room or our bedroom. We'll figure it out."

Jack said, "Unless we start looking at houses."

"I've thought of that, too," Corinne told him. "But I want to economize as much as we can."

"Sweetheart, if I get this writer, really, we'll have money for a house."

"That's some pretty positive thinking."

"I'm serious. This guy is for real. That's why I need tomorrow night, Corinne. This is really important."

"I know it is. Jack, you're okay with this, right?"

"Corinne, yes! I'll paint it. I don't want you breathing paint fumes."

"I mean having a baby."

He saw it in her eyes. "Sweetheart, no, no, I am *ready* for this," Jack insisted. He stood and walked to her and gave her a hug. "The timing is right. Trust me."

"I intend to."

"Trust me," Jack told her again. "That's all I ask."

"I do."

"Then we're fine."

CHAPTER SIX

When Jack got to the office the next morning, his file folders of stories by the Mysterious Writer were on his desk with a yellow Post-It note from Emmett on the top one. No words, just a large bang, an exclamation mark: !

Going down the hall to get his first cup of coffee, he passed Emmett's office and saw him talking on the phone. He was still on the phone as Jack came back, but as Jack turned his computer on, Emmett tapped on his door and walked in.

"You were right," he said.

"As usual."

"This guy of yours, this writer. Brilliant."

Jack said, "Did you read them all?"

"Straight through last night. He's everything you said, Jack. You have to try to find out who he is. We have to go to bat for this guy because this is really good work."

"Hey, I agree."

"I want to talk with Linda. I checked her calendar. She's free this morning."

"Emmett, no, not yet. What are we going to tell her?"

"Whatever you know about this guy."

"I don't know *anything* about this guy!"

"You know he writes like nobody's business. And you're talking to him tonight."

"And that's all I've got."

"You'll get more. Come on."

"To see Linda?"

"Just bring those." He meant the file folders.

Emmett led Jack down the hall to Linda's corner office and knocked on her door. Linda, focused on her computer screen, waved them in.

When Jack was hired to be an editor at Everson Publishing, he got lucky, and he knew it. He'd joined a publishing house that had been doing everything right for years. This was because of Linda Stark, the director. A short, feisty dynamo, at sixty years of age she had spent more than half of her life at Everson, helping it grow into a top-notch brand. She'd shepherded it from a modestly successful paperback house responsible for a series of middling romance novels, Westerns, and science fiction titles into an aggressive marketer of new talent. Everson had its share of rock-star authors—the modestly talented horror scribes and semiliterate thriller writers who sold in the millions—but Linda had also worked hard to get popular scholars under contract, thought leaders, people in the news, and talented midlist writers waiting to break out.

A large part of why she was so successful was because she was a good judge of character. Her motto? If you want to produce the best possible work, pick the best possible people to do that work. So Everson was populated by bright, energetic employees who liked what they did and were happy to be where they were. Linda had hired Jack after a single interview, having sensed the potential in him, and she'd encouraged Emmett to mentor him. Jack was grateful to both of them for that.

Now she turned to face Emmett and Jack, who sat in the comfortable chairs in front of her desk.

Emmett placed the file folders on her desk. "You want to publish this guy."

"Who is he?"

"We don't know."

"You don't *know*?"

"Funny story," Emmett told Linda. "Jack found him."

"Actually," Jack explained, "he found me."

Linda sighed. "Just tell me what's going on here." She reached for the file folders and began leafing through the manuscripts.

"I started getting these anonymously about a year ago," Jack told her, and explained how he hadn't even talked to the author until yesterday, when the guy had phoned him out of the blue.

"You've never met him?" Linda asked.

"Apparently *he* met *me* when I was giving a talk at a library or something, but that's all I know."

"Although Jack's meeting him tonight," Emmett said.

Linda shook her head. "I thought I knew different, but this is different."

Jack told her, "He knows I want to talk to him about getting him published."

"Tell me about the stories," Linda said.

All of them were short pieces, Jack told her, of five or six thousand words, and the writing was out of this world, easily equivalent to the best stuff out there, but definitely in a singular voice. Dark stuff, almost primal in its energy. He synopsized a few of the manuscripts for her.

Linda looked at Emmett. "Have you read them?"

"Every one. Kept me up all night. The guy's brilliant."

Linda made a sort of smile. "Then find out who he is. We should have a name before we go any further."

Jack told her, "I'm meeting him at a bookstore. I'll let you know first thing tomorrow where things stand."

"Fine."

Jack got to his feet as Emmett reached for the file folders and gave him a big smile, as if they were partners in crime or something.

Jack arrived at the bookstore a little before seven-thirty. He'd stopped at home briefly, had had a quick sandwich, and asked Corinne to wish him luck. Then he drove west as fast as he could to meet his genius.

Heading for the corner of the store that sold coffee and pastries, he walked past the racks of recent releases and saw two that he'd worked on earlier in the year. Good for you, he thought. I'm glad you're selling. But you're about to be outclassed, my friends.

He glanced around, trying to spot anyone who looked like he might belong to the voice on the phone, but no one seemed obvious. He walked up to the coffee counter.

The slender young woman there with rings in her eyebrows asked him, "And what for you?"

Jack ordered a regular coffee and sat at one of the circular tables. He kept looking around the brightly lit store as he waited, finished his coffee, continued to wait, restlessly walked over by the magazines to see who might be standing there, and, at twenty after eight, returned to the coffee counter.

"I was supposed to meet a man here," he told the slender woman. "I wouldn't know him to see him, but maybe middle-aged? He writes?"

"Hold on."

She stepped into the back and in a moment returned with a homemade brown-paper envelope that bulged slightly in the middle. She looked at the writing on the top and asked Jack, "Jack Mathis?"

"That's me."

"He was here this afternoon." She handed him the package. "He said I should give this to you."

"Is that all?"

"Well, yeah."

"You remember what he looked like?"

"I don't know. Middle-aged guy. A little taller than you. It was just a guy."

"Thanks."

"He didn't smell too good, though."

"Really?"

"I don't think he took a bath." She waved her hand in front of her face as though clearing the air.

Jack carried the package to another table, sat, and opened it.

There was the new manuscript, as promised, as well as a cassette tape, a regular old-fashioned plastic audiotape. Nothing on it, no labels or writing. Just the tape and the story.

And this story didn't even have a title.

Jack put the paper and cassette back into the envelope. He had a tape player in his Toyota, an old-fashioned audiocassette player in the console next to the CD player. No Blue Tooth, nothing from the Cloud, just old-fashioned technology. So did the mysterious writer know that somehow?

Or had he simply figured that most people still had tape players around somewhere?

No matter. He left the store to sit in his car in the parking lot and listen to the tape.

"Hello, Jack. I'm sorry I couldn't meet you in person this time. I guess I'm kind of careful about going out in public. Basically, I think I'm rather a shy person."

It was definitely the same voice as that of the man who had phoned him. Jack heard the crinkly sounds of cellophane, and then the metallic click of a cigarette lighter opening and closing. The man drew in a breath, smoking.

From other sounds in the background, Jack surmised that the man was driving. He didn't seem to shift gears, but Jack heard muted traffic noises—the occasional horn being honked, loud music fading in and out as someone passed by.

"The main thing is that I didn't want to embarrass myself in case you didn't show up. So if you did show up, Jack, and if you're listening to this, then please understand. I'll phone you tomorrow at your office so that we can talk about this story. And I do want to talk to you about any other plans you have. I suppose I simply feel that I have to be sure that I can trust you. Does that make sense? That's the only—"

Harsh coughing, very loud, and the man seemed almost to struggle for breath. Then Jack heard the clanging sounds of a railroad crossing, followed, about thirty seconds later, by the whooshing noise of a train passing by, presumably a commuter train. More clanging, and then Jack heard the guy's truck or SUV or car or whatever he was driving accelerating and making noises as it bumped over the rails. The man cleared his throat heavily.

"I think you're a bright man, Jack. I'm going by the sound of your voice, of course, and just the little bit of conversation we had, but it's important to me that the right person work with me on these stories. These stories mean everything to me. They *are* me, aren't they? You can probably understand that if anybody can. When I heard you talk, I had that feeling, that you were someone who would immediately understand what I was trying to do. I'm a good judge of people. I read people quite well, Jack. It's a gift. So I could tell, even that soon, that you and I were the same kind of person underneath. I need that if I'm going to trust you with my stories."

The sounds of traffic were gone. The background of the tape was all quiet. Then Jack heard crunching and popping. Clearly the guy was driving on gravel. Perhaps a gravel road? Then Jack could tell that the engine had been turned off.

"Anyhow, we met one other time and we talked for just a minute. I'm sure you don't remember, but that settled my opinion of you. So I think that this could work out for both of us. Anyhow, that's all for now, Jack. I'm glad you're the one who likes my stories. I'm glad we talked about meeting. I'll phone you tomorrow, and we can talk some more."

Click.

Silence.

Jack sat for a minute, thinking.

Something else came up on the tape, more of the man talking, although it sounded now as though he were talking to himself. He was. He was talking out loud to himself about stories or his story ideas. Interesting.

But after thirty seconds of that, the tape went silent again.

Jack hit the button to rewind it and put his car into reverse. He intended to listen to the tape again at home and read the new story, too.

"I think you're a bright man, Jack. I'm going by the sound of your voice, of course, and just the little bit of conversation we had, but it's important to me that the right person work with me on these stories. These stories mean everything to me. They are me, aren't they?"

Yeah, they're you, all right, Jack thought.

Whoever *you* are, and however I'm going to explain *you* to Linda and Emmett tomorrow.

"And that's all he said?" Emmett asked Jack.

"That's it."

"And he never showed."

"He had no intention of showing," Jack told him, very disappointed.

"Well, I'm sorry."

They were seated at a small table in 65, the crowded little Chinese restaurant on West Madison that piles the rice high but charges reasonably for it.

Carl was with them. He asked Jack, "But he's still giving you stories, right?"

"Oh, sure," Jack replied. "And they're better than ever. And still anonymous."

He told them about the one he'd read last night. A little boy playing in a junk yard accidentally locks himself inside an old refrigerator. He suffocates. Naturally, his parents and friends suffer guilt and remorse, but the little boy is happy, now that he's dead. His spirit makes friends with a man who died fifty years earlier in an industrial accident, when there was a factory standing where the junk yard is now. They become best friends and help each other move on into the next world.

Emmett frowned. "Tell me again what's on the tape."

"He's shy and feels awkward in public. And he butters me up and says that I'm the only person who understands what he writes."

Carl said, "You must feel very proud."

"I feel very weird. And I'm not sure what—"

His cell phone rang. Jack took it out of his shirt pocket.

Corinne. Jack listened for a moment, then told her, "Sure. No, it's fine. I know. Yes, tonight."

When he closed his phone, he told Emmett and Carl, "We're going for paint. To paint the baby's room."

Emmett asked him what color.

"A soft green. Sage green."

"Hey, that's very practical. Corinne's idea?"

"Yeah."

"Very restful. But Corinne's a sensible person. You got lucky with her. Jack, let this *go*," Emmett ordered him.

"I was counting a lot on last night. Maybe it's moving too fast. But I really wanted to talk to this guy. I promised you, and I promised Linda."

"Linda doesn't care," Emmett told him. "If he comes through, he comes through."

"I know."

"He phoned you once," Carl told Jack. "Maybe he'll call back."

"Yeah. Maybe." But Jack sounded glum.

Carl, however, Jack decided later that afternoon, needed to apply for his license in the official association of prognosticators and psychics because, sure enough, when his phone rang a little before three, Mystery Man was there.

Jack was alone in his office, although he glanced through his open door every minute or two to catch Emmett in case he walked by.

"I apologize again for last night, Jack."

"You disappointed me. I really wanted to talk about publishing your stories and meet you."

"I understand. What do you think of the new one?"

"It's excellent. As always. But very dark. Your material is getting darker."

"I keep digging deeper, and I keep finding out more things about myself. That's good, right?"

"Absolutely it is." Jack looked up as someone went past.

Amy. But she waved at him and was gone before Jack could signal her to come in or collar Emmett.

"Jack, you're being a good sport about this. I've been giving some thought to how we should best proceed. I do think you're the person I should be working with on my stories."

"Thank you. Does this mean we can make an appointment to have coffee again?"

"Yes."

"And maybe you can leave the tape recorder in your car and we can do it face to face next time."

"I'd like it to be tonight."

"Tonight?"

"Yes."

"Not tonight. I can't do it tonight."

"Tonight, Jack."

"I have an appointment."

"Break it."

"No!"

"We're talking about *my stories*, Jack. Break your appointment."

"We can do it—" He thought quickly. "Tomorrow night. Do it tomorrow night."

"Do what?"

"What do you mean, 'do what'? We can— Sir, listen, please. We can meet tomorrow night."

"Who's your appointment with, Jack?"

"I beg your pardon?"

"Who's your appointment with?"

"Look," Jack said into the phone, becoming uneasy. "That's getting a little personal. Let me ask you: Who are you?"

"Is it with your wife?"

"Excuse me?"

"Jack, is the appointment with your *wife*?"

"How did you know I have a wife?" There was an edge now to his voice, he couldn't help it.

"How do I know? You're passably good-looking, and you're intelligent and ambitious. And you can be funny. Women love that!" the man chuckled.

Despite himself, Jack smiled. "You're right," he admitted, and decided to find out more from the other end of the line. "Are *you* married?"

"I was. She died."

"Is she in your stories?"

"Every single one of them. She's why I do this, Jack. You know, people don't live. We all have to die. But stories live. Am I right?"

"Yes."

"That's why I write. The people in my stories—they're real. I knew them. But, of course, there's something of me in them, too."

"I understand."

"I think you do, Jack. I really think you do. We're all in this together. Nobody gets out alive, but we're all in it *together*," the man insisted, "and we're just trying our best to understand. I call it looking into the abyss."

"That's from...Nietzsche. Nietzsche?"

"Correct. And that's what we all do, Jack. We try to avoid looking into the abyss. Or, maybe if we're brave enough, we take a peek. Just a little peek. We look into that abyss. And the abyss looks back. It always does. Tonight, Jack."

"Tomorrow night. Come on."

"I'll be there. Eight o'clock. And just to intrigue you, here's where we're meeting. It's in the woods. I'm going to give you directions. It's remote. Get a pencil now. You have a pencil?"

"Yes."

"Here." He gave Jack detailed directions. "And I'll be there this time. Trust me. If you come, then I'll know we understand each other, and I'll send you more stories."

"Please. Make it tomorrow. You can—"

Click.

Jack frowned.

There was light knocking on his door. He looked up and saw Amy.

"Bad time?" she asked him.

"I'm a very bad person," Jack told her.

"Really?"

"I'm going to do something tonight to really make my wife angry."

"Then you *are* a bad person."

"No, I mean it. I'm really going to tick her off."

"Then I'm sorry I know you because you're such an evil guy. Only don't tell me what you're going to do."

"I won't. Amy, talk me out of it."

She smiled and told him, "Jack, don't do it. You'll disappoint Corinne, and she'll be pissed at you, and you'll hate yourself."

"Yeah, I know."

"Only, before you go, initial this memo. Then you can go be evil."

CHAPTER SEVEN

Dusk, the daylight being taken away, is how it felt to Jack as he drove slowly down the long gravel road that led to—Well, where?

He didn't know where in the hell he was. Miles from home. Farther west than he'd ever been in the whole time he'd lived northwest of Chicago, and at the end of miles of old roads that turned into gravel as they came here.

Wherever here was.

Damn it, he thought. The son of a bitch. The fucker's done it again.

He let his Toyota coast still and then pressed the brake. Ahead of him he saw only woods. A stretch of grass, untended, and some brush, and a wall of trees.

He was still upset because of the argument he'd gotten into on the phone with Corinne over this. So now Jack had made the wonderfully wise decision to piss off his wife and come all the way out here for this character. And for what?

Lights hit him, bright lights suddenly in front of him flashing on, then off, on again, and off again.

Headlights pointed at him from within the tree line.

Mystery Man signaling him?

Then Jack noticed a light-colored object, a rectangle, ahead of him and just off to the right, in the grass.

It couldn't be. Could it?

Jack turned off his car engine, got out, and walked over to the object.

Incredible. It was one of Mystery Man's homemade envelopes, tightly bound in clear packaging tape and with Jack's name—no address, just his name—handwritten in black Sharpie ink on the front.

Looking up, Jack noticed another one in the grass about forty feet away. He retrieved that one and saw a third homemade package just beyond, at the tree line heading into the deep woods.

Jack picked up that one, too, and looked into the woods.

The sun was gone now, the sky was purple, and the woods quite dark. Jack saw no trail or path before him, just a carpet of dead leaves. The trees here were large and tall, not as big as they grow in Ohio, which is where Jack was born, but sizable, nevertheless, and with nothing but darkness hanging between them.

"Jack?" A man's voice from way back there, and it was him, the guy, Mystery Man calling to him.

Jack said, "You're here?"

Coughing, and then, "Yes, yes! Come on, Jack!"

A bright yellow light appeared, the brilliant light of a flashlight. It was waved back and forth on the ground several hundred feet ahead.

Jack walked toward the light, barely able to distinguish behind it a man in jeans, a little taller than average, and wearing a bulky padded coat, a winter coat, and a baseball cap. He couldn't see much of the man's features, just enough to glimpse deep-set eyes and a full face, almost a moon face.

Jack asked him, as he stepped carefully within the darkness, "How'd you get here? Where's your car?"

"That's far enough. Stop, please."

Jack did so.

The flashlight was pointed directly at him so that Jack had to turn away. It burned his eyes. Then the man pointed the light at the ground again.

"You got the stories?"

"Well, the ones you left on the ground. Are there more?"

"We're going to write one tonight."

"What does that mean?"

"This is how I work on my stories. I told you we need to collaborate. Well, Jack—we're collaborating."

"You've lost me."

"All will be made clear. Like the blind carpenter, I reached for my hammer and saw. You will, too."

"Is that—?" He was trying to distinguish as well as he could whatever was in front of him among the trees, the guy and also a hulking object back there, a little behind him. "Is that a truck?"

"That's my truck, yes."

"You drove your truck into the woods?"

"Sure, yeah." He cleared his throat, hunh hunh.

"So what're we— Hey." Now Jack more clearly made out a long object at the man's feet. He thought at first that it must be a large rolled-up rug, but it made a sound. "What is that?"

Another sound. It could have been someone's voice, someone waking up and mumbling or trying to speak in a slurred way.

The man said, "She's coming around," and shined the light straight down in front of him.

"Jesus Christ!" Jack yelled, "What are you doing?"

It was a woman, maybe in her twenties or thirties, wrapped in a thick blanket that itself was bound by lengths of silver duct tape. Her face, too, was wrapped in duct tape, her mouth covered and her eyes, but not her nose.

She has to breathe, Jack thought.

He said to the man, "I do not know what fucking game this is—"

"It's not a game. Here." The man tossed something toward Jack.

Jack jumped back but looked down as whatever it was landed in the leaves, making noise. He bent forward, kneeled down.

A revolver. A .38. Like an old service revolver police would use.

Jack took hold of it and stood, holding the .38 but pointing it at the ground.

The man told him, "Go ahead and use it, Jack. I want you to."

"Use it for what?"

"Well, use it on me. I want you to, actually. I've written enough stories, and I'm tired. I'm not afraid to die. And if I'm right about you, then you're made of the right stuff, too. If I'm right, then I've just made you angry enough and scared enough that you'll do what I know you can do."

"This is fucked." Jack started backing up.

"Or help me kill *her*, Jack!"

"What?"

"Shoot her. Help me." He reached behind him and produced a baseball bat. It must have been leaning against the tree there. "This is where the stories come from, Jack!" Coughing, he lifted the baseball bat and, as the bound woman made more puling noises and tried to move within the blanket, the man brought down the baseball bat, striking her directly on her side, then brought it down again as she sobbed, hitting her squarely in the stomach.

"Fucking son of a bitch!" Jack dropped the stories and brought up the .38, aimed it quickly and almost—

Almost—

"Jack, do it!"

"Back away and let her go!"

"Shoot, Jack! Shoot me or shoot her! Shoot!"

"*Let her go!*"

"No!"

"I'm calling the police." He threw down the .38 and the packages he'd been holding and pulled out his cell phone. It shook in his hand. Jack tried three times to punch in 9-1-1, failing each time because he was so scared.

"Bastard!" he swore.

"Come on, Jack!" the man yelled, and brought the bat up again and swung it down.

Directly onto the woman's head.

A loud crack. She made no further sounds, and she no longer moved.

Jack wanted to cry. Uncertain and afraid, trapped, he looked around but saw only darkness and trees. He pushed the cell phone back into his pocket and backed away. He wanted to try to dial 9-1-1 again but he didn't, he couldn't do it, when if he started and then this maniac had another gun and shot *him*? Or ran at Jack with the baseball bat?

Get away, is what he thought. Just go now and call the police later. Save yourself is what you have to do first.

The glare of the flashlight hit him in the eyes again, and he felt pain from it.

"Come on, Jack!"

He turned to run away. Moved his feet, and they felt heavy, almost impossible to lift. He was aware that he was dizzy and wasn't breathing. But then, yes, despite all that, Jack was indeed running, or at least he thought he was, at least he was moving his feet—

"Jack! You're really pissing me off!" the man yelled.

He reached his car, opened the door, heard the voice behind him from the woods—

"You have *really disappointed* me, Jack!"

—and got inside, started the engine, put the car into Reverse and turned the wheel as hard as he could. He heard gravel flying and felt the car bump as he bounced over grass and brush and stones, shifted into Drive, and went down the gravel road—

But stopped.

What was this? What kind of fucking game was this?

Think, think, Jack told himself. Think. The guy... this guy—

"The people in my stories—they're real. Nobody gets out alive. I call it looking into the abyss."

A fucking *abyss*?

Is that what this was? A fucking *literary symbol*?

"Shoot, Jack! Shoot me or shoot her! Shoot!"

And he wants to die? Jack thought. Could that even be possible? The guy wanted to die? Why? He's killing people, but he wants to die?

This is so nuts, so nuts, so nuts...

Jack told himself that he should go back, get the .38, aim it at this man and force him to stay there as he phoned the police.

But then there were sounds from the woods, from way back there, an engine, his truck engine.

Was he leaving?

Was he going to come here from the woods, across the grass and attack Jack now with his baseball bat or, what? Say, Hey, Jack, why don't you shoot me *now*?

And then the sound was gone. The truck, gone.

But the stories were still there.

Jack thought, The stories, the packages.

And the .38. Still there?

This is insane. I cannot go back there for, for the *stories*.

He shifted into Reverse and backed the car up, got to where he felt he had parked before on the gravel, and insanely, not sure who it was or what it was that was making him do this, shifted into Park and got out of the car and stood there, listening.

Silence, nothing.

Go into the woods, or at least get the stories?

He remembered that he had a small flashlight in his glove compartment. He reached back in to get it, checked it to make sure it worked, then walked carefully into the grass, not turning on the flashlight but going toward the tree line, trying to remember as well as he could whether this was where he'd been before.

Complete silence, and complete darkness.

Jack continued, went into the woods, and now took a chance and turned on the flashlight. He aimed it around and decided that this was, yes, where he'd been before. He poked the light ahead and saw the envelopes on the ground.

But no .38.

He picked up the packages and held onto them tightly. Shined the light ahead of him and continued walking.

Pointed the light toward where he thought the man had been, and the woman and the baseball bat.

No one was there.

Jack walked closer.

There was nothing. Shouldn't there have been blood from where he hit the woman in the head? The leaves were scattered, all messed up, probably from the guy picking up her body and carrying it away, probably to his truck to drive away with her *fucking body*.

Dear God.

But no blood?

But Jack seen him *hit her with a baseball bat*.

He backed away, and as he got near the tree line, he turned his back at last on what had happened, where he had been, and jogged back toward his car.

Threw the packages onto the car seat, returned the flashlight to the glove compartment, closed his door. Started the engine.

And took out his cell phone.

Call the police or not?

What would he tell them?

I was going to meet this guy who writes stories and I saw him kill a woman? Only there's nothing there now?

Is that, Jack thought, what I tell them?

What do I tell them?

Call the police or not?

As soon as he got home, making it up the stairs and down the hallway and inside his and Corinne's condo, Jack immediately locked the door behind him and, not knowing what else to do, went into the living room and fell onto the couch. He turned on no lights but sat in the darkness. He stuck an index finger in his mouth, bit on the knuckle, something he hadn't done since grade school or maybe college, and did not move.

He heard Corinne come down the stairs from their bedroom. She turned on a table lamp, and he could see her reflected in the glass of the sliding doors leading out to their balcony.

She said, "Is that you?"

"Yeah."

"I'm not real happy with you tonight."

"I saw him kill someone."

"What?"

"This writer, the genius! He was there. He killed a woman right in front of me."

"Jack, wait, wait." Corinne came into the room and turned on one of the lamps on an end table. "Who did he kill?"

"I have no idea."

"You *saw* this?"

"Yes!" Now he stood and, not knowing what else to do, walked toward the patio doors. Jack didn't open them, but he looked outside. A corner of the parking lot was visible from this angle, cars and some trees, and he almost expected the mad genius to walk out of the woods again down there and look up at him, maybe wave a baseball bat to let Jack know he was there.

Or just wave at him, or tempt him with a new package of stories.

Jack turned and saw how anguished Corinne was.

She said, "Tell me what happened."

"I went there, you know, after I talked to you. I get there, and nobody's there, only I find those packages"—he had dropped them onto the couch and now pointed to them—"he has them lined up in the grass so that when I pick them up, they lead right to him. He's in the woods."

"All right."

"And I get there, I get there—"

"Jack, just *tell* me."

"And he has a .38, a revolver, he throws it to me and he wants me to kill him. He wants me to shoot him."

"What?"

"And I'm not, I can't do that, I tell him no, and he says something like, 'Look, this is how I write my stories, you have to help me,' and he shows me this woman on the ground. He has her tied up inside a rug or something, and he's got her with tape around her mouth, duct tape, and she's really scared. Corinne, it was not an act."

"Okay. I believe you."

"And I'm scared shitless, I keep telling him, 'No, no,' and I try to back away, and he kills her with a baseball bat. Right in the head."

He stared at Corinne, shaking, and tried to smile or show an expression. But the best Jack could do was to go back to the couch and sit there.

He picked up the packages and put them on the coffee table next to some magazines and books about babies that Corinne must have bought, pregnancy and your first year, baby books.

Corinne walked over and sat beside him. Very quietly and carefully she said to him, "You know you saw this? For real?"

"Jesus, *yes*, I saw it!"

"What else? Did he do anything else? I mean, Jack, you're here, did he try to attack *you*?"

"No, no, no. Nothing like that. He said something like, 'We have to collaborate.' I just ran, Corinne. I got in my car, and I wanted to leave, but I couldn't. I went back. I thought I heard him leave, and I went back, and he was gone, and so was the woman. Only there was no blood or anything. I can't *prove* this. I brought back the stories. That's it. That's what happened."

"Nobody else was there?"

"It all happened in like three minutes. It was dark."

"And you're sure you saw this?"

"I'm not lying, Corinne!"

"I'm not saying— Did you call the police?"

"No."

"You didn't call the *police*?"

"I tried. I couldn't see the phone. My hand was shaking too much."

"Jack, you have to call the police right now and tell them about this." Corinne got up and started walking toward the kitchen.

Jack said to her, "Wait."

Corinne turned. "Wait for *what*?"

"Let me...think, let me think for a minute."

"Jack, you witnessed a *murder*!"

"I know."

"Didn't you?"

"Yes!"

Corinne came back. "You saw him hit her with the, with a baseball bat, and he killed her."

"Yes."

"Then you have to tell the police."

"And what if they think I was there helping him? Or they find the gun?"

"Jack, you tell them *exactly what happened*."

"I know, I know." Still, he didn't move.

Impatiently, Corinne asked him, "Is that what happened?"

Jack didn't answer her. What to say to that, what to do? He was looking at the manuscript packages on the coffee table.

"Jack?"

"I know."

"I'm getting the phone." She started again for the kitchen.

But Jack said to her again, "Wait."

"Now what?"

"I want to be sure."

"About what? Killing her?"

"I want to be sure."

"Jack..." Corinne returned to the couch and sat beside him, put a hand on one of his, and, more carefully now, asked him, "What did you see?"

"Him. The baseball bat. The gun. I held the gun, I know the gun was there."

"And the woman was there?"

"I thought it was a woman. It looked like a woman."

"Was she there or not, Jack?"

He didn't answer. He bit on his finger again.

And looked at the manuscript packages.

"Jack," Corinne said, "you better be right about this."

He cleared his throat and told her, "I know."

"What did you see? What did you really, actually see?"

"Him with the bat. And a flashlight. And all the things he said."

"And the woman."

"Maybe not the woman," Jack said.

"Are you *sure*?"

"I think so. I'm not sure. Yes, I'm sure."

"You better be. You came in here saying he killed someone."

"That's what it *looked* like, Corinne!"

"And is that what it was?"

He stood again, walked again to the patio windows, looked outside, turned, and said to his wife, "I have to be sure, and now I'm not sure."

"Is that the truth?"

"Yes."

"You thought he killed someone, but he didn't?"

"I know he was doing something to play with my head. To get me out there and give me the stories and play with my head. I think he sincerely wanted me to shoot him."

"And that's why he did that? Like it was an act?"

"That's all I can think of." He looked Corinne in the eyes.

She held his stare, uncertain, then went into the kitchen.

Jack listened. She opened a cupboard. Didn't go for the phone. Turned on the tap and filled a glass of water, and it sounded like she drank it. Then she came back in.

She handed Jack a glass of water and told him, "Sweetie, I'm tired."

"I know." He took the glass and sipped.

"What are you going to do?" Corinne asked him.

"I don't know. I have to think some more. I have to think. I need to be really sure about what I saw."

"I'm just— You've worn me out."

"I don't even know who this guy is. He had his fucking, his fucking *truck* in the woods, Corinne. And he keeps saying, 'Shoot me. You can do it.' What kind of sickness is that?"

"I don't know. I have to go lie down."

Sincerely, now, he asked her, "Are you okay? Are you feeling okay? I mean, the baby?"

"I'm fine. I'm tired."

"I'm sorry, all right? I really wanted to go look at paint."

"Yes, Jack."

"But I wanted to meet this guy, and I did."

"Jack, honey—" Corinne walked to him and kissed him, held his hands for a moment and told him, "It's fine. Whatever happened, you'll figure it out. Okay? Now, I'm tired. Let me go lie down."

"Sure."

"Come in when you're ready." She yawned.

Jack watched her go up the stairs to their bedroom. He heard her get onto the bed.

He looked at the manuscript packages and felt sick to his stomach. He told himself that he sincerely was not sure, now, what he had seen. It had *sounded* like a woman. It had *looked* like a woman. It had. It had.

So he had seen the guy kill a woman, right?

He went to the coffee table and got onto his knees, reached and touched the manuscript packages and rested his fingers on them as though touching them would immediately make clear to him what had happened, would tell him the truth.

Right?

CHAPTER EIGHT

"But I heard *sounds*," Jack told Emmett. "There was someone in there, in the, in the blanket, and I *heard* her, Emmett."

"Or you thought you did."

They were in Jack's office, just the two of them. The morning, gray, hung outside his window and over the city skyline like something Jack had dragged with him all the way downtown, his mood, his fear. He put his head down, then sat back and looked at his shivering hands. "Jesus," he whispered.

"What did Corinne say?"

"Emmett, Emmett... Look, be honest. Do you think he's weird enough to do this? Kill people like this?"

"Everybody's weird enough to kill people like this, but not everybody does it and writes the way he does. Did you read the stories?"

"Jesus, Emmett. Am I that cold-blooded?"

"You are and I am. Did you read them?"

"Yes. After Corinne fell asleep."

"And?"

"They're brilliant."

"Make me copies."

"Emmett, this guy is too fucking strange even for you and me. 'Meet me in the woods, Jack. Shoot me with the .38, Jack. Now I'm going to beat a woman to death, Jack.'"

"And you think he was serious about wanting you to kill him?"

"Who would joke about that?"

"The same kind of guy who would pretend to beat a woman to death with a baseball bat and put his stories out there like an Easter Egg hunt for you to find to get you completely off balance."

"But *why*?"

"Because he's *fucked up*, Jack! And that's what makes him a good writer! There's no answer to *why*. You know that. If I thought this guy was really doing this, I'd feel differently. If he was killing people and raping kids or whatever he does in his stories, then, 'No thank you, keep your stories.' But there's no law against being a fucked-up individual who writes well."

"Except that I don't know what to do now. Should I call the police?"

"No. Because you don't know what happened, and what're you going to tell them?"

"That I agreed to meet a nut who writes great stories, and he asked me to kill him, and could you please help me now find this guy?"

"And what are the police going to say?"

"They're going to say, 'What drugs have you been taking, young man?'"

Emmett asked Jack, "So what drugs *have* you been taking?"

"All I want to do is go back to how things were."

"Before *el* genius started sending you stories? Or do you want to keep the stories?"

Jack frowned and didn't answer. He swiveled in his chair and looked out at the Marina Towers.

Emmett lifted the story manuscripts from Jack's desk. "I'm making copies of these."

"Be my guest."

"And you didn't answer my question."

Jack told him, continuing to look out at the towers and the overcast sky, "I want to keep the stories."

"That's my boy," Emmett said. "I trained you well."

So what do I do now, Bobbie? Cordell asked of his wife's ghost as he sat late in the morning the following day, smoking a Chesterfield and sitting at his kitchen table. Bobbie, the man let me down. I pushed him too fast, but I'm impatient, so what do I do now?

He was looking outside the kitchen window at the trees. Rain was gently falling. It was hardly more than dew, hardly more than a mist or fog, this rain, but Cordell appreciated it as he might a familiar suit of clothes, a comfortable old coat.

As he sat smoking, he considered the next story he would need to write but, more than that at this moment, he thought of Bobbie and talked to her as he habitually did, in his imagination, with his mind, with his heart, his wife long gone, his heart long broken.

Bobbie, he and I need to have a serious talk, Cordell told her.

Jack simply needed an education. That's what was apparent now. Cordell had expected too much, too soon from him. You don't take someone from their warm environment and yank them out into the cold world and expect them, despite the shock, to do what's necessary, not immediately.

Although it surely would have saved time and saved Jack a lot of trouble if he had been up to it, if he had pulled the trigger.

Cordell had had everything ready to go. He'd left the stories for Jack to find, and once Jack had shot him, everything anyone needed to know was in his truck—diaries, notebooks, a letter explaining that he had goaded Jack into killing him by attacking Jack first. Everything Jack would need to clear his conscience and yet continue freely to explore what Cordell had written and make clear to the world what was in those stories.

But Jack had failed.

Well, it hadn't been easy for Cordell to come around, either, to see things for what they are, to look into the abyss and see life for what it is, to see people turned into garbage, and then from the darkness of that abyss learn that the only thing that matters in this world is the stories we tell each other in order to remain human, the cohesion and beauty that come from stories. Without them, we *are* garbage, we are mud on the edge of a river bank, we are leaves flying under an anonymous sky ignorant of itself.

Jack wants those stories.

The world wants those stories.

So what do I do now, Bobbie? Cordell asked of his wife's ghost.

Well, you have to tell him the truth.
She was right. Tell him the complete truth.
Tell him this: *I'm sick, Jack.*
And he will say: *You're sick all right.*
No, really. It's serious. I'm sick.
Bobbie, should I tell him?
Yes.
Is it time to tell him?
It's time, Cord.

The phone on his desk rang just as Jack had anticipated, and at about the time he'd expected it to, as well, at a little before three.

As surprising as this guy was, at least he seemed to be predictable in *some* ways.

"Jack?"

"I've been waiting."

"We must talk."

"No, we must *not* talk."

"Don't hang up! Jack?"

Silence.

"Jack?"

"I'm still here."

The guy sounded truly relieved. He cleared his throat and said, "I'm afraid I pushed things a little too fast last evening."

"Listen, look. I don't know who you are, and I don't want to know. You're sick. You're a sick fucker. I don't—"

"What about the stories?"

"Fuck you and fuck your stories."

"Well, Jack, that hurts, but I don't think you mean it. You came back last night to get the stories, didn't you?"

Further silence.

The man chuckled. "It's all right! I understand. I surprised you, I startled you."

Jack told him, "I'm not here to play games. I like your stories. They're good stories. But that's all they are. I cannot afford to waste—"

"Well, I'd like to send you more stories."

"Then send them."

"I will, I will. But this is why I said we need to collaborate. I need to stretch my voice, Jack. This is where you can help."

"By standing around while you fucking hit some woman with a *baseball bat*?"

"I put her out of her misery, Jack."

"Don't even say that! I am not fooled! There was no woman, there was no—"

"What do you mean? You saw her. You heard her."

"It was a trick."

"Jack, it was a *demonstration*. People die and get killed and get sick, and if somebody hits them with a baseball bat, then that's just how things happen. I'm an accident waiting to happen to them, Jack, nothing more and nothing less. If I don't do it to them, someone else will. Or *something* will."

"See, I'm not going to talk about this. Keep the stories."

"Jack, I need your help." He coughed lightly.

"You need *somebody's* help."

"You say it like it's a joke but, Jack, I really *am* sick. I'm dying. I have cancer."

"I've heard enough."

"It's the truth. What am I supposed to do? Be pissed off? Be angry at God? Jack, I'm trying to write as fast I can. I want to get as much done as fast as I can, and I have to be able to trust you because, Jack, when I'm dead, I'm going to be like everyone else. I'll be garbage. But the stories will be there."

"And what does this have to do with killing that woman? Is that what you do? You kill people?"

Now there was silence on the other end of the line.

"Hang up," Jack said. "Do not call—"

"If I don't do it, somebody else will."

"I want nothing more to do with this."

"You didn't shoot, did you?"

"Last night?"

"I gave you your chance. If you'd hated what I was doing, why didn't you stop me? All you had to do was pull the trigger."

"I don't do that."

"Well, yes, you do, Jack. All of us learn to pull the trigger, sooner or later."

"Not me."

"Not even when you were growing up in Ohio?"

"How did you— How do you know I grew up in Ohio?"

"Jack, I've been paying attention to you ever since I saw you speak at the library. You're not hard to know. I like you. I poked around a little. It's not hard. And that's how I decided to send you the stories. Hey, Jack, you're the Chosen One, all right?" The man laughed.

"Leave me alone." Jack's voice had changed. He was sincerely frightened. This guy was poking around to find out about where he was *from*?

"This means a lot to me, Jack."

"Leave me alone!"

"You don't get left alone, my friend. You're the Chosen One. I chose you to help me with my stories, and you're doing it. You could have shot me last night and put me out of my misery and yourself, too. And saved that woman's life. But you didn't! So *you* helped kill her, *too*, didn't you?"

Jack hung up. Slammed the phone down and swallowed. He was breathless.

He knows where I was fucking *born*?

The phone rang again.

He ignored it.

But only until the third ring.

Picked it up.

"What?"

"You don't get left alone, Jack. You're going to help me. You want more stories, and I'm going to teach you how to write them. A lot of stories just happen. They're not on paper. They're between people, like you and me. We're the story now, Jack. You get the stories, but I get you. I'm your *future*, Jack. You're the Chosen One."

Jack slammed the phone down again. Hard.

Still shaking, he walked into Emmett's office. Carl was there, sitting in one of the chairs in front of Emmett's desk.

Jack took the other chair. "I need a drink."

"It's three o'clock," Emmett told him. "Do you usually start this early?"

"I do now."

Carl said to him, "Dude, you're upset."

Emmett asked Jack, "What? Your writer?"

"He's spying on me, Emmett. Or finding out things about me, like where I'm from. And now he says he has cancer."

"Full of surprises, this one."

"Which is why I was supposed to kill him. Or not. It was a test."

Carl asked him, "What kind of test?"

"To see if I'm worthy or something. Only now I can't get out of it anyway because I'm the Chosen One and the only one worthy of working with him on his stories."

Carl said, "Dude, you must feel very proud."

Jack looked at him as though a piece of wood had just found voice. "Carl, he's insane."

"He sounds it."

Emmett told Jack, "Stories or no stories, we don't need this."

"No," Jack said to him with a sick smile. "*We* don't. Emmett, what the fuck do *I* do?"

"Did he say anything else?"

"Sure. He's going to teach me how to write stories, or how *he* writes them, only they just happen and they're not even on paper. So now we're going to write stories together, and they just happen. And he claims he really did kill the woman lat night. Emmett, he's an accident waiting to happen. His words. So what do I *do*?"

"Ignore him, Jack."

"You think this guy is going to be ignored?"

"Absolutely. I've seen it before. He's really talented, I grant you, but he's just like every other case history out there who insists that he's the next great genius and starts dictating to us like we're supposed to take him seriously. Don't answer next time he calls."

"Just let it ring."

"Let it ring. He'll get the idea. Clam up and ignore him. Pretty soon he'll start bothering someone else."

"It's not going to be that easy with this guy."

"Jack, it will be. They're all the same. I admit this guy got my hopes up, and he's definitely talented, but he's too fucked up."

Jack said, "Maybe I *should* have shot him."

Carl looked at him. "Dude, really?"

"Carl, he wants to die. Or says he does. Or he wants to die, and he still wants to write. If you can figure it out, tell me."

"I think I'd rather just back away. I don't want to know him."

"Neither do I," Jack said, downcast. "But he sure seems like he knows *me*."

Jack told Corinne when he got home that night that the guy had called again and had sounded as though he were this close to actually threatening him. Her response was the same as Emmett's: ignore this creep. Trust Emmett on this one, she told him. I'm sure he's been down this road before.

Jack moodily agreed, and the two of them sat through a quiet supper. Corrine didn't push him. Jack was hurt and disappointed. What he'd wanted for his career had gone bad, and she sympathized.

After supper, Jack moved to the couch and sat quietly there with only one table lamp on and no music, no television. He sipped a glass of Drambuie on ice.

Corinne left him alone until the middle of the evening. When she came in and sat in the wingback chair catty corner to the couch, it was to tell him, "Jack, I know you like the stories, and maybe this man does have real talent—"

"He's past that. He doesn't just have talent. He's better than that."

"Fine. But you have me worried. It's like he has some kind of hold on you."

He looked her in the eyes and said to Corinne, "Do me a favor."

"What?"

"Read the stories."

"Oh. Okay."

"Not all of them. Some of them. Read the ones from the other night, the ones I went back for. I do want his stories, and he knows it."

"Then give them to me."

Jack got up and went down the hall to the spare bedroom he'd turned into his office. He opened the deep file drawer on the right-hand side of his desk, retrieved his file folders with the original manuscripts that had been mailed to him, and dropped them onto the table.

"You might see things I can't," he told Corinne.

"Maybe."

"Like with your kids." He meant from her days as an art therapy instructor.

"Jack, I don't know if that's pertinent."

"Corinne, please. Just tell me if you think of anything. I'm feeling boxed in. I don't know what I'm feeling, I am so fucking angry."

She rose and lifted the file folders. "Then let me read them."

"Thank you."

She made a kissing sound at him and left, heading up the stairs to their bedroom.

CHAPTER NINE

Saturday morning.

In the living room of his parents' farmhouse, Cordell sat cross-legged on the floor with many sheets of blank paper spread out before him. He had arranged them neatly, several rows deep, several columns wide. Blank sheets of paper.

Cordell imagined that if he waited long enough, simply waited, words would appear by themselves on the blank sheets of paper without his doing anything more than observe as this wonder occurred.

He lifted a sheet of paper from the ream at his side and placed it carefully on top of a sheet resting before him. By doing this, he had caused an upper level highway to collapse onto the one below it. By doing this, he had sacrificed lives so that he could enter into their hearts and hear the song of their screams and write well. Blank pages falling upon blank pages, small lives crushed and removed to make way for the next round of blank pages, the next round of lives.

Jack had a wife, Cordell knew. He'd established that already, had driven by their condo any number of times, sat parked in the lot for long stretches and watched as Jack and his wife had entered and exited the building. He knew her name, too. Corinne. He'd established when their mail was delivered every afternoon and then had come by every few days to see whether packages had been left in the vestibule for either of them. Corinne, he learned, frequently ordered products by mail.

Corinne.

Almost like Cordell, with the *Cor* sound.

She didn't work, Cordell surmised. He'd sat there during mornings and afternoons and seen Corinne come and go without any apparent timetable or schedule, so she was at home and didn't have a job, or at least a fulltime job, or perhaps worked from home.

It was so important that Jack understand, and starting with the wife was logical. It had started for Cordell, after all, with his wife.

He took one of the sheets of paper and tore it apart as though it were Bobbie's body being turned randomly into garbage, or the woman from the other night.

She made it too easy for him. Like the guy he'd found in the park and burned in the cellar. People don't pay attention, they don't know where they are, people don't know *who* they are. All of this life, and people sleepwalking through it.

Corinne was no different. Cor-eeeeeen.

He followed her to the Aldi's in the Deer Park shopping center off Dundee in Palatine, close to her and Jack's condo. Corinne in her little Mazda, him in his big red truck. She glanced at him once or twice as she drove, him behind her or two cars behind her while he trailed her through suburbia, but she didn't recognize him, didn't know him for what he was, a kindred soul of her husband's.

It was a warm day. Cordell waited for her in the parking lot. Found a place to park several rows away from Corinne's car—close enough that he could get to his truck handily afterward but sufficiently far away that it would blend in with all of the other trucks and SUVs and cars everywhere. He sat at the wheel of his truck and smoked Chesterfields. Two, three of them. Thinking during this time, waiting. Four, now.

He looked at all of the shoppers going into the other stores, and he looked at the concrete and blacktop as if the whole world now belonged to concrete and blacktop. Cordell had occasionally found himself in this strip mall years ago, a decade or more ago, a long time ago now, when there had been money and everyone shopped all the time and everyone had been young, when he and Bobbie had been young, when buying things meant everything. Now the world of everything was gone. More recently, Cordell had bought some pens and paper at the Target here and then had followed an elderly woman out of the parking lot and captured her and taken her to some woods seventy-five miles away, in Wisconsin, and opened her there to get at the story he needed.

Finally, Cordell sees her walking out of Aldi's. He gets out of his truck, closes the door, throws down his new cigarette, and goes around to the passenger side door of his truck. He stands there, watching, and hears Corinne beep her car doors open.

He waits. Does she notice him? He's standing there, the top of his head just a little below the roof of his truck cab, his red truck. Corinne opens the back door of her Mazda, puts the things she has bought on the back seat, a bag of groceries and a rotisserie chicken in a plastic tray, and then she closes the door. Cordell starts walking. Corinne opens her driver's side door and gets in. And as she does, Cordell pulls his big hunting knife from the oversized pocket of his heavy jacket, steps up, pulls open the passenger side door of the Mazda, gets in, holds the knife up so that the point is aimed at Corinne's face, at her right cheek, and closes his door.

"No noise."

Of course there will be no noise. The truly frightened are silent, always, like the abyss itself.

"Or I will stab you. Do you understand?"

"Yyyy."

She is sweating. She is extremely pretty.

Some people walk behind the Mazda, Cordell sees them coming, an old woman and a middle-aged man, so he lowers the knife. He doesn't want people to see the knife if they look through the back window of the car or through the front windshield.

He tells Corinne, "They don't care. You know that, right?"

"Yes." Quietly. She looks at him but quickly looks away.

"I need to tell Jack something, and you have to tell him what I have to say because he's *not listening*! Do you understand?"

She nods. Her head shivers.

"I can kill you, but I won't if you stay quiet and tell Jack what I need you to tell him. Okay?"

"Yyyy. Yes."

He is filthy. He smells of cigarette smoke and gasoline and dirt and moldy leaves, a pungent mixture of odors, he smells like garbage, and it makes Corinne nauseous. Her stomach is prepared to rotate or jump and move hotly up the inside of her throat like a balloon, but she keeps her teeth pressed together. She thinks, Yes. Whatever he demands or says or asks, Yes is the answer.

She looks at him again. He is perhaps an inch or two taller than Jack, heavier and older, maybe early forties. Filthy, yes. No hygiene at all. And she knows who he is.

She says to him, "Are you the one?"

"The one what?"

"Stories. With the, with the stories."

"Yes. Corinne, right?"

"Yes."

"You're not going to be like my wife, are you?"

"What...did your wife? Do?"

"She said she wanted to hurt me, she wanted to kill me because she was so worried, I made her so nervous. Corinne, your husband is an important man. Jack gave me my life back. He gave me...he pointed me in the direction I needed to go in. He needs to know that. Because I want to help him the way he helped me. He *understands*. Do you know what I'm talking about?"

"I think so. I think so."

"Then what am I talking about?"

She looks in the rearview mirror, but it would be hopeless to do anything, although she has to think it, of course, at least entertain the idea that *she can live through this.*

"Tell me," he insists, while the knife shakes in his hand.

"Stories. Stories," she says.

"Stories live," he tells her. "People don't live. Look around. *Look.* Over there. People don't live. Stories live. Does Jack understand that?"

"I— Yes. Think so."

He sighs. "I'm not being as clear as I could be. Your husband's a very intelligent man. I understand Jack. We understand each other. I actually talked to him at the

library about this. What Jack said about art is so important. It's so important. Am I right?"

"Yes." She is looking straight ahead.

"We forgive people anything when they make great art,
and that is so *true*. I thought I was losing my mind! But I
wasn't," he says. "Only, the people who give us important
work, it's not an accident, the kind of people they are. Jack
said that, and he is absolutely right. My parents died. Are
your parents dead?"

"No," she whispers, "Please, please don't—" Her mouth
is so dry, her throat and the top of the inside of her mouth,
it's not possible to move her mouth, it is stuck. Her tongue
is dry and swollen.

"My wife was killed."

"Please , please."

"Why do these things happen? And Jack says, These
things don't matter. What matters is *what we do with them*.
Find your *voice*. Anything can happen, it's waiting for us,
anything, anything, we, we invite anything to happen,
it's like what's waiting to happen is really us, another us,
it's waiting for us. It knows who we are, and we go and we
meet it. It opens our eyes so *much*. Like when Bobbie died.
It's a *gift*. But we have to learn to *see*. Pity, terror, these
wonderful, wonderful ideas. Did you ever read Euripides?"

Euripides? Corinne looks at him now, really looks at him.
"No. *Yes*. Yes."

"Euripides," he tells her, imparts to her, reminds her.
"*The Bacchae*. Am I right?"

"Yes."

"You remember when the prince, the king—Pentheus—
is going through the city, and Dionysus, who's the god, has
convinced him to dress like a woman and go to the mountain
to see the ritual. You remember what Pentheus said? He was
seeing double. *He was seeing double*. Which is what is absolutely necessary, as Jack knows. He was seeing right through
the, all the bullshit and seeing *life*. Who does that? *Artists*.
Jack taught me that. So after that, I could see both things at
once. Life the way it seems to be, the way people want it to
be, and in fact life the way it is. Am I right? Like Euripides!"

She thinks of the stories she read last night. You might see things I can't, Jack had told her, and what Corinne had seen was this man's anguish and his soul. Not the striving that she'd seen in her students, the handicapped children who gladly struggled to prove themselves to themselves. This man's soul was not struggling in that way. She had jotted down notes. *Everybody dies and is reborn as a spirit of some kind*, was one of her notes about one of his stories.

And, *All of the characters in his stories float around and accidentally bump into each other. Marbles—children playing marbles. No one feels connected to anyone else.*

And, *He uses violence to purify things. In one story it is like a ritual. Is there literary symbolism or a term for that?*

The Bacchae? Crazy people tearing other people apart on top of a mountain because they've been driven insane by some god?

Is that what this is?

She thinks, What's he going to do with me? Beat me to death with a baseball bat? *Tear me apart or cut me apart right here?*

"There's just so much in us that needs to find a way out," he says, and then coughs loudly from deep in his lungs. He is clearly very sick. And he continues. "As much as it hurts us to suffer, whatever happens to us, that doesn't last. We meet it, we invite it, it's us, and that's okay. What lasts is the spirit. It's so important to remember that. Jack understands that." He asked Corinne, "Do you remember the earthquake in Oakland, California, that happened in 1989?"

"No."

"Part of the highway collapsed and crushed the people who were underneath it, I mean, it smashed them in their cars. They're listening to the radio and one second later, they're flattened, they're...flattened. Now they're not human anymore, they're garbage. What does that do to us? Did they ever deserve to have that happen to them?"

Corinne whispers, "I don't know."

"They didn't do *anything*, Corinne, to, to deserve that. They didn't do *anything*. But it comes for us, it's always waiting for us. And we always meet it. It was like getting rained on in a storm or like falling down for them. I do that. I come and I make people fall down, I'm the rain, I'm like a storm, I'm waiting like the storm, only so what? It doesn't mean anything until *I write the story about it.*"

Something in his voice at that moment. Corinne closes her eyes. This is it, he's doing something, he's going to do something—

The car door latch makes a sound. Him, opening his door.

"Keep your eyes closed," he tells her, and he pokes her in the side with the point of his knife.

She makes a sound then like a baby sound, mewing.

"Just them keep closed," is his order, "and tell Jack."

The door opens on his side, air comes in, and she can feel the sun. He leaves the door open.

Corinne waits, her eyes closed, waits—

Opens her eyes, expecting to see the knife right in front of her and coming at her.

But he was way over there, off to the right, walking hurriedly through the rows of cars, walking away, hurrying.

Or *was* that him?

What just *happened*?

Had any of this even *happened*?

Tell Jack.

Dear God, dear *God.*

Had this even happened? What was this? It hadn't happened, she had blanked out, now she smelled the rotisserie chicken in the back seat, she could still smell *him*—

Corinne felt cold. She was cold, the car seat was cold.

She looked down.

She had wet herself, urinated on the seat of the Mazda, and it had gone down her legs, so that now she realized how cold it felt, cold on her legs and on the seat underneath her.

Her scream, before it came, built powerfully inside her, coiled there and soon came out on its own, a *howl*, as Corinne abruptly pounded her fists on the steering wheel, felt the cold seat underneath her, and *howled* in her car in the parking lot.

CHAPTER TEN

As soon as she could manage to open her purse and hold her cell phone and not drop it, Corinne pressed 9-1-1. Almost dizzy, trying to breathe, she told the dispatcher that she'd almost been murdered, here's what happened, this is the truth, a man with a knife got into my car and sat here with a *knife*, yes, this is where I am right now, I'm outside the Aldi's, *yes*. Yes, I'll wait for them, I'll be here. And she gave them the description of her car and what she looked like and what the man looked like and how bad he smelled.

Then she phoned Jack.

"It was him! Your *writer*! *Yes*! He was— Jack, it was *him*! Just please *get here*!" And she remembered to tell him, "Bring me some *dry clothes*!"

Two patrol cars arrived quickly, but the guy was long gone. Maybe the security cameras would show something. They'd see. But who knew? If the guy was mostly in Corinne's car and then got out and simply walked away—

Well, they would check.

"He knows us," she told the Palatine officers. "Or he claims he does. He knows my husband."

"Who is he?"

"I don't *know*! He's some *maniac*. He *writes stories*! My husband is an editor and this man sends him his stories. That's what he says. Dear God."

Jack reached the parking lot just as the last of the officers was finishing with Corinne's report. He had been running some errands—to the post office, to the hardware store—but had left everything in his buggy at the Ace Hardware and driven as fast as he could to get home for some dry clothes and then over to Dundee Road. He parked awkwardly and jumped out of his car and ran to Corinne and grabbed her. And she held onto him.

After a minute, he looked at the police officer, a tall red-haired woman, Officer Kelly, and asked her, "Did you find him?"

"No, sir."

Corinne told him again, "It was the same guy, Jack. It was him!"

"You know him?" Officer Kelly asked Jack.

"No. Yes. Kind of. This is very weird." He explained what he did for a living and about how packages had started showing up a year ago from this guy. He wrote, he was a very good writer, but his stories were strange, and he claimed he had actually killed people.

Officer Kelly said to Jack, "Your wife said you met him last week? Or recently?"

"Yes."

"In one of the forest preserves, or where?"

"Not the forest preserve. Shit, it's way out there, Officer."

"Can you show me where?"

"I can try. I'll try." He looked at Corinne and told Officer Kelly, "I'm scared. I was scared before, but I told the people I work with, and they figured he was just a nut. It's insane because he writes well. I mean, he seemed rational. He's a writer."

"Your wife says he tried to kill someone with a baseball bat in the woods."

"That's what it *seemed* like. It was dark, it was late, he threatened *me* with a *gun*."

"Let's go take a look, Mr. Mathis."

"It's pretty far out, like I said."

"I have a full tank of gas, sir."

Once Corinne had changed clothes in the restroom of Aldi's, it took them more than an hour to reach the forested area. It was nearly all the way out to Harvard, which is the end of the Northwest Metra line and as rural a community as one can find in that corner of Illinois. Jack did the best he could, but he'd been out here in the evening, of course, so the light was different, and now that he was trying to find out exactly where the guy had been—

"Here," he told Officer Kelly.

"You sure?"

"It's got to be. It was right after that bend back there. We're here."

Corinne had been silent during the drive. Annoyingly so, for Jack, who wanted her to go through every detail again and help him figure out who this madman was. Now, as Officer Kelly eased her patrol car down a gravel road that dead-ended where Jack thought that it should, Corinne, in the back seat with him, told him, "Euripides."

"What about Euripides?"

"He quoted Euripides to me."

Jack lost his breath for a moment. "Oh, Christ."

He saw Officer Kelly looking at him in her rearview mirror.

Corinne said, "He talked about *The Bacchae*."

As she put the car into Park, Officer Kelly asked Jack, still looking at him in the mirror, "What's the 'bahkee'?"

"It's a play. Eurpides is an ancient Greek playwright. It's a play he wrote."

"What kind of a play?"

"It's about people who go crazy and kill other people."

"Is it, now?"

"I know who he is," Jack told Officer Kelly and Corinne.

"Good."

"Only I don't know his name. He never gave me his name. He gave me that book of plays. When I was giving my talks. But that's been...five years ago."

"And you don't remember his name?" Officer Kelly asked.

"No."

"Well, please keep trying."

But she sounded as thought she didn't believe him.

He walked forward slowly, keeping his eyes on the trees in front of him and paying attention to any other landmarks he could remember, even though it had been dark when he was out here. Jack stopped then and nodded slightly.

"This is it," he told Corinne and Officer Kelly. "Over here."

He walked them across the field to the tree line, pointing at where he thought the .38 revolver had been.

"About right here. I'm sure of it."

But there was really no indication that a firearm or any-thing else had been thrown onto the grass there recently. It was just grass.

Jack led the way into the woods, took a wrong turn once, and swore out loud. He said to Officer Kelly, almost angrily, "I am *not* making this up!"

"I never said you were, Mr. Mathis."

"He was here. This is where we *were*."

"Take your time, sir."

He found what could have been tire tracks, two long ruts about the right width and dug into the soft earth there, where the trees were spaced widely. They looked like tire tracks, Jack told himself. But they went for only a few yards and then moved onto heavier ground.

"It was a dark truck," Jack told Officer Kelly. "Black. Red. Purple. Shit, I don't know."

"Purple?"

"No, not purple. Do these tracks help?"

"They could be from anything, Mr. Mathis. It's been raining out here. I can't tell you for sure that they're truck tires or anything else."

He walked around in a wide circle, looking for anything, signs of duct tape, pieces of a baseball bat. When he'd fin-ished and looked squarely at Officer Kelly, he nearly had tears in his eyes because of his frustration and anger.

"Am I going nuts?"

For the first time that afternoon, Officer Kelly showed a hint of a smile, a slight one. "I can't really say, Mr. Mathis. You sure this is where you think it happened?"

"It *did* happen."

"And you're sure it was here."

He walked back to Corinne and took one of her hands. "If it happened," he replied, looking at his wife, "this is where it was. And my wife is not making up the story about this guy pointing a knife at her in her car."

"No, sir. I'm not saying she is."

"I will find out who this maniac is," he promised.

"That's the very next thing I want to talk to you about."

On the drive back to Palatine, Jack did his best to recall whatever he could about the people who'd attended his lectures, but it had been so long ago, everything was vague. He kind of remembered a big man, middle aged, who seemed never to bathe, and he'd talked with him a few times. But that man hadn't been the only wannabe writer who'd given Jack manuscripts, hoping he would critique them, or who had passed along books of inspiration, classic novels by important writers.

"They were writers' groups," Jack repeated, as though that alone should make everything clear to Officer Kelly.

And that was it. He was drained and could come up with nothing more.

Officer Kelly left them by Corinne's Mazda in the parking lot, passed along her business card, promised to follow up with the police departments in both Palatine and Harvard, and urged Jack to get back to her just as soon he could with any other information he might be able to remember.

"I will, Officer."

But he didn't mean it.

Corinne insisted that she'd be fine driving herself home if Jack promised to follow close behind. When they parked in the condo lot, though, she looked around suspiciously during the short walk across the blacktop, and she regarded everything warily once they were inside their building—the hallway there, the metal doors of other people's homes. And even though security precautions made it necessary for anyone visiting to be rung in, so that it was unlikely that anyone was waiting around a corner as they made their way up the stairs to the second floor, Corinne remained nervous until they both got inside the front door.

Even then, she locked it as quickly as she could.

They hadn't eaten anything, and it was nearly eight o'clock in the evening, now. Jack put the rotisserie chicken she'd bought in the microwave to warm it up, then set it on the table so that they could pick at it. But he heard Corinne crying loudly and cursing angrily in the living room.

He went in and sat beside her on the couch and tried to hold her, but Corinne pushed him away. When she was done, she coughed and took in deep breaths, lots of air, and walked into the kitchen, ran cold water on a tea towel and wiped her face with it, then dropped into one of the chairs at the kitchen table.

Jack carefully came in and asked if she wanted anything.

"A glass of water. God, all I want right now is a glass of water."

He brought it to her and sat catty corner, cut some of the white meat from the breast of the chicken and chewed on it.

Corinne didn't even pretend to want to eat. She gulped down the glass of water, though, as if her ordeal had dehydrated her.

"Jack, dear God. I am so scared, I can't tell you how scared I am. This is not why I married you. This isn't why I'm here. Not to have this in our lives."

"I know."

She looked at him squarely and said angrily, "Find out who he is! Tell the police! Tell Emmett or whoever you work with to *find him*."

"I will, we will."

She got up and went to one of the drawers under the kitchen counter. She took out a tablet of paper that was there and a pen and brought them back to the kitchen table.

"I'm going to write down everything I can remember," she told Jack. "Everything I told the police and anything else I can remember."

"Good."

"But you call some motels and find out who has the cheapest rates because I cannot stay here tonight."

"All right."

"I cannot, Jack."

"I understand."

"Please. At least for tonight. He knows my *name*. He's *watching us*."

"Not tonight he's not. Not after that stunt."

"Just go call some places. I know what to take. Please. I want to write this stuff down."

"Eat something, too."

She didn't anything to that. Staring at the tablet of paper, Corinne said, "I could be dead right now. Buried in the woods somewhere. Because of some character who kills people and then sends you the stories. Because of fucking *Euripides*, Jack!"

He nodded, took in a breath—

Went down the hall into the spare room he used as his office and turned on the ceiling light, turned on his desk lamp, and from the middle drawer removed the phone book. Quickly enough he located a motel and took out his cell phone. Yes, just for tonight. My wife and me. We did some painting and just want to leave the windows open so that the place will air out overnight.

Then he went to the big bookcase he had against one wall, actually a couple of bookcases set up side by side. The titles once had been neatly arranged but now the rows of books were overwhelmed with companions stacked horizontally all across their tops.

He took down the Penguin Classics edition of *The Bacchae and Other Plays*, the Vellacott translations. Two dollars and fifty cents. It dated back to the 1970s.

Jack opened it and looked at the inside front cover. There, on the yellowing paper, was an inscription:

You inspire me, Jack. Thank you. C. E. B.

"*I know who he is.*"
"*Good.*"
"*Only I don't know his name. He never gave me his name.*"
"*You don't remember his name?*"
"*No.*"
But of course he did.

CHAPTER ELEVEN

They went to a motel just a few miles away, sufficient for Corinne to try to relax, at least somewhat, but close enough that either of them could return home for any reason if need be. Corinne waited in the car as Jack paid for the room. By the time he'd gotten their key card and carried Corinne's overnight bag into their little room on the first floor, she was past exhaustion and deliriously tired.

"I can't move," she told Jack. "I can't even think." She dropped onto the bed, curled up, and closed her eyes. Within a few moments, she seemed to have fallen asleep.

Jack turned on the light in the bathroom, just around a corner of the wall, so that it would brighten the main room sufficiently for him to find his way around, but he kept the remaining lights off. In the dimness, then, he sat in one of the two chairs positioned across from each other at the table in front of the heavily draped window.

He was as tired as Corinne, or nearly so. He looked at his wife and couldn't take his eyes off her. He loved her, and he knew that he loved her. There was no question about that, correct? But he sat there and looked at the wife he loved and whom he had shared so much with, and he thought about what she had told him and the police officers, and he thought about what he had said to her and to the police officers, and about what he had not said.

"Fucking Euripides, Jack!" and what that meant.

He knew what it meant.

You inspire me, Jack. Thank you. C. E. B.

Cordell Burgess.

He was sure that that was the name. It was too odd a name not to be him. As soon as Corinne had mentioned Euripides, it came back to Jack. Carl...Calvin...*Cagliostro*? And then the name had come right back to him, just like that, although he hadn't thought of the strange man, the strange smelly man, in years.

Cordell. And the last name was like Burke only with two syllables, maybe three syllables. Burkett. Burgett. *Burgess,* he had remembered.

C.E.B.

Funny name. Uncommon name. Jack had never done anything more than talk to the man twice at the library gatherings back when he'd talked about writing and publishing. There were a few of these groups in the northwest suburbs, and people from time to time had worked to get aspiring writers together at these meetings. Having local published authors and professional editors attend was a plus, so Jack had made it a point to attend a few of these, talk about what he did, offer some insights and advice.

And that was all.

He'd never coached any writers. Never led any workshops. Had had no desire to do so. At that time, a few years ago, he had still thought that he himself would continue writing, and he'd really had no interest in putting the personal effort into getting together with others once a month or once every other week.

There were a few people he remembered, though, who had shown promise, who talked intelligently, who paid attention to the markets and thought in commercial terms. He remembered a few of their names, the Ariels and Courtneys and Joshuas and Seans, some of whom without doubt were probably being published right now, if not by Everson then by someone else, because they had demonstrated talent and initiative and understanding of the business.

And then there had been the poets and the less commercially minded, the talented few who wrote and wanted to continue to write contemporary literary fiction, who wanted to offer their insights into the grand adventure of our being human, put into words of their own measure and mindfulness what they took to be the truth of us.

Cordell Burgess had been one of those.

Odd man. Middle aged, big, overweight, with the most singular eyes Jack had ever noticed in anyone, eyes that had depth and no depth at the same time, if such a thing were possible. Eyes to look right through you one minute, as flat and unemotional as a dead animal's, and then in the next, abruptly go deep, as if a trap had been lifted or a damper undone, and there was the depth behind the eyes, the hurt and emotion and honesty and pain. It was the damndest thing, standing there talking with such a man, passing the time, making small talk, and having this person look at you with dead eyes one moment and the next, regard you piercingly like some priest or poet or scientist, someone that compelling, that alive in the moment.

The eyes, and the size of him, and the fact that he had no yet joined the rest of the modern world in finding it necessary to bathe regularly, if at all. He'd had the hygiene of a street person and the vocabulary of a cosmopolitan littérateur, and how was one supposed to forget such a person—or his name?

Cordet, no, Cordell, yes, Burgess.

And that had been years ago, and Jack had moved on and had had no contact whatsoever with any of the other young writers he'd spoken with briefly back then. It had occurred to him over the years that you'd think that one or another of them would email him to follow up with a proposal of some kind or just touch base, but no.

The years had gone by until last year, when he'd begun getting the stories in the mail, and it had never occurred to him, not once, that Cordell Burgess could have been the author. He'd never actually *read* anything by Burgess at those library meetings, just spoken with him, and Burgess had never actually given Jack the intention that he had wanted to write, only that he was a literate, large, hygienically challenged man who, of all things, appreciated good writing. Of course, he had probably wanted to write someday. Everyone wants to write, or has tried it.

But to begin receiving remarkable little masterpieces in the mail and make the connection, years later, that the Smelly One himself had written such things?

Not likely.

But here it was.

You probably don't remember me, but thank you for inspiring me.

You inspire me, Jack.

"We must talk, Jack."

"I'm dying. I have cancer."

"You're the Chosen One."

Chosen for what?

To have his wife attacked and almost raped at knife point?

Chosen for what?

"If you'd hated what I was doing, why didn't you stop me? All you had to do was pull the trigger."

"Why didn't you stop me?"

"He's fucked up, Jack! And that's what makes him a good writer! There's no law against being a fucked-up individual who writes well."

Corinne, sleeping, grunted and began mumbling in her sleep. Mumbling, and moving her face around, only Jack couldn't tell what she was saying. Sounds, and she was angry as she said whatever she was saying with those sounds. Angry and afraid.

Jack looked at his wife and couldn't take his eyes off her. He loved her, and he knew that he loved her. There was no question about that, correct?

"Why didn't you stop me?"

So why don't you stop him, Jack?

He fell asleep in the chair and awoke just as the room was turning gray, the very first light of morning coming through the heavy curtains. Jack adjusted his posture—his neck hurt and one of his shoulders, too—but he didn't have it in him to get up and walk over to the bed and crawl in beside Corinne. Even as he thought about doing it, he knew it was a dream, and in a moment, he was asleep again, in a twisted posture as he sat in the chair.

When he woke up again, his neck and shoulder still hurting, he saw Corinne staring at him from the bed. He thought he'd had a dream in which he'd heard her crying, and now he realized that it had not been a dream, of course, but had indeed been his wife, crying. Her face was red, and her eyes. She was lying on her right side with her head up on the pillow, watching him.

His wife said to Jack, "I'm afraid of you."

He looked at her. Still not entirely awake, either of them.

Corinne repeated what she'd told him the night before. "I can't tell you how scared I am. This is not why I married you, Jack. This isn't why I'm here."

He said, "I know. I know that."

"He knows who we are."

"I understand that."

"Jack, how long has he been *watching* us? He acted like he knew *me*."

"I don't know."

"'You don't know.'" Her tone was snide.

He said, "Please, Corinne."

"He's been, he has been *watching* us or watching *me* and following me, and he knows who you are, apparently he knows *a lot* about—!"

"Corinne, *enough!*"

"No, it is *not* enough, Jack!" she said angrily, and sat up. "Enough?"

But she said nothing more, and Jack stood and rubbed his neck. It hurt like hell, now.

He went into the bathroom, and Corinne heard him urinating. Then he came out and rinsed his hands and dried them.

"I'm afraid of everything now," Corinne confessed. "What am I supposed to do? I'm going to have a *baby*, and this maniac is fucking following me with a *knife*?"

"He didn't—" Jack stopped himself.

"He didn't what?"

"Never mind." He stood there. Didn't move.

"What, Jack? Kill me? He didn't *kill* me?"

"Yes."

"That's fine. That is brilliant."

"He didn't kill you, Corinne, because it's me, he wants me. Whatever he wants with the stories and the, and his phone calls—"

"And the knife. Let's not forget the knife."

"Corinne, I *don't know* what he wants!"

"He wants stories, Jack! He wants his fucking stories! Whatever that means to you and him, *that's* what he wants! And you're supposed to understand that, okay? That's what he said!"

He walked back to the chair and sat in it again, stared at the floor.

"I read the stories, Jack. I read some of them. Okay?"

"What about them?"

"All of these people in his stories are completely lost. They're losers. They're...they die and they get to be reborn or they turn into ghosts. He means that life is like that. *His* life is like that. Jack, this is what he said to me, okay? His wife was killed. So it makes him crazy. Anything can happen. That's what he said. So if anything can happen and we're all going to die horribly, the only thing we can do is write stories about it. That's what he *said* to me. Is this what you and he talked about at the library? Because that's what his fucking stories are about."

Before he could stop himself, he told Corinne, "They're not 'fucking stories.'"

"What?"

He regretted saying it, or saying it in that way. But it was the truth. "They are not *'fucking stories.'*"

"Dear God."

"They are fucking *brilliant* stories. Okay? Corinne? And the fucker who writes these fucking stories is *insane.* But they are *not 'fucking stories'!*"

Quiet.

Quiet in the room, as his wife stared at him.

"Will you listen to yourself?"

Jack said, not knowing what else to do, trapped between his wife in this room and— What? Trapped between his wife and the fucking stories?

He stood.

Corinne asked him, "Where are you going?"

"I don't know." He turned and looked at her. "I'll get us some coffee."

"Get me breakfast. Because I am not going out there. Not yet."

"Corinne, you can't stay in a motel room forever."

"Not forever. Just until he and his brilliant stories get caught by the police or until you decide what you're going to do with him and his *brilliant stories*."

Tears started again, and Corinne tried to stop them, keep herself from really letting it out. "Jesus," she said, and looked away from Jack, embarrassed, and wiped her face with her hands. "I am not a person who gets afraid. I do not let people do this to me. I am not this way, Jack."

"I know that."

She looked at him again. "But this is like it happened on the news. Someone gets raped in an alley. Or people die. I don't want to be on the news. I want my life. I do not want this, this *fucker* out there tracking me down and sending you stories and—"

Terrible. A terrible stretch between them, as though the air itself, there in a motel room, was disturbed and they could feel it, like water being stirred up, maybe their souls or their psyches becoming disturbed, stirred up, becoming more and more unsettled, and certainly their marriage, now, as well.

Dear God, Jack thought, even their marriage?

"He will be stopped," he promised Corinne then. "One thing at a time. I just want this to be one thing, and then one more thing, and we'll do it that way."

"This is not a story, this is my life, and you better change your mind about what a goddamn story is and what my life is."

"I can tell the difference."

"Can you?"

"Damn it, Corinne! Now let go! Back up! Please!"

"Jack, get me some coffee. I'm ready to throw up. I have a headache."

"So do I."

She rolled over and curled up under the covers, and Jack undid the door and went outside and listened for the motel room door slowly to fall closed and to lock, which it did. Loud steady automatic powerful proud sound of the door locking and keeping killers out here and his wife in there, as good a sound as any and as good a sound as any that had ever happened or been described in a *fucking story.*

He walked to his car.

He needed breakfast.

He needed to breathe without Corinne's being there.

CHAPTER TWELVE

Jack picked up some bagels and orange juice and coffee and left them for Corinne in the motel room, on the table by the window. She was sleeping, or pretending to be sleeping. Then he drove to their condo simply for the sake of being there, to look around and assure himself that nothing had been disturbed, that Cor—

No.

He didn't want to think of that clown's name right now.

He needed to look around and make sure that the *writer*, the *maniac*, the *man with the knife who had been in his wife's car* hadn't broken in and done whatever he intended to do next.

It was fine. The condo was fine.

Jack went into the kitchen and took down the cordless phone handset from the base that hung on the wall, sat at the table, and phoned Emmett at home.

Emmett picked up, yawning and drinking coffee.

"We stayed at a motel last night," Jack told his boss. "She's scared. And really angry. At me."

"I don't blame her," Emmett told him. "Jack, he didn't molest her or hurt her, did he?"

"No, no. He was trying to get to me. I mean, by using Corinne, by scaring her or something."

"Do you have a gun?"

"I have a Swiss army knife and whatever's in the kitchen drawer. Now I wish I'd kept the .38."

"You told me you grew up in the country. And you used to shoot."

"I did."

"Then you need to have some firearms hanging over the fireplace. This is why we all need to go around armed. Jack, I'm serious. With this guy? Go out and buy a damned gun."

"I'll consider it."

"You going to be around later?"

"Why? You want to have some target practice?"

"I'm coming out by you to pick up something Sandy has at an antique shop. She does all this shopping online."

"Okay."

"Have some coffee ready."

"That we can do."

He undressed and took a shower, got into some fresh clothes, jeans and a shirt and sweater, and made himself a short pot of coffee. He thought about phoning Corinne to tell her what he was doing, that he was sitting and thinking, and maybe apologize to her for whatever he needed to apologize for. He decided that after he'd finished his coffee, he'd pull out his old files, things he kept in a bankers' box in the closet in his office, old book reviews and newspaper clippings, and make sure that this character really was who Jack thought he was.

But he had just finished his coffee when the phone rang. Of course it would have to be Corinne. Jack decided to rinse out his cup in the sink and let voicemail kick in so he could listen to her, see what kind of mood she was in.

After four rings, it clicked over, and Jack heard a masculine voice say, "Corinne? I know you must be there. Pick up the phone, please."

Trembling, Jack took down the handset. "It's not Corinne."

"Jack, is that you?"

"I know who you are!"

"Of course you do."

"Cordell...Burgess? Am I right?"

"You do remember me."

"And you're trying to *kill* my *wife*?"

"No, Jack."

"*No*?"

"I'm leaving that for you to do."

"Shut up!" He yelled it and slammed the handset down on the base.

In a heartbeat, the phone rang again. Rang and rang.

Jack watched it.

The recorder kicked on. "Pick it up, Jack."

Jack didn't move.

"Pick. It. Up. Jack. I was speaking metaphorically."

Jack took down the handset. "Don't you *ever* say that to me."

"And don't you ever pretend you don't know what I'm talking about. It took you long enough to figure this out. I've been hiding in plain sight, Jack!"

"Then where are you? Tell me where you are."

"Sitting at home. Talking to you."

"This is so— This is so fucked, you are so fucked up."

"We both are, Jack. But look at what I'm sending you."

"Don't send me *anything* more, and stay away from—"

"Seriously? No more stories?"

"No more, Cordell!"

"You don't mean that."

"I absolutely mean it."

"This from the man who took stories from me that I threw on the ground like they were garbage. From the man who thought I was so wonderful before—"

"*No more!*"

"Jack, you care about those stories as much as I do. I'm a sick man. I told you that. You're my last hope."

"Stop it."

"You are, Jack. Now listen to me. I do not want to die without having my say." His voice rose. "I absolutely will not put up with this, this *bullshit* from life without *having my say.*"

Jack waited. Cordell Burgess had gone into a sudden rage. That's all you could call it. Rage.

Shortly he calmed down, or seemed to, and Cordell asked, "Are you still there?"

"I'm still here."

"Jack, you helped me, and I want to help you. What I do is not normal, I know that. There is no normal. There's nothing, really. There's life, but so what? Am I right?"

"I've read the stories."

"I want there to be peace between us, Jack, because you're all I have. I'm a proud man. I come from *nothing.*

I come from *nothing*, Jack! And even that gets taken away from me. What lives?"

"Stories."

"Stories. I'm not insane. I simply see through the bullshit. I present the truth as clearly as possible. You can touch it. You feel it. Am I right?"

"*Enargeia.*"

"Yes. You know the term."

"Of course I know the term! It's a fucking literary—"

"Do you understand what I could have done yesterday to Corinne? And I didn't? What hurts more, Jack? That I *could* have? That I *didn't*? What's *real* to you? Wake up, Jack! That's the whole point! What do I have to—"

"Shut up, Cordell!"

"What else do I have to do for you?"

"I'm not you! You want me to be *you*!"

"You're me."

"*Never!*" he yelled, and banged the handset down again, hard, loud.

Now Jack couldn't breathe. His chest hurt. He was dizzy. He couldn't breathe. He went to the kitchen table and sat.

Not a heart attack. At least he wasn't having a heart attack.

"Do you understand what I could have done yesterday to Corinne? And I didn't?"

But he couldn't breathe...

"What's real *to you?"*

Cordell Burgess.

Cordell Burgess.

Jack went into his office, turned on the desktop computer, and as soon as he could, with his fingers shaking, searched for Cordell Burgess's first name and last name under as many different spellings as he could devise.

He went by city, by area. Burgess was not an uncommon name. He tried to recall where the manuscripts had been sent from, where most of them had been sent from. A pattern there?

Just look for Burgess.

But there were so many of them.

Fine, then. He'd track down every Burgess he could in the northwest suburbs, in Chicago, in southern Wisconsin, wherever. He'd find them. Phone them. As soon as he heard the voice on the other end of the line, he'd know whether to be suspicious or not.

And anyone who didn't answer the phone, he'd drive there.

Which was nuts.

How was he realistically going to do that?

Maybe it would be better just to sit at home and wait for him to show up, come around again? Apparently he couldn't keep away. Jack could tell Corinne to sit by the window with a camera and when she saw him, take his picture, get his license number.

This was nuts. This was all nuts, nuts.

Jack turned off the computer and stood still, trying to decide what to do with his frustration and anger. Hit the wall? Hit the computer?

The phone rang.

He ran into the kitchen, nearly tripping in the hallway, and almost yelled into the handset.

"*Hello*?"

"Jack?"

"Corinne."

"Where are you?"

"Home. I'm home."

"Is everything okay?"

"Everything is fine. I'm trying—"

"Well, not *fine*."

"Corinne, I'm sorry. I'm just trying to think. Please. I need to think."

"Jack, whatever you think you're doing...the police are handling this."

"Are they really?"

"Just come back here. It's too far for me to walk. I want to take a shower and get something to eat."

"I know. I'm coming."

"Now, Jack!"

"*Now*! I got it!"

He hung up, still not certain what to do, and decided the best thing, yes, was to get something to eat, calm down, get some fresh air, go out, get his wife.

"Don't you ever pretend you don't know what I'm talking about. It took you long enough to figure this out. I've been hiding in plain sight, Jack!"

If you're hiding in plain sight, Cordell, thought Jack, then I am finding you, I will find you, I will.

He opened the motel door quietly on the chance that Corinne might have fallen back to sleep.

She hadn't. She'd showered and was in her robe, standing in front of the big mirror in the back and combing her wet hair. Without turning around, in a flat voice, she said, "Food."

"Right now. We coming back here?"

"I don't know." She threw the comb into her overnight bag, which sat on the fake marble counter top, and turned and looked at him. "What do you think?"

"I'll do whatever you want. But Emmett called, and he wants to come over later on."

"Emmett?"

"He's worried about you. I can tell. And he's picking up an antique for Sandy. He wants us to have coffee ready for him."

"I can do coffee," Corinne said.

She went to the bed, where her overnight bag was lying open, and started putting her clothes and things into it.

Cordell smoked a Chesterfield as he sat in an old wooden Adirondack lawn chair once painted green and now with the paint peeling. He was in his back yard, just a few steps from his back porch, and could see the old barn from here, where he parked his red truck every day and where his dad had had his old band saw and wood-working tools and other things, and where his parents' '99 Taurus was, covered by any number of blue tarps to keep it relatively clean. Cordell started up the Taurus once a week, every Sunday, to keep it going, and it still ran well. And he could see the woods from here, where he had put the people he had freed, and once a dog, too, an experiment.

Storm clouds were coming in, the temperature was dropping quickly, and now the first fat drops of rain came. Cordell finished his cigarette and dropped it onto the ground, and he began to cry. The sound of the thunder and the storm coming did it to him, took him back to his childhood and made him cry. And the fact that Jack didn't understand him and that there was so little time left, so little time left. He leaned forward in the old chair and sucked in a great breath, then put his hands to his face and powerfully sobbed.

He could not help himself. Tears came, and great pushes of emotion that had been within him, like those storm clouds coming open, like trees losing their leaves in a fury. The sobs came and came and were the only sound in the back yard, as empty and dark as it was now, his old old sobs that disturbed the quiet of the back yard, and everything came back to him, his life, everything that he knew, his aloneness, his living sadness.

He was afraid. He was so afraid—of the dark, of the abyss, of the aloneness, afraid of the rain, the thunder, afraid of the wet grass, afraid of the chair he was sitting in, afraid of the trees around him, afraid

He thought of words, and of what he might yet write, what he might yet tell others, to those with the ears to hear. The pain he would speak of, the anguish within the mysteries that must be deciphered, the rumors about living that needed to be confronted, and the deep truths that come with our passing, the deep truths that come with trying not to be afraid of the dark, every truth.

The terror passed, and Cordell wiped his face.

But the afternoon was now cold and the grass wet, the air heavy with wetness, and the rain was coming down, all of it, and there was only him and what he held within him, what he desperately tried to free with words and their tricks, tried to confront and make sense of.

CHAPTER THIRTEEN

Lunch passed quietly. One-thirty on a Sunday afternoon at Café Fourteen in Palatine, a friendly crowded family place, lots of people and children, and John, the owner, as pleasant as your grandfather, welcoming everyone who came in with a smile and a handshake, noise coming from the kitchen in the back and laughter and smiles from the waitresses and the young Mexican-American guys busing the tables and refilling coffee cups. Jack watched Corinne as she ate as though she were an eggshell, thin and delicate, brittle, that was suddenly going to crash to the floor, her in pieces all over the floor.

"Is your omelet okay?"

"It's fine, but I think I'm getting a headache."

"We'll get you home."

"I can't believe how *exhausted* I feel. It takes everything *out* of you."

When they came into the condo, Jack went in first—maybe Corinne would feel better or safer if he did—and then carried her overnight case upstairs.

And got a chill in his stomach when he heard call up to him, "Jack, who called?"

He'd forgotten to erase the Cordell Burgess phone call. She'd seen the number on the readout on the phone, a big 1. One call.

He ran downstairs, yelling, "No one! Emmett!"

"Emmett's not 'no one.'"

He got into the kitchen just as she pressed Play.

"Corinne, it's no one. *Delete it.*"

At first she smiled when she looked at him—and then she understood and lost the smile. "Oh, God."

"*Please*, it was—"

"Corinne? I know you must be there. Pick up—"

She said, "He *called* here?"
Jack hit the Erase button.
"What did he say?"
"I told him—"
"You *talked* to him?"
"What am I *supposed* to do?"
"I don't know! Only don't *talk* to him!"
"Corinne, listen!"
But she was gone. "Jesus, Jack." Out of the kitchen, up the stairs, into their room.
He heard the door slam behind her.
Fuck it, he thought.
And, Fuck you, he thought.
What am I supposed to do?
Jesus, Jack...

As promised, Emmett came by a little after four. Jack let him in. Corinne had already come downstairs and started a half a pot of coffee, and she took a frozen coffee cake out of the refrigerator and warmed it up in the microwave. She seemed to be steadier, if not clearly in a better mood.

Emmett had walked in with something in a plastic Jewel grocery bag, but Jack didn't ask what it was. He assumed it to be whatever Emmett had said he was going to pick up for Sandy.

They sat at the kitchen table, the three of them in a circle. Ate cake. Sipped coffee. Emmett was careful about what he said and how he said it. He asked whether Jack thought he'd be coming into the office tomorrow, and Jack said, Yes, he probably would. Then the small talk dropped to nothing, and it was so quiet for a long minute, they heard the coffee maker sigh as though it were disappointed in them.

Finally Corinne said, "This has totally worn me out."

Emmett told her, "I can only imagine."

"The thing is," she said, "I'm lying down, and I'm trying to turn my brain off, and I can't. I start thinking about what he was saying when he was in the car. I was remembering things. It's as if I didn't hear them at the time, but now they're coming back."

Emmett asked her, "What did he say?"

"What he seems to say to Jack. That only Jack understands him. But here's what I started wondering about. Here's my question. What do writers want? I mean, not him, but writers, you as a writer."

Jack said, "To write stories."

Emmett said, "To get published."

Corinne looked at Emmett. "Exactly. Why write if you're not going to have anybody read your story?"

Jack was intrigued—and happy that Corinne was getting out of her bad mood. "But," he said, "some people would still write if they were on a desert island, even if there was never *any* chance that anyone would read what they wrote."

"You're right," Emmett agreed. "It's something they have to do. If Beethoven was on a desert island, he'd keep hitting a stick on a rock just to make some kind of music."

"But that's what this man is doing," Corinne told them. "It's like the kids painting in my class. They enjoy painting. Only maybe this man tried to get published and got turned down, so now he writes because he has to. But he's always been writing. If we want to know who he is," she said to Emmett, "then maybe he sent you some stories years ago, and you turned him down. Would you still have them?"

"God, no," Emmett told her. "If we kept every bad novel every writer sent us, we'd have to build a warehouse from here to Lombard."

Jack said, "But Corinne's right. He still keeps writing. Because he has to. Because...he's past worrying about readers reading him. He's too good for that, now, anyway. He knows no one's going to understand what he's doing. Maybe a few people."

Corinne said, "How many people even know what an en-jee-arr-uh is?"

Emmett was puzzled. "A what?"

"*Enargeia*," Jack told him. "Sophocles. Euripides. The Greeks. Awareness. Unbearable awareness. The artist wakes you up, you see life for what it is, and it scares you shitless. It's too much. He's doing that with his stories."

"Pity and terror," Emmett said.

"Pity and terror. It happened to him," Jack said, "and he's doing it to other people now, scaring them, killing them, and then he's putting it in stories so that anybody who reads his stories is going to feel it, too. They wake up. They look into the abyss. They can't stand it."

Corinne said, "Only he still doesn't have any readers. So who's he waking up?"

"He has Jack," Emmett told her. "And me. And now you. Apparently we get it. There are plenty of literate readers. Only he has to find a way to reach them."

Jack said, "Everybody else turned him down. They didn't see what he was doing. He was sending his stories to people who want the next big bestseller. They're not looking for art. They're looking for money. He's casting pearls before swine."

"And then you show up and you talk at the library," Corinne said, "and you tell him exactly what he wants to hear."

Emmett nodded. "He finally finds an editor who understands what he's doing."

"So he sends *me* his stories," Jack said. "Only he doesn't know whether he can trust me or not. So he's careful. He's anonymous."

Corinne said, "But he's dying of cancer. What about that?"

"He didn't always know he was dying of cancer," Emmett suggested. "Maybe it's a recent diagnosis."

Corinne said, "If we could find out who is doctor is, we could find him really fast. Only they can't tell us because it's against the law, right?"

"At least against their code of ethics," Emmett told her. "My guess is that he found out a little while ago that he has cancer, and that's why all of a sudden he's pushing Jack really hard. He's running out of time."

"Which is exactly what he told me," Jack said. "He wants to have his say. Here's what I think. He thought he had enough time for me to get the word out. Help him get into print. Reach an audience."

Emmett smiled. "Because he thinks you're as crazy as he is."

Corinne made a face

"My wife is not amused," Jack said to Emmett.

Emmett looked at her. "Corinne, I'm not serious. Come on."

Jack told him, "She takes this seriously."

Emmett was befuddled. "Really?"

Corinne said, "Emmett…please be careful here."

"I will! I didn't know!" He held his hands up in a gesture of sufferance, but he seemed truly puzzled.

"How would Sandy be?" Corinne asked him. "I married this guy because I love him, and I want him to succeed. He's a good writer. But he talks this guy's language. I'm supposed to feel comfortable with that?"

Jack said, "Corinne, *I'm* not comfortable with it."

She regarded him steadily and said strongly, "But that's what he's doing, Jack. It's sick, but he doesn't think so, and he thinks you understand."

"Well, I don't."

"Methinks you doth protest too much," Emmett said, but then: "Jack, seriously. We know that. Corinne, we all love Jack because he's just a mickle odd, as my grandfather would say."

Jack told him, "'Mickle' means a lot."

"No, it doesn't."

"Emmett, it does."

Emmett shook his head. "Seriously?" he grinned. "All these years, and I didn't understand what my grandfather was saying?"

"Did your grandfather have a mickle of things to say?" Jack asked him, smiling weakly.

"Yes. And now I feel a mickle dumb," Emmett confessed, and glanced at Corinne.

She was frowning.

"Sorry," Emmett said to her.

She shrugged. "I need a mickle bunch of advice on what to do next."

"Understandable," Emmett nodded.

"He wants us to feel what he feels," Corinne said. "And I do, now. What do rape victims do? They get raped, so how do they go outside their house anymore? The whole world is out there waiting to rape them again. That's what he's talking about. That's how he sees his world."

"But not exactly," Emmett told her, and faced Jack. "I mean, he did this to get to you. You weren't listening. Maybe you'll listen to Corinne?"

Jack said tensely, "This is between him and me. My wife has nothing to do with it. I don't even know what I did to set him off, and now he drags my wife and my, my future child into this. It's beyond sick."

"You have to look out for yourself and your lady, here," Emmett told him as he reached down and picked up his plastic grocery bag. He'd set it on the floor by his chair, and now he pushed his plate aside, set the plastic bag on the table in front of him, and took out a medium-sized box, brown with the printed design of wood grain. He lifted the lid to show the .22 Colt semiautomatic inside and a box of rounds.

Corinne looked at Jack but said nothing.

Jack asked Emmett, "Where'd you get this? At the antique store?"

"No, no, no. It's not even mine. It's my brother's. He didn't want it anymore. He gave it to me. I've never even shot it. I wouldn't know how to load it or clean it or anything."

Jack lifted it out of the box and released the clip from the handle. There were rounds in the clip. "Emmett, this thing is loaded."

"I didn't know that."

"It's been loaded all this time, guy."

Emmett made a face and went for another piece of cake.

"Jack," Corinne said, "I'm not sure I'm comfortable with this."

"You're not going to shoot him," he told Corinne. "And you're not going to carry it in your purse. But at least we have something."

"Just hide it," she told him.

"It's the Chicago way," Emmett said. "He brings a knife, you bring a gun."

Jack said, "Christ, Emmett, please."

"Once again, I don't know my boundaries," Emmett apologized, and raised a hand as a peace offering to Corinne.

"I know what you're doing," she told him. "I appreciate it. I do. But I'm not sure this is what I want to do, have a gun in the house."

Emmett asked Jack, "How about you?"

"Hey, I'm a gunslinger from way back in my frontier days in Ohio. Corinne—" He looked at her. "I'll hide it in a closet. Or under the nightstand. You won't know it's here."

"You really want to keep it?"

"Just until this is over."

She shook her head, said, "Fine, whatever, only I don't want to look at it," and picked up her and Jack's empty plates and walked them to the sink.

With her back turned to them, Emmett smiled at Jack and raised his right hand with the index finger out and thumb up, the way kids pretend they have a gun. He pushed his thumb down and lifted his hand as though it had recoiled.

Jack pursed his lips and replaced the Colt in the box. He took out the box of rounds and counted twenty bullets remaining, .22 longs. Then he put everything back in the brown plastic bag. "Thanks," he told Emmett.

"If I have your thanks, then my work here is done." He stood, picked up his own plate and coffee cup and walked over to the sink, where Corinne was rinsing the dishes. "No offense," he told her.

She smiled up at him. "None taken." She kissed the tip of her index finger and pressed it to his cheek.

Emmett told Jack, as he started to leave the kitchen, "Take tomorrow off if you need to. If Corinne feels better with that."

"We'll talk. Whatever she wants."

Not turning around, Emmett called back to Corinne, "Thanks, C!"

"Any time, Emmett!"

He and Jack went into the living room, and Jack opened the front door for him. Then he turned and called to Corinne, "I'm walking Emmett down to his car!"

"Okay!" from the kitchen.

Emmett was uncertain what Jack intended. "What's up?"

"When we're outside."

They took the stairs and went through the first-floor vestibule and across the blacktopped parking lot to Emmett's Lexus. The afternoon was cool. The breeze chilled them. Emmett opened the door behind the driver's side and lifted out a small box to show Jack what was in it.

"Three hundred and fifty bucks," he told Jack, displaying a cut-glass candy bowl about ten inches across. "We could get a candy bowl at the Dollar Store." He replaced the box on the floor behind the driver's seat.

Jack told him, "Emmett, I know who this is."

"Really?" Emmett closed the door and looked straight at Jack.

"It's a guy named Cordell Burgess."

"Doesn't ring a bell."

"We never *published* him, Emmett!"

"No, no, I'm thinking maybe someone said something somewhere."

"Nobody said anything. He's nobody."

"He doesn't write like 'nobody.'"

"I want to find him."

"Ask the police."

"*I* want to find him."

"Jack, no. Leave this to the professionals, okay?"

"As soon as I know where this fucker is, I'll tell them. I can't— It's hard to explain."

"It's not hard to explain. It's personal."

"This fucker played me, Emmett. He sucked me in with the stories, and he's a maniac."

"He didn't play you. Maybe he did. I think he knows you, Jack. He really does. Like I do. And Linda. And he's pushing you past the point where you want to be when it comes to this stuff, and it pisses you off."

"It's more than that."

"Look, he's trying to make you feel like a hypocrite because you won't kill somebody and then write a story about it. You have to admit, it's novel. No pun intended."

"Emmett, he attacked Corinne!"

"I know, I know. Jack, just look at his stories."

"I've read his stories, come on."

"No, *look* at them. You're the one always telling me that writers are all in their stories, and that's why their stories are so bad. *You* taught *me* that, Jack. Like every Stephen King protagonist is another fucking writer, and why can't he actually make the guy a circus clown or a fireman?"

"Because all of Stephen King's readers dream about being successful writers, too. They like reading about writers. They don't dream about being circus clowns."

"Really?"

"Sure. Only this guy isn't Stephen King. This guy is *good*. He's a *genius*."

"He's still a writer. And he's writing about himself."

Jack said, "The clues are in his stories."

"You don't need me to tell you this. You didn't think of it because you're so scared about what he did to Corinne."

"This is a good idea, Emmett."

"Which is why I have the office I have and you're still a lowly scrivener."

"Thanks."

"Not at all. Look, take tomorrow off. Come in on Tuesday. But be ready to get back to work, okay? Best therapy in the world. Corinne will be fine."

"What about this guy?"

"He'll call you. Or he'll send you another story, and then he'll call you, like he always does. And you can talk to him and do whatever you need to do to find out where he is and tell the police. Make it a conference call. Include me in."

"That's redundant."

"And tautological."

"I appreciate this, Emmett."

"Not a problem. You're my best editor, and I want you to stay safe and sound so you can keep editing those really bad novels that make us so much money."

"Thanks. I think."

"Hey, maybe we'll publish you someday."

"My stuff might be too tautological."

"Or this Burkett character. That would be strange."

"Burgess." Jack stepped back as Emmett opened his door and got behind the wheel.

"You just take care of your little girl and talk to the police. You're a scrivener. You're not a hero."

"I'm also as crazy as he is."

"Not quite. But that's why you're a good editor."

"See you Tuesday."

Emmett nodded, closed his door, and started the Lexus.

Jack waved to him as Emmett pulled out and drove down the lot. Then he walked over to the lobby door to his condo.

Three hundred and fifty dollars for a candy dish? he thought. Really?

He wasn't even sure that he and Corinne had a candy dish anywhere in their condo.

CHAPTER FOURTEEN

Jack had had one of the editorial assistants scan in and clean up every typewritten story this weird genius writer Burgess had sent him, going back for a year. He'd saved them on a disc at work and also on his thumb drive. Now, with Corinne upstairs once more, lying down again to rest before supper, Jack went into his office and took out the thumb drive, always there in his pants pocket.

For the next hour, Jack scrolled through the stories on his desk top. Did word searches in them, compared story documents side by side, shrank them and dumped them into the tray at the bottom of the screen to retrieve later, and tried to see whether any of these dots could be connected in any way, whether Cordell Burgess was telling more about himself than he realized, whether he was really actually honestly telling Jack who he was, Cordell Burgess.

Roads. Crossroads. Trees. A pair of tall old oaks. These appeared over and over in Cordell Burgess's stories. Trees and crossroads. Every story in the world has trees in it, probably, and every third story ever written has two roads intersecting.

But how many had two gravel roads way out in the middle of nowhere intersecting in the same vicinity as the pair of tall old oaks?

And a few miles down the road from a small country store?

Cordell had three stories with those elements in them. And two with just the country store.

The two old oak trees that stood tall and gray like dead bodies with their arms stretched out, like long tree arms—were they the same trees that Jack had noticed near the woods where Cordell had directed him, where Cordell had dared Jack to shoot him, where Cordell had killed a woman with a baseball bat?

Thirty-seven stories. That's what Jack had, some of them only four or five thousand words long, a few of them twenty thousand words or more.

One of the earliest ones had the crossroads and the trees in it. So did one of the recent ones. Jack had never before noticed this because the stories were not, after all, about trees. The stories were about a man in pain dying or meeting ghosts or learning to fly or separating into several separate people or about something else happening, something fantastic that felt real, like a myth or a fairy tale, shockingly and frighteningly and abruptly real—*enargeia*.

And yet...they were indeed stories set in the woods near an intersection.

The same woods, Jack realized.

The same trees.

And the small country store? He'd never noticed it when he'd driven out to see Cordell kill a woman, but that had been at night. And he'd been very distracted, obviously, when he'd gone out in the same direction in the back of Officer Kelly's patrol car.

What else?

Colors appeared endlessly in his stories. The man wrote in Technicolor, but the effect was subtle until you slowed down and just started counting the number of colors on each page.

But that wasn't going to help.

Neither were the insights into human nature and all of the fear and anger and rage in the stories.

There was a well in somebody's cellar in one of the recent stories. How do you check to see if there's a deep well inside somebody's house?

But if where Cordell had asked Jack to meet him was in the general area where Cordell lived, where a *Burgess* lived—

The tape.

The stupid tape that Cordell had left for Jack at the coffee bar in the bookstore.

Jack ran out of his office, out the front door of the condo, and down the stairs to his car. Got in, tried to remember what he'd done with the tape—

It was still there, on the seat on the passenger side, underneath the old copy of *Scientific American* he kept there in case he had to wait in traffic for a long time and needed to occupy himself with something better than brain-numbingly bad local radio broadcasts.

He put in the tape, listened, Fast Forwarded, listened, hit Rewind—

"...simply feel that I have to be sure that I can trust you. Does that make sense? That's the only—"

Harsh coughing, very loud, as the man struggled for breath. And then, right there, Jack heard the clanging sounds of the railroad crossing warning bells, followed, about thirty seconds later, by the whooshing noise of that train passing by. More clanging, and then Jack heard Cordell's truck, it really was an old truck, absolutely, not a van, accelerating and making noises as it bumped over the rails.

Railroad crossing.

More sounds. Traffic. Cordell talking—

"I'm a good judge of people. I read people quite well, Jack. It's a gift."

—and then the crunching and popping of the truck tires on gravel, and the engine being turned off.

"That's all for now, Jack. I'm glad you're the one who likes my stories. I'm glad we talked about meeting. I'll phone you tomorrow, and we can talk some more."

Click.

Silence.

Jack sat. Thinking.

Crossroads. Trees, those trees. The woods where he had met Cordell. How close could that be to railroad tracks, to the Metra line. Was it a Metra line? They'd been nearly all the way out to Harvard, the end of the Northwest commuter line.

Now he got out of his car and hurried back inside, up the stairs, through the door, into the office.

Corinne was still upstairs. Totally quiet. He didn't hear her. But he could feel her, her presence, almost as if she were in the room with him. It was a kind of pressure in the room.

He went online and did his search again for Burgess and looked to see how many Burgesses there were around Harvard, Illinois.

Only a few, and none of them named Cordell. A Gary. A Robert. An Anna Rose.

So who were these people? Relatives? No relation at all? The name was common enough for a dozen Burgesses to live in the same place and never be related.

Jack pulled up a map of Harvard and clicked on the scale marker a couple of times so that the image on the screen pulled back. He found the road he'd directed Officer Kelly to take to get him to the woods where Cordell had killed the woman. He found the woods.

He clicked on the map and slid it around so that the cartoon woods and downtown Harvard both were on the screen.

He enlarged the map. The woods and downtown were still on the screen. So they were close together, the woods where Cordell had *killed a woman in cold blood with a baseball bat* down here in the lower right hand corner and Harvard up here, at about nine o'clock or ten o'clock on the left hand side of the screen.

And there were the railroad tracks, the Northwest commuter line cutting right through the middle of Harvard, Illinois, way out there in farmer land, barn land, soybean land.

Jack enlarged the map, coming in close so that he could estimate where the Metra crossing in downtown Harvard was in relation to any of the Burgess addresses he'd written down.

There was only one.

Robert Burgess lived on a country road not far at all from downtown Harvard. If you were driving your truck and you had to wait for the Metra train to pass, you'd be sitting there listening to the bells and the rush of the train, and then when the train had passed, you'd bump over the rail lines and go down the road to the right, make a left, make another right, make another left, and follow this road while you're talking into your old tape recorder—

"That's all for now, Jack... I'll phone you tomorrow, and we can talk some more."

—and by the time you were saying, Hey, we can talk some more, you'd be at this part of the old road, and there was a long driveway there—at least on the aerial view it looked like a long driveway—and at the end of the driveway was an old barn and a house and so many trees that Jack couldn't see anything else on Google earth satellite.

This is where the man driving the truck *Cordell Burgess* had crossed the railroad line and driven while he talked to Jack *"That's all for now, Jack"* and then had parked his truck and turned off the engine, just a few days before he drove back down his driveway and down the road and across the railroad tracks and found a woman and drove with her here, here in the lower right hand corner, and baseball-batted her into a nasty fearful brilliant cold delicious terrifying insightful human story.

Killed her, actually.

This had to be the place.

But...*Robert* Burgess?

Who was *Robert* Burgess?

The father? An uncle? A fake name?

Jack wanted to leave now. He wanted to leave before Corinne came downstairs to make supper, before anything else could happen, and drive out there to make sure.

He had no phone number, there was no phone number for a Robert Burgess or a Cordell anywhere online. Private number, clearly.

Jack would have given anything at that moment to have had Caller ID on his office phone or the phone in the kitchen.

But it didn't matter.

He was sweating, yet he was cold. He was afraid. But he was happy, almost, and not sure what else to do.

He felt it in his gut, felt it to be absolutely true, that he knew now where Cordell Burgess lived. The fucker actually had an address, and he lived there.

He was real, or still real. Always had been real, the person behind the stories. The man in the woods. The man in Corinne's car.

"That's all for now, Jack… I'll phone you tomorrow, and we can talk some more."

Yeah, we're going to talk, mother fucker, Jack thought. We're going to talk some more, you can bet we're going to do that.

All through supper, he thought about finding some excuse to tell Corinne something, anything, because Jack wanted to go out there, go to the address he'd found online and find out for sure that Cordell Burgess was there and confront him.

And shoot him, perhaps? With Emmett's gun?

He allowed himself to fantasize about that for a few moments, but that was all.

Corinne was very quiet, too, through supper, but when they were done with their microwave meatloaf and mashed potatoes, she told Jack, "I want some fresh air."

"Okay."

"Just walk around. For ten minutes."

"Then let's go do it."

She didn't want much to talk. It was past twilight, almost night, and the street lights had come on throughout the complex where they lived, a dozen buildings with apartments and condos. They walked down the main driveway until they came to a path that cut through tall trees and then behind some buildings, and there was the pond they liked to sit by when it was warm. A retainer pond, actually, Jack thought, but here they could relax, watch the ducks with their little ones in the spring, and sit on the wooden benches that were there under the lights.

So they sat. Jack had on a light jacket and Corinne had thrown on a sweater because it was chilly and damp. The rain from this morning was still wet in places on the grass and in depressions on the walkway.

After a minute, Corinne said, "This is what I needed."

"You want to get some ice cream or anything?"

There was a quick-stop market nearby.

"No. This is good. What I really want now is a cup of tea."

"Then let's go make you some tea."

As they walked back to their condo, Corinne looked around. Jack watched her as she did it. He could tell that Corinne really wanted to watch the pavement and relax, but she'd look up, look around, look at trees, look at buildings, look back at the trees.

Is he there? Or there? Or hiding over there?

As they reached their condo, Corinne wordlessly put out her right hand and touched Jack's left and held it, and so they walked, holding hands.

Later that night, after tea, after turning the lights off and checking every door and window twice, they went upstairs and lay beside each other. Corinne didn't want to make love, but she wanted Jack to hold her, and so they fell asleep that way.

He was more tired than he realized, and he needed the sleep.

He found himself wondering, though, weakly, as he rolled over in the middle of the night and came half-awake, whether Corinne was holding onto him because it felt protective, as if he were protecting her, or if she were holding onto him to stop him for some reason, prevent from leaving or going somewhere or doing something.

He thought it, and realized that it was part of the funny imaginings that come when we are half-asleep, and so dismissed it.

Stop him from doing what?

And he went back to sleep.

He got up at his usual time Monday morning and told Corinne that he felt like going to the office. Really? she asked him. Half a day, he told her. I'll be back after lunch. But I want to.

He gave her no more reason than that and actually left with his briefcase. Corinne watched him from the living room window as he came out of the building and crossed the blacktop to his car. After all, she thought, apparently he really is going to the office.

She sat for a moment in the kitchen, finished the cup of coffee she'd started, then went upstairs to their bedroom and from her purse took out Officer Kelly's business card.

It was already showing signs of wear. Corinne had thumbed it several times in the motel room, and last night when Jack thought she was sleeping, and now here she was, looking at it again.

You're going to wear the ink off it, she told herself.

Then she reached for her purse again and lifted out her cell phone.

CHAPTER FIFTEEN

Nine-thirty-five in the morning. Right on schedule, the 640 Metra train came through downtown Harvard on its way into the city. Jack sat in his Toyota, first in line to cross the tracks once the bells stopped dinging and the gate arms rose.

It had been drizzly all morning, but now the rain started falling heavily. With the overcast skies, it felt like deepening twilight instead of the middle of the morning.

As the 640 passed, Jack hit Play on his dashboard audiotape player.

Cordell said, "I think you're a bright man, Jack."

If he was right about which house Cordell Burgess lived in, he should be able to follow the map he had called up online and time his driving to the sounds on the tape. Hit the gravel driveway at the same time that Cordell did in his truck.

Jack moved through one intersection and almost missed the turn at the second, but he braked hard, slid slightly on the asphalt, and ignored the driver honking behind him.

This narrow two-lane road very soon became hemmed in with trees on both sides, heavy woods exactly like the denseness of the forest preserve. There was just enough daylight, even under the heavy rain clouds, for Jack to see well enough ahead of him and guess that he must be coming up on the Burgess farmhouse.

"I read people quite well, Jack. It's a gift. So I could tell, even that soon, that you and I were the same kind of person underneath."

And this should be it. He should just about be there...

"That's all for now, Jack. I'm glad you're the one who likes my stories."

As he heard the sounds of gravel under truck tires, Jack pressed Stop and took his foot off the accelerator so that the Toyota gradually slowed. The road took a slight bend to the right, and as it did, Jack saw ahead of him, silhouetted against the gray and purple stormy sky, a line of trees that was precisely as Cordell Burgess had described it in one of his stories.

And there was the gravel driveway, on his right.

He pulled in very slowly and turned off his headlights as he did.

A rural mailbox sat on top of a rusted metal post that leaned slightly. Jack couldn't see the writing on it from behind the wheel of his car. He got out of the Toyota and unzipped his jacket so that he could pull the top of the jacket over his head as a hood, then walked through the puddles of water in the gravel and leaned close to the mailbox.

The painted numbers were almost completely worn off, and some of the letters of the name, but it was clear enough who lived here: BU GE S.

Jack got back into his car and continued slowly up the long gravel driveway. The rain continued, running in long streams down his windshield, and in his mind he saw this driveway and the house and old barn and trees up ahead, coming into view, as he had more or less imagined them when looking at the aerial Google Earth view on his monitor screen last night.

The driveway ended in a wide area of gravel and mud. There were grooves in the gravel, well-worn ditches caused by the same tires moving over the same path, the truck, no doubt, as Cordell Burgess drove it up here and then into the old barn off to the right.

Jack stopped his car, put it into Park, and opened his door. He stepped out and stood behind the open door and held his left hand over his head to act as an umbrella, to keep at least some of the slow rain from getting his hair too wet.

To the left was the farmhouse, larger than he thought it would be, but it was in the desiccated condition he had expected: white paint peeling off the old clapboards, sunken wooden steps leading upward to an enclosed back porch that, startlingly, was not the same color as the house but instead was a bright yellow, of all things. Jack could see a large French window on this side of the enclosed porch up there. The window had been lifted so that only an old screen was there, an old screen so rotted that it had a dozen holes in it. Probably Jack could have put a finger through that ancient screening and it would have gone straight through like going through dust.

But was Cordell Burgess here?

Jack didn't know what to do now. Walk up onto the back porch? Go around to the front of the house and knock on the front door? Assuming that there *was* a front door around there, facing the wide lawn that Jack had seen from the driveway. Or just leave?

He told himself to get back into his car, close the door, make a U-turn, and go back down the drive—

Except that there he was now.

Cordell Burgess.

Coming around the barn, a shovel in his right hand. Dirty, with mud on him, and dressed in jeans and a flannel shirt, no jacket, and wearing a worn John Deere baseball cap to keep the rain out of his eyes. He coughed. Jack heard the cough coming through the misty air just as he saw Cordell Burgess, the heavy middle-aged man Jack remembered, coming around through the grass and stepping onto the gravel and then stopping.

He stared at Jack.

And smiled.

He was perhaps fifty feet away, across the wide gravel area, and smiling as though genuinely happy.

"Here we go," Cordell said, and cleared his throat again. "Is that you, Jack?"

Jack didn't say anything.

Cordell started walking forward.

Jack told him, "Do not! Just stay right there, stop right there."

"Understood." He kept his smile going. "Now you're like one of the characters in my stories, am I right?" Cordell asked him. "That's what this is. My characters get into situations and it's like they're in a dream. Is this like a dream for you, Jack?"

"I don't know. Just stay there."

"I'm not moving. How'd you find me?"

"You leave clues in your stories."

"Do I? Clues? Funny." Cordell shook his head. "Then they're clues that you're the only person who's found them. No one knows I'm out here."

"Is your name really *Robert* Burgess?"

"That was my father. You want to come in? Jack, can I get you a beer? You want a Coke?"

"Jesus Christ, no."

Cordell yelled at him then, losing the smile, viciously yelling it, "Then why the hell are you here, Jack? Why are you *here*? You want *me* to tell you why?"

"I know who you are, Cordell! I'll tell the police who you are!"

"Apparently you haven't done that *yet*!" He started walking forward again.

Jack yelled at him, "Don't you come near me! Don't you touch me or my wife ever again, Cordell! You scared my wife and you, you scare *me*!"

"Apparently you're not scared enough! But you're here, Jack. That is a big step."

"Stop!"

Cordell did so, standing in the rain, now about thirty feet away. "You know why you're here, Jack? Want me to tell you?"

"You tell me." And then: "I'm here to warn you to *stay away* from me and my wife!"

"Jack, we're connected, okay? You don't want to think about that. It offends you. But it's about the *stories*, my friend! It's not about you *or* me, Jack. We're both scared! Don't you think I'm scared, too?"

Jack watched him. Cordell remained where he was. Despite himself, Jack, still standing behind his open car door as though it were a shield and he were facing an ancient enemy or wild animal with only that shield for protection—despite himself, aware that Cordell was trying to draw him in, Jack asked, "What are *you* afraid of, Cordell?"

"Jack, I'm afraid of the stories. And of you. And your wife. I'm afraid of everything. I'm afraid of rain and the, the clouds, the weather, spiders, everything. Jack, why *wouldn't* I be afraid of everything now?"

"All right, that's all," Jack said, and started to get back into his car.

"Jack!" Cordell walked forward again.

Jack got out and warned him, "Stay where you *are*, Cordell!"

"I was never going to kill Corinne. You know that, right? It's not about her. But I had to contact you. How do I *reach* you? You know? Through your wife, am I right? It's always the wives, isn't it?"

The sky made sounds above them, thunder, and the rain began to lift, not coming down as hard.

Jack asked him, "Did you kill *your* wife, Cordell?"

Cordell coughed—a terribly long cough from deep inside him, a long awful cough, a sound emitted by a dying man. He spat into the gravel, and Jack saw that Cordell Burgess's spit was red with blood.

Cordell smiled, cleared his throat, wiped the back of his right hand across his wet lips, and said, "Did *I* kill my wife? I'm not sure. I mean, since I was in the car with her, and we were arguing—I admit it—and then we got hit by the truck. You know how I am, Jack. I'm like you. I was going on and on about stories and how important they are, and I was drunk, I was a bit drunk, I will admit that. I was talking about creativity and the falling bridge, and I distracted her. Same way I distract you. So...*did* I kill her?"

Jack stared at him. Said nothing. Was powerfully aware of the rain in the air, the rain shiny on the gravel, the thousands of pieces of gravel there in the wide area between himself and Cordell Burgess, aware of every detail around both of them and between them, shiny pieces of gravel, shiny leaves on bushes and flower petals over by the back porch, yellow paint on the porch, and how cool the air was, almost chilly, and so heavy and damp with all of the rain.

"Maybe *you* killed her, Jack!" Cordell Burgess laughed.

"What does that mean?"

"You're going to kill somebody someday, and you're going to take their energy and eat their heart the way cavemen did, and then you're going write something so incredible you won't even know it's you who wrote it. Stories you never believed possible. I read some of your old books, Jack. It's in there. You're that good."

"I am not that good. And I won't kill anyone."

"You want to start with me?" Cordell Burgess asked him.

Jack said, "I have had enough. None of this makes *any sense*! You don't make *sense* anymore, Cordell! Just stay away!"

"Do you want more stories or not, Jack?"

"Stay away from *me* and stay away from my *wife*!"

"You going to tell the police, Jack, or do you want more stories?"

Jack didn't answer him. He got behind the wheel of his Toyota, slammed his door closed, locked it, locked all of the doors, and put the car into Reverse.

Cordell walked slowly toward him, yelling to make sure that Jack would hear him and pay attention. "We're capable of *anything*, Jack! Tell the truth! All the other books are lies! All the other stories are *lies*! We're the only ones telling the *truth*!"

Jack turned the wheel so that the car backed around in the gravel. He looked into his rearview mirror and saw Cordell standing in the rain a short distance behind him, not moving, simply watching him, yelling.

"*Anything* could happen next, Jack! What do you think life is for? Tell them the *truth*!"

Jack shifted into Drive, gunned the Toyota, and steered as fast as he could down the long driveway, kicking up gravel behind him—

"*Tell them the* truth*!*"

—and tried to see as well as he could through the fogged windshield while he turned on the air conditioning to clear the glass inside and continued to get away away away down the long gravel driveway, away from Cordell Burgess Cordell Burgess Cordell Burgess.

Officer Kelly agreed to meet her for an early lunch at the Subway off Northwest Highway in Palatine, the little plaza with the Ace Hardware and the Dollar General. Corinne told her that that would be fine. She'd be there

And she managed it, too. Looking around carefully as she left the condo.

Keeping an eye on traffic in every direction.

And driving through the parking lot until she saw Officer Kelly's patrol car so that she could be sure that she was there.

Officer Kelly, seated in one of the booths, was already working on a salad as Corinne walked in. Too nervous to put food on her stomach, Corinne bought a bottle of water and slid into the booth opposite Officer Kelly.

"You're not eating?"

"I'll be okay."

"Mrs. Mathis? Or Corinne?"

"Corinne. I really appreciate this."

"Tell me what you think is going on."

"Jack knows more than he's telling me."

"About the man with the knife?" Officer Kelly asked her.

"Yes."

"Do you want us to question him? Jack?"

"I don't know." Corinne frowned and looked down the aisle behind Officer Kelly that led to the restrooms as though expecting someone to appear. "He's acting like he sees this as his personal responsibility. He wants to find this man. It's stupid. It's dangerous."

"Is that what you think is making your husband not talk to the police?"

"Yes. What do I do?"

"Corinne, you have your life and the life of your baby involved here."

"Oh, God, I know that."

The radio on Officer Kelly's shoulder talked, and she reached up to it and turned the volume down. She took a sip of her Coke and told Corrine, "Here's what should concern you. This man with the knife knows your husband, or claims he does. Your husband takes me out to Timbuktu to find a place where this man allegedly killed someone. Why is your husband behaving this way? Has he done this before?"

"No, never. All that's happened is that he's been getting stories from this man, and then the man tried to trick Jack. He got him out to the woods. He phones him at the office."

"And you don't know who it is?"

"God, no."

"Whoever he is, are he and Jack doing something together?"

"See, I don't even want to think that. You mean, something illegal? Jack doesn't hurt people. He doesn't play games! Is that even possible?"

"I don't know your husband. Is it?"

"No!"

"My honest opinion?" Officer Kelly said. "Your husband is in some kind of difficulty. It's drugs, or—"

"Jack? Not Jack!"

"—or—listen to me, now—or you're going to have start looking at some other possibilities. I have no reports of anyone missing that hasn't turned up. Unless your husband's friend imported this alleged victim from Canada, something else is going on."

"You think Jack is crazy."

"Look at his behavior. He says he knows this man, and this man accosts you. Your husband has gotten involved in something dangerous. Would Jack deliberately put you and your child in danger?"

"Never."

"But he's done precisely that. He needs to explain to you what's going on, whatever it is about this writer or whoever this is who attacked you."

"Can't you do anything?"

"I can talk to Jack. That's all I can do."

"You can't help find this man?"

"Where do we start? It sounds to me like we start with Jack."

Corinne shook her head and made a sound of frustration. "It all comes back to *him*!"

"If this is someone he works with or whoever this is, your husband needs to make a choice between his job and his family. If he's involved in something illegal, he needs to talk to us right now."

"Dear God. He's *always* been this way about this job. He's great. His boss loves him. They all love him. He's not... crazy!"

"Then this friend of his is, and he's getting Jack into serious trouble. He's no friend."

"I don't like to think of him being that way," Corinne confessed. "He's not deliberately keeping any information from me. He wouldn't do that."

Officer Kelly said nothing.

"I think he wants to be a hero and find this man himself because he's a good writer."

"The man who attacked you?"

"Yes."

"This is why Jack is compromising your safety? Because this other man is a writer?"

Corinne was quiet for a long minute. Then she said, "It's about how this man writes. Jack does this for a living, and this man writes brilliantly. He tells stories about people who are so scared, it's like people in ancient Greek plays."

"I never read any of those plays."

"It's— The ancient Greeks. They created the first stories, the first art. They thought that life was so horrible, we try not to look at it. We want to avoid it. It's like a really bright light. You can't look at it directly. But when things happen, they hit you hard, and then you really do have to face life. It's like looking into the bright light."

"And that's what this friend of Jack's writes?"

"Yes. This is why he thinks Jack is so important and understands him."

"So he's playing on Jack's ego."

"I guess."

"Interesting." Officer Kelly finished her lunch and picked up the loose straw wrappers and bits of lettuce scattered on the table top. "I don't know anything about plays. But I know that your husband is in some kind of difficulty, and before anyone else gets compromised or you get hurt or he does, he needs to tell us who this man is. Have him call me."

"I will."

"I wish I could offer you more than that, but this is what we do. We usually show up after somebody's made a mess. I'd rather prevent the messes in the first place."

Corinne nodded quietly. Officer Kelly stood and adjusted her belt around her waist.

Corinne looked up at her. "Have you ever been married? Can I ask? Are you married?"

"Yes. I'm married."

"Jack and I, we're a team, we're partners," Corinne told Officer Kelly. "We help each other out. We've always wanted to be this way for each other. And I *know* how talented and determined he is. And I support him, no matter what. But I am not prepared to have this character in our lives like this. This was never part of the, part of our plan." She stood and looked Officer Kelly in the eyes. "So...I'm scared."

Officer Kelly told her, "I think you should be."

CHAPTER SIXTEEN

"What do I do?" he'd asked Emmett days ago, a long time ago.

"Ignore him, Jack."

"You think this guy is going to be ignored?"

"Absolutely. I've seen it before. He's just like every other case history out there who insists that he's the next great genius. Pretty soon he'll start bothering someone else."

Not quite, Emmett. Not quite.

He drove and drove and drove, remotely aware that he was stopping for traffic lights when they turned red, automatically slowing down as he steered around bends, driving as though he were under water, everything thick and murky, and with some part of him aware that he drove past the country store that had figured in the stories.

So now he knew where the country store was.

"Do you want more stories or not, Jack?"

"Stay away from me *and stay away from my* wife!*"*

"You going to tell the police, Jack, or do you want more stories?"

More stories.

More stories...

Finally he had to stop because he was nearly out of gas. The red warning light on his dashboard had come on.

How long had it been on? And he hadn't even noticed before now?

What if he'd run out of gas and been unable to leave Cordell Burgess's house?

Dear God.

He pulled into a Citgo station and got out and walked into the store and gave the clerk a twenty-dollar bill and came back out and started pumping gas as he always did.

"You just take care of your little girl and talk to the police. You're a scrivener. You're not a hero."

"I'm also as crazy as he is."

"Not quite. But that's why you're a good editor."

His hand was shaking as he held the gas pump dispenser.

I'm as crazy as he is…

As he reached the outskirts of Palatine and came onto Northwest Highway, almost home, Jack woke up, found himself, felt that he was breathing normally again, but was still not sure what to do next.

All he wanted was for everything to stop, for Cordell to stop killing people and stop bothering him, and if that also meant that Cordell Burgess should stop sending him stories, then do that, please do that, stop sending me stories.

"This guy of yours, this writer. Brilliant. He's everything you said, Jack. You have to try to find out who he is."

"Jack, we're connected, okay? It's about the stories, *my friend! It's not about you or me, Jack. We're both scared! Don't you think I'm scared, too?"*

He got home, parked in his spot across from the condo, turned off the car, but was afraid to get out.

"Jack, I'm afraid of the stories. I'm afraid of everything. Why wouldn't I be afraid of everything now? Anything could happen next, Jack!"

He noticed that Corinne's car was not in the space next to his.

She wasn't home.

Where was she?

"Anything could happen next, Jack! What do you think life is for?"

"Corinne!"

He yelled it as he unlocked the door and came into their living room. Heard nothing. Went into the kitchen to see if there was a note there, or even a phone message.

A phone message with a *blinking red light…*

But, of course, she wouldn't have phoned him at home. She would have phoned him on his cell. So had she tried? And he'd been so distracted that he hadn't even heard his cell phone ring?

He pulled out his phone—

Nothing, no message.

But he couldn't have gotten to her that fast, could he? Cordell? Even *he* couldn't have beaten Jack home in time to—

But he didn't have to beat him. All he had to do was phone Corinne and tell her something that would get her out of the house—

"Corinne? I work with Jack, and there's been an accident! Please hurry!"

—and he would have her, he would have Corinne and this time, with his knife—

"Anything *could happen next, Jack! What do you think life is for?"*

This time—

"Jack!"

Corinne.

She called to him as she came through the front door. He heard a bag in her hand, a shopping bag rustling.

He ran to the entranceway to the living room.

"Jack, are you okay?"

"Yes." But his voice was weak.

"You're pale. What happened?"

"I was worried. I came home, and you weren't here."

"Oh, Jack." She smiled, crossed the room, kissed him—it was rather a cool peck of a kiss, the kind she might have given an acquaintance—and set her bag down in the little hallway leading to the stairs going up to their room. "Did you go to the office?"

"No."

"No?"

"Kind of. I got on the train and got downtown, but I didn't feel like going to the office, so I didn't. I came back."

She looked at him.

He thought, I just lied to Corinne.

"Oh," she said.

Why did I lie to her? What am I holding onto? Why would I lie to her?

Corinne said to him, "Jack, come and sit. I want to talk."

"Okay."

She went around and dropped into the couch and tapped the cushion next to her. "Please," she said.

He nodded and sat beside her.

"Jack, I called Officer Kelly this morning. She and I had a talk."

"Okay."

"I'm so worried. Not just about this writer but about you."

"I guess I can understand that."

"If he *is* a writer."

Now he sat up. "Corinne, if he '*is*' a writer?"

"You know him. Or he knows you. And I'm not clear about any of this. Maybe you two are drug addicts or something. Maybe *he's* a drug addict—"

"Whoa, whoa. *What*?"

"I'm *scared*, Jack!"

"So you think I'm on drugs? Is that what Officer Kelly said?"

"Jack, we don't know! I have to look out for my baby now! She says—"

"*Officer Kelly* says."

"You're in some kind of difficulty! Your friend tried to kill me with a knife!"

"He's not my friend!"

"He *knows* you, Jack! And you know *him*!"

"I don't *know* him!" He yelled it, yelled at Corinne, and stood, his hands became fists as he looked down at her. "I don't *know* him!"

Corinne stood, now, too. "Then what am I supposed to do? Tell me, Jack! Tell me what I should do next with you about this, *this writer you don't know*!"

Silence between them again, as it had been in the motel room, silence like something you could touch, silence that was jelly or some other substance keeping them apart, a substance that would require great effort to push through.

Quietly, Jack said to Corinne, "What else does Officer Kelly think about me?"

"Jack." Her voice was as low as his. "There's no reports of anyone missing. I mean, this woman he killed in the woods."

"She said that?"

"Yes."

"People go missing all the time, right? Dear God, now I'm trying to convince you that he *did* kill a woman."

"She doesn't think you're crazy," Corinne told him.

"Then she's the only one because clearly you do, and Emmett does!"

"Stop it!"

"Okay, then. I will stop."

"Will you talk to her?"

"To Officer Kelly? To the police?"

"Yes."

"Yes. I will."

That surprised Corinne. "You will?"

You will? he thought, and told his wife, "I don't want this guy in my life anymore. I've told him that. I want this to be over. It is going to be over."

"Just talk to her. For me."

"I will."

"They really have no place to go, otherwise. I mean, to try to find this man."

The phone rang in the kitchen, and the extension rang on the end table, right by the couch.

"Thank you." Corinne said it very quietly.

Jack didn't say anything.

The phone rang again.

Corinne took in a deep breath, picked it up, and said into the handset, "No, it's okay. Yeah. He's right here." She handed it to him. "Emmett."

"Really?"

"He wants to know how you're doing. He's worried."

"I worry everyone. That's what I do now." He took the handset and said, "Emmett?"

Corinne walked over to the shopping bag she'd parked in the hallway, picked it up, and took it with her up the stairs to their bedroom.

"You okay?" Emmett asked him.

"Fine."

"Your friend sent you another package."

"Why does everyone think he's my friend?"

"Jack, I couldn't resist. I opened it."

"I suppose there's a story about a man killing a woman with a baseball bat."

"Actually, they're weirder than that. He's got three of them."

"Three of them?"

"You want to hear?"

"Emmett, you don't have to read them to me."

"I'll give you the gist. You're coming in tomorrow, correct?"

"Yeah."

"Then you can read them yourself. But this is what he wrote."

> In the first story, a lonely man who has lost the will to live kidnaps a woman because he senses that the divine is in her, the divine or whatever nameless thing it is that ties all of creation together. But she does whatever she can to escape from the lonely man and elude capture. He chases her into dark woods that are nothing less than his own landscape of despair. Trees grow faces and laugh at him. Roots lift from the ground and try to strangle him. Rocks jump from the ground to strike at him, and birds dart down at him, trying to claw him and strike at him with their beaks. With each nightmarish act of Nature, the woman warns the lonely man that if he will cease pursuing her, the woods will let him leave with his life. Finally, when both are exhausted and seem incapable of exerting themselves further, each turns into a child. The girl continues to run, a nymph in a woods of shadows and watching faces. The little boy can hear her laughing at him. He collapses at last and sees the spirit of his desire, now a woman again, deep in the woods, barely visible in the darkness, waving sadly to him as she moves on. He will never attain what she seemed to have promised him, the spark that he sensed within her. He has become a little boy lost in the woods, and he begins to sob, looking for the woman everywhere, even though he knows she is gone forever.

"I'm not impressed," Jack told Emmett.

"I agree it's not up there with his other stories, but I think the writing is quite good for an insane man. Number two. He's back in the woods."

> A man goes with a tape recorder into the woods to record sounds of nature. When he plays the tape back, he hears not just bird calls and waterfalls but, in fact, voices that do not seem to be human. Spirits of the dead? Ghosts? He returns to the woods day after day and at last establishes to his satisfaction that what he is recording are the voices of the actual spirits of the woods, the animistic forces of the woods themselves, the trees speaking to each other, and the rocks and the waters. His excitement increases until, one afternoon, he sees a trio of strange people coming toward him on the path he is taking. They inform him that they were the ones who made the sounds, who were responsible for the voices on his tape recorder. So sorry that you misunderstood. We didn't mean to trick you. The man is profoundly disappointed. Once he has left the woods, however, the trio turns into shafts of light that rise into the sky. The gods are tricksters. They provide us with wonders, but we fail to see through the illusions around us, the pretense that we mistake for reality. We would rather believe the obvious explanation than trust our own senses that inform us of the wonder surrounding us.

"Where's he coming from with these?" Jack asked.

"One more," Emmett told him. "This one I don't like, and I don't care how well he writes."

> A mysterious author who lives deep in the woods writes stories and sends them to a man in the city. The stories are written in coded language. Only the man in the city is able to translate the code because only he understands the author. The man in the woods also includes token objects with his manuscripts. Each represents someplace along a path that the writer is following through the dark woods. He

sends a length of bone—animal or human? Does it matter? He sends a small plant, a seedling that has been uprooted, and, the next time, grubs and worm taken from deep within the soil. Each of these the man in the city decodes as meaning that the writer is going deeper into the woods, perhaps is going back in time, and is learning how the apparently hollow lives of human beings actually have a foundation in the terror and fear of living in a deep woods, in the pity that is felt when the woods kills one of us, in the fear we acknowledge when we look upon deep shadows and old trees. But then the man in the city begins to lose his ability to decipher the mysterious writer's stories and gifts from the woods. What is the writer to do? How can he shock the man in the city back to understanding what is happening? Words are no longer sufficient. Action must be taken. Deeds must be performed. And so the next gift the writer sends to the man in the city is a piece of cloth taken from a human being, and the cloth has blood on it.

"Enough," Jack said. "That's enough."

Emmett told him, "That's the end of the story, anyway."

"He's losing it," Jack said.

"I thought it was already lost."

"He's sick. Literally. Cancer, his cancer. He can't concentrate anymore."

"That's pretty good, Jack."

"I want him to die. I want him to die right now. He can do it right now."

"And the stories."

"We have enough stories, Emmett. What are we going to do with them, anyhow?"

"I say we publish them. If he has a problem, let him step forward. Maybe it'll get him to come into the sunlight."

"Maybe."

"I've been talking to Legal about it, and I'm serious. No one who writes this well gets to be left alone. The world must have its geniuses, Jack."

"I hear you."

"Talk to you tomorrow."

"Yup."

"I'll leave the stories on your desk."

The man in the city begins to lose his ability to decipher the mysterious writer's stories and gifts from the woods. What is the writer to do? How can he shock the man in the city back to understanding what is happening? Words are no longer sufficient. Action must be taken. Deeds must be performed.

The ride on the Metra commuter train that afternoon was difficult for Cordell. After Bobbie's death, he had sometimes gotten on the train and taken it for a few stops and gotten off on a whim wherever he felt like it, in Mount Prospect or Park Ridge or Edison Park, any of the villages along the Northwest Line where he could relax for a couple of hours in a restaurant or have coffee, or he would go downtown and sit in the Ogilvie station and watch people as they shopped or ate in the food court. But doing that had been so long ago—pleasant, in its own way, but so long ago.

On the train now, Cordell, dying, did not stop on his way downtown. He looked out the window as the train stopped in each of these small villages, and he coughed quite a bit, which was a distraction to the other passengers, but he no longer cared about them. He had seen them all so many times, these people, here on the train and in the food court and in the villages along the rail line, and they were all of them the same, these empty people.

The afternoon was cool. As he walked down Washington Street and crossed the bridge over the Chicago River, Cordell paused and looked down at the water. He had done this previously on his walks in the North Loop, considering a few times that he should simply jump in to see whether he would drown. But once he'd begun writing stories, he no longer had the desire to drown himself or stab himself in the heart with a butter knife while standing at the kitchen sink or to jump in front of the train or do away with himself by any other means. And once he'd been diagnosed with cancer, well—that made all the difference.

Now he no longer had to go out to meet Death. Bright clear Death was coming for him. Which would be fine. It made him want to write all the more, all the faster, all the better.

He walked under the cool cloudy sky until he came to the United Building at 77 West Wacker and went in, crossing the beautiful marble lobby with its Corbero sculpture, "Three Lawyers and a Judge"—tall pieces of black rock, three of them, symbolizing the lawyers, except that the lady lawyer has a shapely leg coming out of her rock, just her leg, a beautiful leg, like Claudette Colbert stopping traffic in that old movie, a leg to get one's attention.

Only where's the judge? There are just those three pieces of rock.

Which makes us the judge, Cordell understood. Each of us is the one looking at the art and judging it.

Perhaps he would yet have time to write a story incorporating the beguiling message of those tall black rocks and that lovely leg.

Yet he'd been doing that all along, setting up pieces of art for people to try to understand because the people are part of the art, too. Only how many people comprehend that?

At the desk, he asked the security guard, "Everson, the publishers?"

"Thirtieth floor. Take the far elevators."

"Thanks."

His ears became somewhat clogged on the way up, so he coughed lightly, and when the elevator doors opened, he got out and saw that Everson was on his left, at the end of the hall, beyond a pair of large glass doors.

Cordell felt as if he were under water.

He opened the glass doors, and before he reached the receptionist's desk, three people walked in front of him, hurrying and laughing. Bright young people, energetic.

"Help you?"

The receptionist, Nancy Something, was an older woman, and Cordell stepped up to the counter and said to her, "William Tull?"

"Who?"

"William Tuill. Bill Tull. He works here."

"Sir, there's no one by that name here."

"I'm sure he said—"

"Can I help you?" A tall man came up to the desk, gray-haired, refined-looking, and he smiled slightly at Cordell, puzzled by this moon-faced man overdressed for the day in his heavy coat.

Before Cordell could say anything to him, the receptionist told him, "We don't have a William Tull here, do we?"

The handsome man smiled. "William Tell? Nope, not him, not today."

"Tull," Cordell corrected him.

"Tull," Emmett repeated, now watching Cordell carefully, as though he ought to recognize him. But: "No. Are you sure you want Everson Publishing?"

"Everson Publishing?" Cordell said. "No. That's not where he works."

"Well," Emmett told him, "that's where you are."

"I apologize." Cordell turned, went back out the glass doors, and pressed a button to take the elevator back to the lobby.

"Weird," Nancy said to Emmett. "And smelly."

"Agreed," Emmett told her, but continued watching as this strange man in the heavy coat waited for the elevator.

As he did, Cordell glanced back through the glass doors and looked Emmett right in the eyes.

Leaving the lobby of 77 West Wacker, Cordell walked around the block, just in case anyone was watching him, then took a position across the street from the main entrance. There was a side entrance, as well, he saw, and perhaps he should keep an eye on that door, too. So occasionally he walked around the block again and did so.

Eventually, around 4:30, people started leaving the building, crowds of them, and did so pretty steadily as the rest of the afternoon went on and the sky became darker with clouds and with twilight coming.

Eventually, Cordell saw the tall handsome man he had spoken to at the receptionist's desk on the thirtieth floor come out of the main doors and turn left. Cordell followed him. Followed him the nine blocks or so to the Ogilvie Station. Got on the same Metra train that Emmett did. Sat in the same coach, several seats behind him. And, when Emmett reached his stop in Park Ridge, Cordell followed him off the train and got into a taxi and asked the taxi to follow Emmett's car as Emmett drove home.

"Why am I doing this?" the cabbie asked Cordell. "Something I should know?"

Cordell reached into his back pocket, pulled out his wallet, removed a hundred dollar bill, and handed it to the cabbie.

"And that's all I need to know," the cabbie said.

"No one who writes this well gets to be left alone. The world must have its geniuses, Jack."

He couldn't sleep.

One in the morning, and he absolutely could not relax. He tried forcing his eyes to stay open. That had never failed before. He'd always finally just conked out, never remembering when he did it. When that didn't work, he tried tapping his thumb on the pillow like a metronome, or listening to Corinne's breathing so that he could get in synch with her and get to sleep that way.

But he was far too wired.

"The world must have its geniuses."

He looked at his wife sleeping soundly next to him, her beautiful face gray and warm in the dimness, and he whispered to his sleeping wife, "Corinne, I don't know who I am anymore. I want to be Jack, but I'm very twisted around. I don't want to be Cordell, but I want to write. I want the stories. I want you and the baby, and I want to keep you safe, but I want the stories. I do, I do. I want those stories."

CHAPTER SEVENTEEN

Emmett awoke to the sound of movment on the back porch. Sandy was still asleep, deep in the pillow and buried under the covers. He lay in the twilit bedroom, trying to pick up whatever noise he could from outside and two stories down.

Nothing.

The old-fashioned alarm clock ticked slowly on his nightstand.

He looked at the clock. A little after three in the morning.

He closed his eyes, started to roll onto one side and reach for Sandy—

—and, again, scratching sounds on the back porch, like stones being rubbed together, or bricks.

As carefully as he could, not wanting to disturb his wife, Emmett slid out from under the covers, pulled on his slippers, grabbed his bathrobe from the leather chair in a corner of the room, and went into the hallway, listening.

Quiet again.

They'd had a dog at the door one time, somebody's dog that had gotten out and started scratching on the back door to get in. The occasional squirrel and stray cat. So that was likely what was making the noise.

That, or a burglar—which was unlikely in this neighborhood, although these days, who could tell?

He went down the hall and through the kitchen to the back door. Pulled aside the checkered curtains over the window and looked outside.

He saw no intruders, human or otherwise, only a lump of something sitting in a corner of the porch by the antique washtub that Sandy had used for twenty years as a planter for her annuals. A pile of rags or someone's stray cat. Emmett turned on the back porch light, unlocked the back door, and pushed the screen door open.

He hissed at the lump, "Go on home!" and, when it didn't move, he stepped onto the back porch and stamped on the concrete a couple of times. "Go on, damn it! It's too early!"

He heard a sound behind him, and as Emmett looked to his right, he saw a man, not a tall man, but a man in a heavy coat moving toward him with his right hand raised. The man held a baseball bat that came down fast through the warm color of the back porch light.

His head had been bandaged, and the left side of his face was wet, presumably with blood. Emmett felt what he surmised to be an extremely large lump on the top of his skull, a lump held in place by whatever was wrapped under his chin and around his head. An ice bag, he imagined, one of those blue ice bags you buy at the drugstore to keep your lunch cold.

He blinked, and the pain was remarkable as it dived inside him, behind his eyes and down nerves or muscles into the back of his neck. What had he been hit with? His stomach was empty, and the pain made him nauseous.

His hands were tied behind him, and his feet were tied together around the ankles. He had been placed in a large, comfortable chair, one of those old-fashioned plush chairs you'd see in movies from the forties. The room he was in was not well lit. The floor lamps were not on, and the ancient, cream-colored window blinds had been pulled down to the sills. It was daylight outside, Emmett could tell that much, but otherwise—silence. He heard no city traffic. He heard no traffic of any kind. He heard no people or animals. Without doubt he was someplace isolated, probably someplace rural. The room looked like the parlor of a country farmhouse eighty years old or more.

"You're awake."

He turned his head to the left, and more eruptions of pain jumped and hurt him behind his eyes and sped down his neck. The man walking into his field of vision was, yes, he had to be, the same man who had been on his back porch, the heavy man, and now holding a large soup bowl. He was eating something with a spoon. The something crunched. Breakfast cereal. He was eating breakfast cereal.

He sat on the couch across from Emmett. The couch was positioned before the two big windows. Against the drawn blinds, the man was backlit by the amber glow, and his features were not easy to discern.

Emmett asked him, "Can I ask who you are?"

The man coughed and said to him, "Would you like something to eat? I'm eating corn flakes."

"No. Thank you." He winced. More pain. "Were you trying to kill me?"

He shook his head. "I don't think you have a concussion, but I put the ice on your head. I know it's wet. I hope it's not too uncomfortable. I used an Ace bandage. I'll take it off if you want."

"If you don't mind."

He set the bowl of cereal beside him on the couch, stood, and approached Emmett, then went behind him. The guy smelled awful. Did he ever bathe? In a moment, the stretchy bandage had been undone and the ice bag removed. Both were dropped onto the floor.

"Can I ask where I am?" Emmett said.

"No. Well, you can ask, but I won't tell you." He came around again and sat on the couch and took up his bowl of corn flakes.

Emmett said to him, "You're the writer, aren't you?"

"That's right."

"Carl Burkett. Something like that."

"Something like that. And I know who you are," Cordell said. "I saw your picture on your website. You're Jack's boss."

"You attacked Corinne."

"I didn't attack her."

"You were going to kill her."

"I wasn't going to kill her. I was sending a message to Jack."

"What do you want from him? Why are you even doing this? He admires you. He thinks your writing is phenomenal. So do I."

"Thank you."

"Are you going to kill me now?"

Cordell remained silent.

"I just want to know what my chances are. Because I'll fight you if you're fair about this and give me a chance."

He sat back, bit on the nail of one thumb, then told Emmett, "What we're going to do is call Jack. We're going to phone Jack."

"Do whatever you're going to do."

"I know you think I'm probably crazy, but Jack and I have a relationship, and I'm trying very hard to make him aware of certain things. He's fighting me, though, which I don't understand. He understands me. Am I right?"

"You're seriously nuts. *You* know *that*, right?"

Cordell sighed. "What we're going to do is, we're going to phone Jack in a little bit. I want to do it soon, but I want you to tell me when you feel you're up to it."

"Good of you."

"I'm afraid I gave you quite a hit on the head."

"Yes. Whoo-oww." More pain jumping through him. "But you have to tell me— Look, you write well. That's all we care about."

"What I care about"—Cordell thought a moment— "is to help people see the world. I looked into the abyss. The world is a horror. What happens when you look into the abyss and see the horror, and you know the world is a horror, how it can be a horror to you—but you can't come back?"

"We have to come back."

"I can't."

"What do you mean, you can't?"

"I'm awake now. I see life for what it is. Shouldn't I be telling people that?"

"But we don't have to be that way all the time," Emmett told him.

"But we *do*!" Cordell yelled. "Otherwise, it's just— It's not being alive! Don't you want to be alive?"

"No," Emmett told him. "I don't know! Untie me! Untie me, and then we'll talk. I'm trying to convince you to trust me. We're talking, this is a good talk."

"And I appreciate that. But I'm doing this for Jack's sake, actually."

"What does that mean?"

"People don't live, Emmett. People are garbage. People die. Stories live. Jack understands." He stood, walked toward Emmett, then crouched as though he were going to pick at something in the worn carpet. Instead, he worked his thumbs together, pushing the nails on top of and underneath each other, back and forth, clicking them, then looked up at Emmett and asked him, "Do you remember when the highway overpass collapsed in San Francisco years ago and crushed all of those people in their cars?"

Nine o'clock. Jack was at his desk when his phone rang. He was surprised when he picked up the handset and Emmett said to him, "Hello, Jack."

"Emmett? Where are you? We're worried sick. Sandy's called here six times already. Are you okay?"

"No."

"I'm— What do you mean, 'no'?"

"I mean, no, I'm not okay, Jack. Let me talk and I'll explain."

"Please."

"I'm here with Cordell."

"*What?*"

"Yes."

"Where? Emmett, where? Tell me! Can he hear you?"

"Jack, slow down. I'd like to live through this. He's trying—"

Now Cordell came on. "Jack, Emmett is here to help us."

"Cordell, let him go. I will do anything you want, please, please. Let him *go*."

"You're the one who has to learn to let go, Jack."

"Cordell, *please*. Where are you? Are you at your house?" He looked up. He'd been staring at the calendar on his desk, staring at it but not seeing it, and now Amy looked into his office from the hall.

Jack regarded her with what must have been fear in his expression because Amy's eyes went wide.

He waved her in and motioned her to come around to his side of the desk.

She said, "Jack, what—?"

Cordell asked him, "Jack, is that someone else with you?"

"One of my coworkers."

"Jack, put them on, too. Put them on—I've forgotten—the speaker phone. Put them on the speaker phone."

"Cordell, this is not about Emmett or the people I work with."

"Put them on speaker phone, Jack!"

"All right, fine," he said, scribbling on his desk pad for Amy, *Cordell Burgess Harvard NW send Police NOW! Get Linda!*

Amy tore off the sheet and ran from Jack's office.

Jack pressed a button on his phone and hung up the handset. "Can you hear me?"

"Yes."

"Cordell, please. Tell me what you want me to do so that you'll let Emmett go. I don't want you to hurt my friends or my wife. This is between you and me."

"That's why we're writing this story."

"This isn't a *story*!" Jack said, losing patience.

Linda walked in. "Jack, Amy told me—"

Over the speaker phone, Cordell asked, "Who is that?"

"It's my boss."

"I can hear her very clearly."

Jack looked at Linda and put an index finger to his lips.

Linda nodded. Silently she pointed out Jack's office door and mouthed, exaggerating the syllables, *A-mee Po-lease.*

Jack said into the phone, "Tell her about the story."

Cordell coughed several times, hacking and hemming.

Linda winced to hear it.

Jack said, "Cordell, you need to see a doctor. This is over. This is *over.*"

"I know. We don't have a lot of time left. But, Jack, you gave me a gift. I want to return that gift."

Amy stepped into the open doorway. Jack and Linda looked up, and she nodded to them—the police, on their way.

Cordell said to Jack, "I'm ready to die. Are you ready to do what you need to do, Jack?"

"Cordell, let him go."

"I mean, what we talked about yesterday."

"We didn't talk about anything yesterday."

"We did, Jack! We did!"

"All right, calm down. Calm down."

"We're all garbage, Jack."

Linda moved into the chair in front of his desk and leaned forward. Amy walked up and stood behind Linda. Linda said into the speaker phone, "Sir, may I ask a question?"

"Yes."

"We're all going to become garbage. What gives you the right to do that to someone? Life will do that *for* you."

"You're very intelligent."

"I'm trying to understand. None of us is garbage. You aren't garbage."

"I *am* garbage!" he yelled into the phone, then coughed for nearly a minute, very worked up, coughing and wheezing.

When the coughing stopped, Linda said to him, "Sir, this is what life is."

"All those books you publish," Cordell said to Linda. "They're not the truth."

"They're not supposed to be; they're entertainment."

More people came into his office. Carl. Two other copy-editors. One of the layout artists, poking his head in.

"Why don't you tell people the truth?" Cordell asked her. "Jack and I know what the truth is."

"Do you?"

"I'm very tired. Jack knows. He understands."

Jack said to him, "I do understand, Cordell. Now let Emmett go. You and I will talk. We will meet and talk—"

"It's too late for that now. You should have listened to me."

"Cordell, I *am* listening!"

"Anything can happen, Jack, right? Am I right?"

"Cordell, *please*."

"I told you I was scared, Jack."

Linda leaned forward again. "Sir, let me—"

But then they heard Emmett, sounding distant because he wasn't talking directly into the cell phone, as he yelled, "Jack, he has—!"

Gunshots.

One, two, three—too many to count.

CHAPTER EIGHTEEN

Jack reached for his jacket as Linda asked, "Where is this?"

"His house, his house!"

"Where?"

"All the way out in Harvard!"

Carl, backing up as Jack hurried across his office, said, "Dude, I'll go with you!"

"Then hurry!"

It was pointless to take the train. That would take forever. Jack hailed a torquoise-and-white 303 cab and told the driver, "Palatine! Please try to hurry!"

The trip cost him eighty-five dollars on his credit card, but the driver got them to Jack's car on the top floor of the downtown parking deck in forty minutes—a record for him.

Then Jack, with Carl in the front seat beside him, drove all the way out to Harvard, a long trip made even longer because each moment, of course, was an hour, a day, felt like the longest time possible, although there was really no time happening at all, just a haze, that same underwater haze Jack had felt yesterday, *only twenty-four hours ago*, when he had looked at Cordell Burgess from behind his car door and asked him, Cordell, what are you afraid of? and Cordell had told him, Everything.

"Jack, why wouldn't *I be afraid of everything now?"*

Halfway there, Carl, who had said very little all this time while looking out the passenger side window, asked Jack, "Why did he shoot Emmett?"

"To provoke me. To try to make me as nuts as he is."

"It's not working, is it?"

"No. But he keeps trying."

"He must really hate you."

"Actually, I think I'm the only friend he has in the world, the way he sees it."

By the time they reached downtown Harvard and drove over the railroad tracks, taken the few roads that led to the old mailbox, and come up the long driveway to the gravel area that Jack had stood in yesterday in the rain, there were five police cruisers and two emergency ambulances by the back porch of the farmhouse. Jack had to park some distance away, and when he and Carl stepped out, an older Harvard police officer approached him with his right hand raised.

"No, sir. Please, now."

Jack told him, "I know that man."

"Which man is that?"

He and Carl both were staring at the gurney being lifted into the back of one of the ambulances—a body under a white sheet, and there was blood on the sheet, Emmett's.

"His name is Emmett Walker."

"Is it?"

"And the man who lives here is Cordell Burgess. He's a writer."

"What else do you know about these men, Mr.—?"

"Mathis. My name is Jack Mathis."

"Oh. You're Jack Mathis."

Jack wasn't sure what that meant. "Excuse me?"

The officer looked from him to Carl, then back to Jack. "Your name's all over the place in there."

"*My* name?"

"Jack Mathis. Wacker Drive. What do you know about Cordell Burgess?"

Jack recounted everything: the story manuscripts that had begun to be mailed to him a year ago, the crazy guy he'd met longer ago than that who he finally realized was the writer of those stories, the taunting phone calls and the dares. The woman and the baseball bat in the woods just down the road. Then Cordell's holding Corinne at knife point the day before yesterday. Jack even told the officers that he had figured out where Cordell lived.

And he'd come out here yesterday to warn Cordell to leave him and his wife alone.

"And what did he say to that, Mr. Mathis?"

"Nothing. He didn't say anything."

"And you didn't call us."

"I didn't know what to do! Can I do that?"

"Of course you can do it."

"I went through this with the police in Palatine. You can't arrest a man just because you think he's a killer, can you?"

"Technically, no."

Jack became upset. "Officer, if I'd thought that you could *technically* wipe the son of a bitch off the face of the earth, I would have *technically* told you whatever I could, okay?"

"Calm down, Mr. Mathis."

"This *is* calm! I *am* calm!"

But he wasn't. Tears were coming. He turned away from the three officers talking with him, and Carl, still standing there beside him, touched Jack on the shoulder.

Carl said, "Dude, it's all right."

"Carl, no, it is *not* all right!" Jack said strongly. "He fucking killed Emmett!"

"You didn't do it."

"All right, I know, I know that. But I should have done *something*!"

He had done something, of course—done everything wrong, without doubt. Maybe not technically broken any laws, but—

Jack looked up at the older officer—Gardner, the name on his badge was Gardner—and asked him, "What about the woman in the woods? Can you look into that? I'm not making that up."

"We'll look into it. Only let me ask you—can you give me any idea where this guy might be?"

"He's not here?"

"Where might he go, Mr. Mathis?"

"God, anywhere. I can't— He scared my wife. He just shows up out of the blue. He's not in the same place twice. Even when he mailed me packages."

Two more officers came from around the barn, walking in the same direction Cordell had taken yesterday, Jack realized, when he'd been carrying a dirty shovel, and one of them called to Gardner, "Hey, Jimmy? We got a grave-yard back here!"

"What?"

"He buried half a dozen people back here! Maybe more! I am not shitting you!"

"What?" Gardner looked at Jack.

New tears started from Jack's eyes. "He really did it, he actually did it."

"Did what, Mr. Mathis?"

"He killed people. He killed people, and then he wrote stories about them. He said he did."

"Did he?"

"The world must have its geniuses, Jack."

"Only we couldn't believe it. We didn't believe him."

Jack stayed for as long as he could stand it, and Carl was patient with that. They waited together, feeling cold and strange, under cloudy skies as raindrops started again, a light shower. They said little but they watched, standing out of the way, as, in answer to calls Gardner made, village employees arrived with digging equipment—tractors to knock down trees and backhoes and shovels and picks to rip up the earth and trucks to move the disturbed earth out of the way—digging equipment to reveal how many bodies Cordell Burgess had buried in his back yard, his private cemetery in his woods.

Finally, a little before two, Gardner told Jack and Carl, "Go home. We have your information, and we'll be talking with you. But you can't be around here for this."

"No?" Jack asked him.

"Go home, Mr. Mathis." And he told Carl, "Get him home."

"Yes, sir."

But Jack drove. He insisted he was fine. He could drive.

Although they did stop at the MacDonald's in downtown Harvard and had a late lunch and coffee, and Jack phoned Corinne to tell her what had happened. Something terrible, he told her, to Emmett. Yes, Emmett.

And she guessed it right away. Was it him?

Yes.

Jack, is Emmett dead?

Yes, he's dead.

He drove Carl to the Palatine Metra station so that Carl could catch the next train heading back to Edison Park, where he lived with his parents. Not wanting to go home immediately, though, Jack sat in the train station with him, sipping Starbuck's coffee and looking at the clock on the wall. And the ticket counter. The Starbuck's baristas. The wall decorations local school children had made. Anything.

And it occurred to him as he looked at the decorations, Dear God, what if they find the body of a child out there?

What if Cordell had killed children?

He wouldn't have killed children, would he?

The bells sounded for Carl's train, and Jack walked him outside the station, where it was still drizzling.

"Dude, I'm really sorry," Carl told him.

Jack said he knew that and watched Carl board the 648, and he stood there until the train was thoroughly out of view.

Then, with nothing else to keep him from doing it, he went home to Corinne.

She was still crying when Jack got home. She let him in and hugged him and asked him, "Why *Emmett*?"

"To hurt me." He went to the couch and sank into it.

"Did they get him?"

He didn't hear her.

Corinne followed him and sat in the wingback chair. She asked him, "Jack, did they get him?"

"No."

"*No?*"

"They'll *find* him. He can't escape forever. Corinne...they found bodies. He had—"

She made a sound in her throat, trying to choke off something coming up. She coughed. "Oh, Jack."

"He really did this. Killed those people. Wrote the stories."

"And they can't *find* him?"

He shook his head and told his wife, "You didn't hear it. Be very, very glad you didn't hear it."

The phone in the kitchen rang, and Corinne went to answer it. In a moment, she walked back into the living room and handed the phone to Jack.

"Sandy," she told him.

"Oh, God." He took the phone. "Sandy, Sandy, what do I say to you?"

Her voice was thick from hours of pain. "The kids are coming over, Jack. They'll be here in a minute. I want you to know that I don't blame you."

"I am so sorry."

"No one can be blamed. God knows why. That's what I keep telling myself. He knows why. But it still hasn't sunk in yet."

"For us, either."

"They'll get the man who did it."

"I know they will. They *will*, Sandy."

"He loved you like one of the boys, Jack. He admired you so much."

"Sandy, I'm sorry. I think I'm still in shock."

"Me, too. Us, too. That's the door. Jack, it's not your fault."

"Thank you, Sandy."

"God will tell us why."

"I know. I understand."

"I have to go."

"We'll be in touch." He pressed off the phone and set it on the coffee table. He noticed then the papers there—Cordell Burgess manuscripts. He looked at Corinne and asked her, "What were you doing with those?"

"Reading them."

"Why?"

"I don't know. I'm trying to understand, too, Jack!"

He reached for the manuscripts but then pulled back as though they were poison, as though by touching them at that moment he would contract Cordell Burgess's disease or hurt himself or...something.

Corinne asked him, "Are you hungry?"

"No. We had lunch. Carl went with me."

She told him, "I can't talk anymore. My brain is numb. I want to throw up."

"Okay."

Corinne stood and asked him, "Did you ever call Officer Kelly?"

"I was going to."

She let out a sigh that Jack could not translate. Was she disappointed in him? Angry? Did she understand that this had been a mistake, that this wasn't supposed to happen but that *anything can happen*, and that this was some kind of awful, a God-awful mistake that was not meant to happen but had happened anyway?

Corinne told him, "I have to lie down."

But had happened anyway, like him attacking Corinne with a knife and his own wife being torn apart in a car accident, and whatever else always happened, like some maze or plot that had gotten turned in on itself because Cordell Burgess was so fucked up and somehow *had caused all of this to happen*, even though anything can happen, which is life.

He looked at the stack of manuscripts. On top of them was a page from a large ruled tablet. There were words on it in Corinne's hand.

Her notes from reading the stories.

Loss, shock, pain, she had written. Then, *Learning— finding people to learn from. And Death, murder… Revelation or epiphany… Misunderstanding… Disappointment… Searching… Needs other people—control or ownership.*

The themes of his stories, the very stories that had convinced Jack that Cordell Burgess was a genius, the very stories he had gone through with a Search button, tearing them apart to make sense of them. And here Corinne was doing it, too. Trying to find him, the monster, the writer, find him in every way possible, his heart, his creativity, his genius.

"Where might he go, Mr. Mathis?"

Where had he gone? Where had Cordell Burgess run off to?

If Jack went through the stories again, more carefully this time, could he figure it out?

"You're going to kill somebody someday, and you're going to take their energy and eat their heart."

Could he find him and kill him, finally kill him, kill Cordell Burgess?

"We're capable of anything, Jack! Tell the truth!"

Finally kill him?

"We're the only ones telling the truth!"

Or should he do what he did two days ago and drive away? Get away from Cordell Burgess, burn these stories and put everything into Reverse and steer as fast as he could and get away from Cordell Burgess Cordell Burgess Cordell Burgess.

That night, as he lay beside Corinne, she rolled over and, in her sleep, put her arms around him again to protect him or to hold him. To hold him. As if to keep him from continuing to hurt himself.

A little before midnight, unable to sleep, Officer Kelly decided that she might as well put her sleeplessness to good use, so she got quietly out of bed, pulled on some clothes and a light jacket and left her apartment to make a run to the nearby twenty-four-hour Jewel-Osco. Pick up some extra cans of cat food, maybe a few frozen dinners, see what else was on sale. Frozen dinners for her husband. He liked chopped steak.

She filled a couple of plastic grocery bags and, on the way back home, unable to get Jack and Corinne Mathis out of her mind after hearing, late this afternoon, about the Cordell Burgess situation in Harvard, took a short detour and went by the Mathises' condo complex. Drove through slowly, looking at the separate buildings, most of them quiet now, a little after midnight.

She stopped her car in front of the building where she knew Corinne and Jack lived and looked at the darkened windows of their home. Officer Kelly understood that she would not interfere, knew that the Harvard officers had established whatever needed to be established regarding this strange young man and his wife. And that was part of why she was here, looking at their dark home in the middle of an October night.

She had been a police officer in Palatine, Illinois, for close to seven years now. Growing up, she had known the village to be quiet, friendly, very conservative. But the bizarre Brown's Chicken murders in January 1993, in which two losers, Juan Luna and James DeGorski, had murdered seven people in a fast-food restaurant simply for their own amusement, had changed the tone of the village. The crime gained national attention and remained unsolved for nearly ten years. In that time, as Officer Kelly grew to womanhood, spent some time in the military, and then joined the police department, her community had enlarged to become more gentrified and more diverse. Meanwhile, there had been no more late-night, fast-food restaurant massacres.

But now there was this. Cordell Burgess. And there were this strange young man and his wife. And Office Kelly wondering about all three of them. Because she had become thoroughly aware of what can occur on the other side of darkened windows and behind closed doors and inside locked buildings. There are so many little rooms everywhere, all over the world, in fact, odd corners, closets and basements, alleys and attics where everything peculiarly human takes place. Blood and yells, drugs and guns, pain and violence. Sometimes love and laughter, but more often than not, in these odd little places, blood and yells, drugs and guns, pain and violence. She had learned long ago that you never can tell what will happen. It's always the same story in that way.

She sensed potential tragedy with the Mathises, and she hated that feeling. But doctors deal with cancer, soldiers deal with terrorists, and cops deal with whatever it is that they confront behind closed doors, inside locked buildings, on the other side of dark windows.

Officer Kelly yawned and, tired, now, drove on. Time to go home. Get some sleep.

Get some rest to deal with whatever would be behind the closed doors tomorrow, and the tomorrow after that.

CHAPTER NINETEEN

The next day, Wednesday, at the office, Jack was fiercely aware of everyone looking at him as he came through the glass doors, said good morning to Nancy, and walked down the hall to his office. He was a doomed man, and the people in the cubicles he passed were the witnesses to his deserved execution. Amy tried to be friendly enough. Carl said as bright a hello as he could. But the office was no longer a family, or something like a family, and it was Jack's fault.

What have you done? he heard them all ask as he walked to his office.

And, Why, Jack? Why did you make this happen to Emmett? he heard them ask.

He thought that he had come to a crossroads and, without hesitating, had continued through the intersection as though there were no other choices to be made, no other directions to take, no attention to be paid.

He went into his office and sat at his desk, and his telephone message light was on, but he had no interest in seeing what the message or messages were about.

What if one of them were from Emmett from before he died and he had to listen to Emmett's voice now on the phone?

"Jack, he has—!"

As he sat there, Amy came in with something in a file folder and placed it in his In box—probably no more than an excuse to break the ice or get the morning started so that Jack wouldn't feel completely isolated—and told him, "Jack, they will find him. They know what they're doing. The police know what they're doing."

He gave her an expression that was almost joyful and said to her, "Really? This guy? Will you listen to yourself?"

Amy told him, "I'm just trying to help."

"I'm sorry."

"No one here hates you, Jack."

He swallowed and looked at her and his eyes became warm.

Amy left, and Jack went to the kitchen to get himself a cup of coffee, but as he sat again at his desk, the phone rang.

Linda.

"Come by," she told him. "We need to talk."

He carried his coffee with him down the hall to her corner office.

The door was open. He tapped lightly and came in, placed his cup on the table she had in the corner. Four chairs there, and piles of manuscripts and pens and pencils, pads of yellow paper, coasters.

Linda's back was to him. She was looking out the window at the skyline, the windows, the morning, the day that waited. She turned, gestured to the table, and moved toward it herself. "Should I ask how you are?"

"I don't know how I am. Have you ever been in a situation like this before?"

"No one's been in a situation like this before." She sat across from him and, as was her habit, picked up a pencil and bounced it eraser-end in a regular rhythm on a pad of paper. "Have you spoken with Sandy?"

"Briefly."

"I talked to her last night at home. Her and the one son, the older boy."

"And?"

"He wanted to come in and get Emmett's things. I told him we'd pack everything up and get it to Sandy."

"Sure."

"We talked about this madman and the stories, and how you fit into it, and Emmett."

Jack pulled in a long breath. "Okay."

"I took some of his stories Emmett had in his office. This Cordell Burgess."

"And?"

"It's good work."

Jack admitted, "I think he's extraordinary."

"I agree. Despite the circumstances. You and Emmett agreed that he's worth publishing."

"And you're going to do it?" Jack listened to himself as he said that. His tone was judgmental. He was almost surprised at himself.

Almost.

"I've been talking to Legal. There are issues."

"I'll bet."

"I want you to give me all the work of his you have."

"In my office. I have the originals at home, but they're all here."

Linda looked at him. "Do you truly feel he murdered people in order to get...excited enough to write?"

"I do. Those're the bodies they found."

She shook her head as though incapable of comprehending it. "I'm not making any formal decision until I've talked about this more with Peter in Legal, but I want you to know I'm seriously considering it."

"I'll help however you want me to. I can do that. At least I can do that."

"I do want your help, but I'm not sure you should be the editor."

Jack was genuinely surprised. "Linda, that hurts. Who on earth here makes more sense?"

"Can you do it?"

"Yes."

"And be objective? Not...get involved?"

"Involved in what way?"

She frowned. "I'm not sure. I know you and the writer were close. Is that the way to put it?"

"I guess. I don't know how to, myself."

"We do the collection as soon as possible. This is what I'm considering. He can't profit from any of it because of his crimes. He hasn't signed any contracts, so we're potentially in trouble there, except that we're going to make it clear that any money we make, above costs, goes to the families of the victims or to some fund we set up for the families."

"That's good."

"Maybe the publicity will get him out in the open so the police can find him. But I want the sales. I want our name on the book. I want the PR that we're going about this for exactly that reason, for the families of the victims. And I want to get the literary people talking about it, too. I've been putting feelers out."

"It'll be an event."

"But it's nothing more than a stunt if we aren't completely honest about it and if the stories aren't worth it."

"But they are."

"Well, I agree. Emmett had it mapped out. Imagine that Jeffrey Dahmer or some other monster did all of these grotesque things to human beings but also wrote like an angel and left that work to us. What would come of it?"

"People would buy the book out of morbid curiosity. Some people would protest. But if the work was good—"

"It would change the discussion entirely."

"I'm afraid it would."

"We have some good work by a good writer who also happens to be this incredible criminal. We're not the police. We're not psychologists. We're a publisher. That's our job."

"I agree."

"All right," Linda said, and stopped tapping the pencil eraser on the yellow tablet. She stood, went back to her desk, and took her chair behind it.

Jack wondered if somehow she had connived to get him into this position where he was going along with this idea, or if she'd been uncertain herself and had needed to use him as a sounding board to get into the frame of mind to move forward with this.

He took another sip of coffee and stood. "Okay," he said.

Linda looked at him. "What are you working on now?"

"A Peterson thriller."

"Give it to Carl."

"Really?"

"Peterson's terrible, but Carl hasn't been given a complete assignment yet. We don't need to edit Peterson. People would read him if we printed the type backward."

"True."

"He can learn on the Peterson manuscript. How far into it are you?"

"About a third. Do I kiss your hand in thanks for allowing me to abandon this semiliterate bozo?"

"You mean the semiliterate bozo whose made us a major player and could buy this city if he wanted to?"

"That's the one."

"Just monitor Carl while you organize the Burgess stories. Write an introduction or something. But Legal clears it."

"I understand."

"Nothing too personal. Public facts. Talk about the writing style. But not a lot about the Jeffrey Dahmer aspect."

"I can do that." He quoted Dryden. "'Great wits are to madness near allied.' But that would be the extent of it."

"All right." Her computer dinged. Linda looked at her monitor screen. "I have a meeting."

"Okay."

"Are you coming in tomorrow? I'd like to get you back on schedule, as cold-blooded as that sounds."

"I'll be back on schedule. And I want to go to Emmett's funeral. Day after tomorrow?"

"We're all going."

"Sure, of course." He stepped toward the door.

Linda asked him, "I do want to know something else."

He faced her. "What?"

"What was it like to talk to this man?"

Jack thought a moment and then admitted to her, "I actually confronted him. Recently. When I figured out where he was. Where he lived."

"When was this?"

"The day before yesterday."

"Before Emmett was killed."

"Yes. I went out there. I wasn't sure if it was the right house or not. I was so scared, I almost turned around about six times. But I put together some clues I found in his stories—"

"Did you really?"

"He'd mentioned enough things that I made an educated guess. And it was him. I talked to him for about ten minutes.

Then I was so scared, I just got into my car and drove like crazy to get away from him. I was this close to him. If he'd had a gun, he could have shot me—" Jack stopped abruptly, realizing what he'd said.

Linda asked him, "Did you tell Emmett this?"

"No. No. This was...I went out there, and then I came home, and I was so scared, I didn't know what to do. I promised Corinne I'd phone the police and tell them where to find him. But I fell asleep. I came to work, I was going to phone the police, but then this happened."

Linda watched him for a long moment, then nodded slowly, as though deciding whether to believe Jack and at last relenting, having determined that, yes, this sounded correct. "So was he obviously insane?"

Jack told her, "No. When he talked...it wasn't *what* we talked about. But I knew his stories, I knew what he'd done, and when I confronted him— I didn't really confront him. We talked. He was over there, and I stayed here. But the effect was of someone who had discovered something deep, really deep secrets, and he was determined to put them out there for the rest of us. What he did, the things he did, the acts he committed, those are criminal. But to hear him talk in his stories... It's why we love literature, Linda."

"I see."

"It's a terrible thing, isn't it?"

"Yes."

"He talked about *enargeia*."

"Emmett mentioned that."

"Life is so terrible, the truth of it can overwhelm us. He calls it the abyss. And he's determined to confront that. But to do it...these are the things he did."

"Well..." she began, slowly, thinking, and then told Jack again, "I really do have to get to this meeting."

"No problem."

"Pity and terror."

"Yes."

"He actually was trying to create real art."

"Actually, he did it. It makes me sick to admit it, but he did."

He left Linda's office and went down the hall toward his own, passing Emmett's on the way.

Emmett's office door was closed. Linda, or someone, had printed out a sign that said "Do Not Disturb" and taped it to the door.

Too late, Jack thought.

Everything's already become very, very disturbed.

He met with Carl that afternoon and went through the Peterson manuscript with him. Bestseller number what? Carl had asked him. Number nine-hundred-zillion-forty-three? Peterson could turn out mechanical thrillers like a machine cranking out buttons or Twinkies. Every one of them the same. And people read them in the same fashion they used buttons and ate Twinkies; they needed those thrillers, these readers had determined, just as they needed buttons and Twinkies.

Well, maybe they did. Readers often want nothing more than something to read, in the same way that sports fans simply want to watch a basketball game. It doesn't matter who's competing. They simply want to watch basketball. Many readers want simply to read.

Jack had to admit that there was something brilliant about Peterson, his discovering some musical note that everyone was compelled to listen to again and again. It was rather like the note of a dog whistle, arousing those who hear it to react each time in precisely the same way.

But he was, after all, writing stories, correct? Not Cordell Burgess stories or Iris Murdoch or Mark Twain or Leo Tolstoy or Joseph Conrad or Edith Wharton stories or Ray Bradbury stories, but—stories. Jack appreciated that fact. It was like spending a rainy Saturday afternoon watching some light B-movie or old science fiction adventure. Jack had a weakness for those old movies. He couldn't read Peterson, or at least take him seriously, because words on a page meant something to Jack, even though they didn't for most people any longer. But he could see where readers would put away a Peterson thriller in a couple of gulps the way he himself would enjoy watching an old science fiction movie. Something engaging without being too demanding. Something distracting to let your mind relax without actually deepening into a true thought pattern.

But there were novels, stories, products, and then there were words on the page that resolved into something more than product because they were superior words on the page. They were the right words, properly chosen words, and they made sentences that were more than they seemed to be on first reading. They opened the mind, such words and sentences, and, once opened, the mind could explore between those words and beyond those sentences. It was similar to a musician admitting that the real secret to great music is the silence between the notes. The notes are there. The words on the page are there. But what are those infinitesimal moments of silence between the notes? How long does the pianist or the orchestra wait between those notes? Anything could happen within that silence between those notes. The world could end or the galaxy spin out of control during the silence between those notes. But then the next note arrives, the pianist plays it, and the world is still here, the galaxy remains. But what about the next almost incomprehensible moment of silence? We wait for it, it comes, that silence is filled by its own complete silence—an impossibility, but it occurs, silence completed by silence—and the notes continue, creating something more than themselves and something more than the silence and the notes combined. Perhaps they create spirit, or humanity, or new worlds of some sort, or something that exists for a short time and then is gone, having existed only to exist no more.

The same is true for words on the page. Peterson could put words on a page and they were no more than words. They were ants moving in single file to complete some mechanical ant function, the bare minimum required of sentences or of life or sentience or being. But when someone who knew what he or she was doing, when a Cordell Burgess put words on the page, there occurred the silence between the notes as well as the notes themselves. There were words and sentences and a wonder that comes from being more than words and sentences set stupidly on the page. There was spirit, or humanity, or darkness giving way to light, and light succumbing to darkness. Life, real life, unexpected life was there.

You could get lost in the spaces between those words, spaces that were also the moments of silence between the notes. You could explore your own soul or humanity's soul in the space between a *d* and a *c*, or between a *c* and an *s*. You could move into that space, float there and explore, then return, come back out of the page, hoist yourself back up by stepping on the *d* and the *c* and the *s*, climb up them and join the world again but see it for what it is, less than itself and more than itself at the same time, all things possible, the inert and the active, the is and the is not, the becoming and the never to become.

Jack thought—perversely—how Emmett would have reacted to that insight: with a snicker and a smile, as if to say, Well, whatever has happened to me, however the office feels about you, whatever you have allowed to happen— you, Jack—well, is there a good story in it?

And Jack would have said, Yes, there is. Let me tell it to you.

Because that was the part that very few others could understand. No one outside that mindset understands how very special stories are, what they do—really do—in opening souls and in bringing us back to ourselves, in making us human with all of our clichés, all of the true clichés and deep wonders, all of the heart of us, in stories, in stories.

Is there a good story in it?

Yes, there is, Emmett. Let me tell it to you.

Even in stories, or perhaps especially in stories, in which someone you know and respect is killed, killed because of you.

CHAPTER TWENTY

That evening, when Jack returned home, he found Corinne upstairs in their bedroom, putting the last of some things into her suitcase and her overnight bag as she talked on the phone to...her mother, it sounded like.

"No, that's fine," she said into her cell. "I could take a cab. If you want to. It's too early! Okay, then. You, too. Love you, too. I know." She pressed off her phone and dropped it onto the bed and looked at Jack. "Don't be mad."

"Your mom?"

"Yes."

"Is she okay?" He went to the spare chair they kept in a corner and sat in it, sat on top of some of Corinne's clothes from yesterday because that's typically what the chair was used for. It was a clothes hamper.

"Mom's fine. I'm the one who's not doing so good."

"Because of all this?" He started clicking his thumbnails together in front of him, one on top of the other.

"I'm sorry."

"Well, don't be *sorry*!"

"I sat here all day, and I got so nervous. They don't know where he is."

"No."

"Will they tell us if they find him? Is that a priority?"

"I honestly don't know. You think he cares about us anymore?"

"He cares about *you*. And he came at *me* with a *knife*!"

"He's truly a caring person."

"Jack, it is *not funny* and you know it."

"I do know it." He stood and walked over to Corinne, touched her shoulders and looked at her eyes. Her eyes were red and a little swollen. "What are you doing? Going back for a few days?"

"I need to."

"Do you want me to go with you?"

"I want to be with my mom."

"Got it."

"Couple of days. I'll stay for the weekend. Back Monday."

"That's fine."

"I got the train ticket already. If you'll drive me, I still have time."

"Now? Tonight?"

"I told you. On the Amtrak. It's tonight."

Jack stepped back and frowned. "Is this happening kind of fast, or am I missing something?"

Corinne let out a long breath. "It *is* happening fast. You didn't miss anything. Only you love me, and you'll understand."

"And, so...what if he comes back for me?"

"I don't know. I figure you'll call Officer Kelly or something."

"God, Corinne."

"I don't *know*, Jack, all right?" Her hands pulled up into fists at her sides.

"No, it's fine, I'm fine," he told Corinne. "I'm just surprised that it's so fast."

"I tried to call you at the office. Your phone was busy. I was going to call you again, but I forgot. I called my mom."

"It's okay."

"I can call tonight once I'm on the train."

He stepped away again, caught sight of himself in the mirror of her bureau, and realized how tired he looked, almost gray, with gray skin. "What am I doing?" he asked. "Putting you on the Metra?"

"Yeah."

"Okay." He looked around. "Everything ready? You're ready, right?"

She walked to him and turned so that her back was to him and reached and pulled his arms around her waist. He smelled her hair, which was wonderful, and smelled her skin. She'd showered, and the skin of her neck was still damp. Corinne said to Jack, "I don't know what else to do."

He told her, "I'd do it, too. Go see your mom."

She turned around and smiled at him, or tried to. "We still pals?"

"Still pals. Bring me back something from Pittsburgh. That God-awful beer they have."

"Arn City."

"Iron City."

"'*Arn*.'"

"Do you have the charger for your phone?"

"Yes."

"Because I don't want you buying one every time you forget it."

"Jack, I *have* it."

"Okay."

"Okay." She looked at him for a couple of heartbeats. "Honestly, I don't think he wants to hurt you. Or even me, maybe. He could have. But I can't think about Emmett and those other people getting murdered, Jack."

He nodded.

"They'll find him. You're right. Or he's so sick that he'll just curl up and die somewhere. I just need a break."

"Then a break thou shalt have. Come on, or you'll be late."

"I know." She took a last look around.

He grabbed her luggage and then followed her out of the bedroom door and down the stairs.

He got her onto the Metra just in time for her to make it to the Amtrak station in the Loop. He kissed her again on the platform and watched her take a seat with a window on his side of the train, and he waited and waved to her as the coaches moved down the line.

And that was it.

You start your day going to the office where they're all going to blame you for killing their boss and their friend, and you end it coming home with just enough time to put your wife on the train out of town, suddenly, very surprisingly, and then you start the drive back to your condo and it's evening and cloudy and October. You figure you can heat something up but instead you stop at Heng Wing and order pork-fried rice and some shrimp toast and then you go home, only it doesn't feel like home. It's someone else's home or area or place.

A phone call to mom, wife on the train, stop for Chinese, come home, and the place feels emptier than the tomb of the pharaohs. No *life* in it, even though you're standing there and you can smell the aroma of the fried rice. Is that life?

How many times had he and Corinne been apart? Not many. She'd go back to see her mom once or twice a year, but usually they took trips together. So had Cordell gotten to her? Driven her away? Was that what he'd done to his own wife? And is this what Cordell Burgess had felt when he came home the first night when no wife was there?

Or was his plan simply to make Jack as paranoid as he himself was?

Jack sat at the kitchen table and got himself a Coke and opened his carry-out food and put it on a plate and ate, all the while understanding how empty the area or place was around him in the kitchen and wondering to himself how quickly that had happened, how quickly Corinne had decided to leave.

Did she know something he didn't know?

Should he be paranoid?

Or was his wife simply so afraid because of all the hell that broken loose that, understandably, she needed a break, and that was all?

He finished what he could of the fried rice, boxed up what was left, and put it in the fridge.

His cell phone rang.

For a moment he panicked, expecting it magically and uncannily to be Cordell Burgess.

It was Corinne. "I'm on the train. Safe and sound."

Odd way to put it, Jack thought, but maybe she was telling the truth, more so than she knew. He told her, "Get some rest. Take a break. Sleep."

"I intend to. Honey, I'm very sorry that I sprang this on you so suddenly."

"It's okay. You can go back and see your mom whenever you want."

"But I should have told you before you got home."

"Corinne, get some rest."

"I will. I love you."

"Do not be afraid."

"No, I kind of am. For you. I didn't think this through."

"Get some *rest*, Corinne."

"Right now." She blew him a kiss and clicked off.

He tried to watch TV but could not. Got on the computer and checked his email, mainly bank reminders to pay some bills. Thank God, there was nothing from Emmett sent before he had been murdered.

Jack tried to imagine what to do next.

He opened some folders on his desktop, then went ahead and displayed a few Cordell Burgess manuscripts.

Because, as he had told Linda, "*I put together some clues I found in his stories.*"

The stories had helped Jack figure out where Cordell Burgess lived.

Now the stories could help him figure out where Cordell Burgess was, whether he was hiding or running or...wherever he was.

Soon enough, looking at Cordell Burgess words and Cordell Burgess paragraphs, thinking of Cordell Burgess driveways and trees and intersections and country stores and ghosts and fathers and spirits and demons, Jack decided that Cordell wasn't hiding anywhere.

Wherever he had gone, he hadn't stayed there long.

Cordell was home.

He was back at his house, Jack decided. He'd gone somewhere to hide, waited out the police, and then come back.

Jack felt it, he sensed it as surely as he had ever sensed anything he knew to be true.

Cordell was afraid of everything, and wherever he had gone, he would have been afraid, so now he was back at the farmhouse because of course he would be there. Where else would he go to die or hide or be? He couldn't stay there forever. He'd have to be afraid that the police would come back there, or the loved ones of someone he had killed, and in that case, he would be too weak to defend himself, at least eventually. But at this moment? Right now?

Jack breathed it in, enjoying the feeling of this, of truly understanding Cordell Burgess.

Then he went upstairs to his and Corinne's bedroom, knelt and reached under the nightstand on his side of the bed, and took out the Colt semiautomatic Emmett had given him. He made sure there were rounds in the clip and took it with him, wrapped in a plastic shopping bag to hide it, as he left the condo and went outside and got into his car.

He reached Cordell Burgess's driveway a little after nine-thirty. The sky had filled with clouds and, as it had a few days earlier out here, a drizzle began to fall. The night now was cool—cold, in fact. And all Jack had brought with him was a light cloth jacket.

He'd also brought a flashlight with him and had loaded it with two fresh D batteries he had in a bag of some stuff in the trunk of the Toyota. He had no intention of using the flashlight to give himself away, but if he needed light, at least he would have the flashlight handy.

And the .22. That he had placed on the front seat beside him. The safety was on, but Jack told himself that he was ready to use if he needed to.

He turned off the Toyota's headlights as he pulled up the driveway, mentally commanding the tires to move as quietly as possible over the gravel. Finally he pulled onto the wet grass and parked in order to make no sound at all.

As softly as he could, he opened the driver's side door, picked up the .22 automatic in his right hand while holding the flashlight in his left, and stepped out onto the grass. He bumped the car door closed with his right knee and continued alongside the driveway on foot, staying in the grass.

He could see just well enough to make his way. Jack thought it interesting that, even allowing for the rain clouds, night out here in the country could still be this dark. Night in the suburbs no longer was, not truly dark. Maybe that was part of what had made Cordell Burgess so crazy, being so far out and away from everyone under night skies that were so thoroughly lightless, they seemed primitive, premodern.

He reached the large gravel area that served as a kind of parking area between the back of the farmhouse and the barn across from it. There was no way he could stay on grass. Bushes came right up to the gravel on Jack's left, so he made his way as quietly as possible across the stones, heading toward the back porch.

He moved up the porch steps, putting each foot down carefully in case the old wood made any sounds, but nothing gave him away. It was all right.

The back door was right there at the top of the stairs, the back door and a screen door. Jack expected the screen door to be closed the old-fashioned way, with a hook and eyelet inside. But there was nothing to hold it closed. In fact, it swayed in the wet air as though exhaling under a breeze. Raindrops had collected on the dark mesh screen of it in a congregation of tiny diamonds.

Jack put the .22 into his jacket pocket and, with his right hand, pulled the door back as slowly as he could. The hinges squeaked. To stop them from squeaking, he spat on them, as the kids had done in *To Kill a Mockingbird*, he remembered. Then he tested the damp metal doorknob of the back door itself, turning it.

The door opened.

Had Cordell Burgess or the police forgotten to lock it, or been unable to?

Jack pushed the door inward and had a sudden panicky expectation of a dog barking and jumping at him. Maybe Cordell Burgess had had a dog all this time?

Or, if he ever had, perhaps he had killed it, too, for inspiration?

He stepped slowly, very slowly. Left no sound. He was in the kitchen. It was full of old smells—dust and damp wood and perhaps the odors of food, and the tired odors of cigarettes and coffee and beer. There was a window to his right, at that end of the kitchen, which let in whatever light could make it inside from the cloudy skies outside.

Jack heard a sudden scraping sound and flinched. A cough? Cordell? He almost bumped into the back door, which would have made more noise. But the sound was from outside—a tree branch bouncing in a breeze against the kitchen window.

Jesus...

Jack waited until his eyes adjusted as well as they could, and he saw an entranceway to a room farther on. He negotiated his way past the kitchen table and chairs and around the stove and made it into a small dining room. The light was better in here. A window to the right had been left uncovered, and so this room was not completely dark. Dozens of blank sheets of white paper, copy paper, had been tacked or glued onto the walls of the dining room, not in any order or in any sensible fashion, but randomly, some vertically, some put up any which way. A few old paintings or framed prints had been defaced with blank sheets of white copy paper attached to them. Why? What sick symptom was this? Blank sheets of paper for all of the stories that Cordell was never going to write? Or for stories that he wanted Jack to write?

Still walking carefully, seeing as well as he could in the dimness, Jack passed through the dining room and into the room beyond, a sitting room.

More sheets of paper everywhere. The room was nearly covered with them, blank sheets of paper filling every wall, glued onto the ceiling, taped onto the couch and onto the window shades, pasted onto the shades of the two standing lamps—blank paper. There were two tall, crowded bookcases placed against the far wall, their shelves filled with books. White sheets of paper had been glued or taped the spines of all of these books, as well.

There was a plush chair in the center of the room—

It had bullet holes in it, bullet holes from when Cordell Burgess had shot Emmett, absolutely, they had to be. Jack could just make out dark stains on the cushions, on the seat, and on the arms. And where Cordell Burgess had pressed white sheets of paper onto the plush chair, the brown stains came through.

Emmett's blood.

Jack let out a sound. He couldn't help it. His eyes became hot, and he closed his eyes as tears came. He breathed deeply several times, despite how bad the place smelled—dirt, dust, dried blood, whatever else was here, scents from whoever had lived here before Cordell himself, his wife or his family, dead people, more dead people—

The blinds had been drawn against the two big French windows in this front room. Jack crossed toward them, knelt on the dirty old sofa, and reached to pull back one of the amber-colored shades. He hoped that he wouldn't loosen it and send it clattering back up to its roll at the top of the window, making a racket the way loose window shades always do in old cartoons. But the shade was fine—and he was able to see a wide expanse of front lawn and some trees, perhaps part of the driveway, and, to his left, a low wall and a pillar of a front porch.

Jack back off the couch and, still holding the flashlight in his left hand and protecting the .22 in his jacket pocket with his right, headed left. Another entranceway led into a small vestibule or entry area with a closet door and a hall tree. To the left was a staircase going to the second floor.

Jack started up the steps.

CHAPTER TWENTY-ONE

It was so dark on the stairwell that Jack, at last, clicked on the flashlight. As he did, he aimed it at himself, so that the light would not be too bright but instead would bounce off his light cloth jacket.

It helped, providing him with sufficient ghostly light—illumination, really—to guide him up the stairwell and onto the second floor.

Three doors here—two for bedrooms, presumably, and one opening onto a small bathroom—plus a fourth door at the opposite end of the landing, which Jack surmised must lead up another flight of stairs and into an attic. That was the floor plan of all of these old houses. He remembered an uncle's farmhouse from when he was a child in Ohio. The attic had been a kind of playground or wonderland for him and his cousins, full of junk and therefore full of everything a child's imagination could conjure, pirates and soldiers and monsters, everything.

He wondered whether Cordell, growing up here, had ever enacted such imaginary adventures in the attic.

But of course he had. All children do.

And all storytellers do, without exception.

Jack kept the flashlight pointed at himself as he moved quietly down the hallway. He glanced into each of the two rooms, both of them bedrooms, as he had guessed. One, the first one, was more of a storage area now than a true bedroom. Perhaps the parents or grandparents had slept in here? It was more or less in order, with a couple of standing bureaus, one with a tall mirror, a bed, and a small secretary in a corner with an old chair in front of it and a standing lamp beside it. Boxes were piled neatly on the floor, taking up most of the old carpet, and, on top of the boxes, neat piles of books stacked on their sides.

Jack couldn't resist. He stepped in and leaned close enough to make out some of the titles and authors' names on the book spines. He was surprised. The range was encyclopedic. Several of the books were quite old. Had they been in the family for generations, or picked up at flea markets or second-hand shops? An ancient collection of Tennyson sat atop a number of Jack London novels and an old hardcover edition of *Lorna Doone*. Above those were the short stories of Tagore, then *Le Petit Prince* and plays by Molière and Cocteau, published motion picture screenplays of Ingmar Bergman, a biography of Alfred Hitchcock, and novels by Iris Murdoch, William Faulkner, F. Scott Fitzgerald, and Edith Wharton, topped by a paperback edition of *Shakespeare's Bawdy* and Eldridge Cleaver's *Soul on Ice*.

Another stack—a history of classical Greece, Victor Davis Hanson's history of the Peloponnesian War, Homer's epics, and, as though to establish to any intruder that there was no meaning or sense whatever to these random piles of literature, several books of essays by Sidney J. Harris, John Keegan's *The Face of Battle* and *The Mask of Command*, Star's definitive edition of the *Tao Te Ching*, Marina Warner's books on folklore and fairy tales, and a short history of the people of Appalachia, crowned by paperback collections of the *Peanuts* and *Calvin and Hobbes* cartoons.

Further eclecticism in a third stack—hubris, genius, and kitsch. Stephen King. Chaucer. A pictorial encyclopedia of motion pictures atop an illustrated history of twentieth-century calendar pin-up art. Germaine Greer. Volumes of Nietzsche, Schopenhauer, and Bertrand Russell. Essays by Montaigne, novels by DeLillo, and the short stories of Edgar Allan Poe, Alice Munro, Raymond Carver, Andre Dubus, Kurt Vonnegut, Ray Bradbury, Charles Beaumont. Several histories of the American West. Huston Smith's *The World's Religions*.

Had Cordell read any of these? Had he read *all* of them?

"I came from nothing, Jack!"

He backed out of the room and looked into the bedroom at the end of the hall. Clearly, this was where the writer slept. It was a mess, but even the disorder, or what Jack could discern of it in the refracted low light he allowed himself, was itself in a kind of order. The bed was unmade but the covers not crumpled or in disarray. There was a large, antique desk with a green slate top and an old wooden swivel desk chair. There was a chest of drawers, a large closet, several antique barrister bookcases, and books—everywhere, books. Books and loose papers, file folders, magazines, stacks of newspapers and bankers' boxes filled with who knew what?

Atop one of the barrister bookcases were some framed photos. Jack walked in just far enough to get a glimpse of the people in the photos. Cordell Burgess's wife and parents and grandparents? They had to be. Only one of the images was in color and showed Burgess as a younger man—and thirty pounds lighter—standing in front of a farmhouse with a slender, extremely attractive auburn-haired woman. His wife? The parents and grandparents were posed a little more formally, or least were standing at attention and looking at the photographer.

On the desk was another small framed photo, again of Burgess and the auburn-haired woman at about the same ages as they were in the other image. And books—more books aligned tightly across the back of the desk, against the wall. Joseph Conrad. Mark Twain. Tolstoy. Chekov. Dostoevsky. A biography of H. L. Mencken. Goethe's *Faust* in one volume, very old. Milan Kundera. Leonard Shlain. Freeman's *The Closing of the Western Mind*. Culler's *Literary Theory*. Translations of Greek drama—including a copy of the Vellacott Penguin paperback of *The Bacchae and Other Plays*, the same edition Burgess had given Jack.

And stories. A small pile of typed pages—short stories by Cordell Burgess. Jack lifted the first few sheets. He had not seen these before, and they were not drafts of manuscripts that Burgess had already sent him. These were new stories, or at least other stories.

More stories.

By Cordell Burgess.

Jack picked up the whole stack, perhaps a hundred and twenty-five sheets of paper, and slipped them inside his jacket, pressed against his shirt.

He left the bedroom and looked at the door that likely led to the attic upstairs. Could anything be up there? Or anyone?

If Cordell were here, what better place to hide?

He stepped to the door, eased it open, and leaned in to give himself a bit of light, continuing to hold the flashlight toward his jacket. It was indeed a narrow stairwell leading up to the attic.

Something caught in Jack's throat then. Before he could resist the impulse, he coughed lightly—and at the same time, looked at the top of the attic stairs. If Cordell were there, he would have heard, right?

But...nothing. Silence.

Jack moved up a few steps. One of them squeaked slightly, and he took the next few as softly as possible. He also placed his right hand into the right pocket of his coat and held onto the .22, keeping his finger off the trigger but holding onto the grip.

As his head and chest cleared the top of the stairs, the light reflecting off his jacket showed the area near him to be clear, the door to the attic open. Farther back were large objects—an old chest of drawers, a kitchen table and some chairs, and cardboard boxes labeled as containing Christmas decorations. If there were anything farther back, Jack could not make it out in the darkness.

He moved up two more steps, and the area behind the stacked cardboard boxes appeared, filled with large, plump black plastic garbage bags—old bedclothes shoved into them, no doubt, or used clothes.

But no one was in the attic.

Jack came back down the stairwell. He had seen a door in the kitchen that must lead down to the cellar. He'd look there.

Passing through the kitchen, Jack opened the tall wooden door and, still guarding the brightness of the flashlight, moved down the steps as they made a corner and then let upon the large cellar itself, perhaps thirty feet across and at least forty feet long, clearly stretching the length of the farmhouse. Cordell's work station was in a corner just opposite the bottom of the stairs—a desk and swivel chair, a computer and an old file cabinet, all on a dais set on the damp cellar floor. The floor here was cement, but Jack saw that elsewhere it was nothing more than packed earth, in a few places covered with old brick or wooden one-by-sixes.

A well was in the center of the floor, and it smelled of oil or gasoline. Jack wondered if Cordell burned trash in it, or perhaps stories, manuscripts that displeased him. Or people?

In one of the stories, Cordell—or whoever the character was—had killed a man in a well.

Had it been *this* one?

Off this main room of the wide basement were other rooms, some of them almost like tunnels. One small room behind Jack served as a laundry area. Others were for storage. In an old alcove lined with brick were shelves that held canned goods.

Noise, suddenly—a dehumidifier coming on. Jack jumped, almost dropped the flashlight, and saw the portable dehumidifier in a corner near one of the tunnels. Its white electrical cord led up a damp, cement block wall to an old metal outlet near the ceiling.

Nothing here interested Jack more, however, than what might be in the filing cabinet or in Cordell's desk. He took out the papers he'd kept inside his jacket and set them on the wooden desk next to the computer keyboard. He looked through two small stacks of papers sitting in plastic trays to the right of the keyboard. Typescripts, yes, of stories, some of them with handwritten notes or line edits on them.

Jack added them to his stack, then pulled out both of the drawers of the desk.

Nothing. They were empty except for reams of printer paper.

He turned to the tall, three-drawer wooden filing cabinet, an antique. There were file folders and well-worn stationery boxes stacked in the top one—more stories!—along with spiral-bound notebooks filled with handwritten notes. Jack added these to the pile he was building on the desk. Then he pulled out the middle and bottom drawers—not much there. If there had been, maybe the police had taken the material as evidence. What had Officer Gardner said to him?

"Your name's all over the place in there."

Maybe there had been envelopes filled with material Cordell had meant to mail to Jack and the police had taken them for evidence or something.

Shit. Could those people even comprehend what it was that they were handling, what they'd taken, the significance of it, the artistic value of it?

Enough. There was nothing more he could do here. How long had he been in this house, anyhow? A half hour? An hour? And what was he doing here? Hunting for Cordell Burgess? Wasn't that the original plan?

Or, Jack asked himself, was he now going to be a thief and steal the man's property, take these several hundred pages of stories, and the stationery boxes, and the notebooks, and leave with them?

Well? He considered. What else can you do? Leave them here? For the cops to take? Or for Cordell to take with him if ever comes back here? Or to be forgotten and disintegrate?

How would you feel if you left here without these papers? he asked himself, realizing what it was you'd found and then abandoning it? How far down the road would you get before you turned around and came back for this stuff? How would you explain to Linda tomorrow morning that, Oh, yeah, I had a fucking *stack* of Cordell Burgess material, but I just couldn't bring myself to, you know, take it with me after *I broke into his house with a gun* and had this vague idea that if I ran into him, I would, you know, shoot him.

With my gun.

Right?

Jack looked around for something to wrap all of the papers in but saw nothing, not even old newspapers or a paper grocery bag. So he held onto the material as tightly as he could, pressing it against his jacket with his right hand as though he were a primitive man guarding his child against danger, and made his way back up the cellar stairs, still aiming the flashlight against his jacket, and then moved across the kitchen floor to the back door.

He opened the door and stopped. Listened.

Anything?

The house remained incredibly silent. Not even the sound of a clock ticking anywhere. He heard the dehumidifier humming in the basement and then even that turned off, so that the old farmhouse in the rain, house of time, house of death, house of souls, house of—what? genius?—the whole ancient farmhouse in the rain, in the misty night, in the cold, was impossibly silent.

Jack went out, closing the door quietly behind him as though he were shutting the door on an archaeological site or a remote outpost that he would never see again, that no one would ever see again, a place to be abandoned, and he opened and closed the screen door just as carefully, then went down the damp porch stairs, tiptoed across the gravel, and made it into the wet grass. Here, he turned off the flashlight at last and moved as quickly as he could, in the drizzle, to his car, still sitting where he had left it.

Had he expected it to be gone? For someone to come along and take it?

Jack didn't know what he had expected, this was all so unusual for him.

He put the stack of papers and boxes and notebooks carefully on the passenger side of the front seat as though he were depositing critically important archival material in a world-class museum or library. Then he got his keys, started his car, eased ahead so that he wouldn't sink his tires into the wet grass, made a wide U turn, and headed back down Cordell Burgess's gravel driveway to get away.

And he didn't breathe again, it seemed, until he was a mile down the road heading into Harvard.

Jack looked at the clock on the dashboard. Ten-fifty-nine.

He'd been in there for nearly an hour and a half, in Cordell Burgess's house for that long.

And now he had escaped, just like that, just as easily as that, with an untold fortune's worth of Cordell Burgess manuscripts on the seat beside him.

He wondered if he would have dared to do this if Corinne had not spontaneously decided to go her mother's, and Jack determined that he would not have.

Thank you, he thought, sending the message by mental telepathy to his wife in Pittsburgh. Thank you, Corinne.

I love you, and wait until you see what I have.

As Jack steered his Toyota in a U turn over the gravel to return down the driveway, someone in a cold corner of Cordell Burgess's barn coughed, coughed loudly, hacking and retching. Cordell Burgess himself.

What had awakened him? The need to cough? The cold? He was curled up in a dirty corner of the barn, not having dared to retreat into his house, and wrapped in old blankets that he kept in the back of his truck, lying atop a mattress he had made of old plastic tarps.

Rest. All he needed was rest. Then he could move on, go somewhere, stay here for tonight—much safer and drier than trying to stay outdoors—and then, in the morning, take some clothes, take some of his papers, take some books and leave, go, drive as far as he could, as fast as he could, escape—

Escape.

And die somewhere in silence, alone, with no Jack, no wife, no anyone, simply die, having come from nothing to become nothing once more.

Or had it been the sound of someone's tires on gravel that had awakened him?

Cordell stood and wrapped the old blanket around him as though it were a cape and he a superhero. He walked the length of the barn in the darkness, knowing his way, and pushed open one of the tall doors and looked out at his cold unlit wet farmhouse and the damp grass and trees and the gravel and at the length of his long driveway.

If someone had driven up the driveway, looking for some-thing or simply because the person was lost way out here and needed to turn around and get back on a main road—

Well, that person was gone now.

Long gone.

Like Cordell himself, he decided.

He went back into the darkness, coughing and clearing his throat, to curl up in the corner of the barn to sleep as well as he could.

CHAPTER TWENTY-TWO

The next morning, the *Daily Herald* carried a notice on page 2 that nothing new had developed in the investigation of Cordell Burgess, the Harvard, Illinois, man suspected of murdering at least twelve people over the course of several years. The police welcomed any helpful information from residents of the northwest suburbs.

Jack spent the day at the office, dividing his time between assisting Carl on getting started with the Peterson manuscript and reviewing the tall pile of material he had taken from Burgess's house the night before. Jack didn't tell anyone, not even Linda, what he had done. Better to wait. Better to let them think that Burgess had somehow sent him this material from wherever he was hiding. Better to stick with the material that he'd already shared with Linda and Emmett.

The afternoon mail run, however, brought him another of Cordell Burgess's carefully wrapped packages. This one had two stories inside—and both of them, Jack realized, were final drafts of manuscripts he had found last night at the writer's house. Jack had stayed up late just sorting through the papers and notebooks, and he immediately recognized the similarity between the two newly arrived manuscripts and the earlier drafts he had taken.

Excellent. He was able to compare the versions side by side the way any good scholar or editor would, and so he followed Burgess as the genius crossed out passages here, recast sentences there, even reworked one phrase six times until he had had to draw an arrow at the top of the page to indicate that the final sentence, the perfect sentence, had been penciled on the back of that sheet of paper.

And it was indeed perfect.

Both of the stories were perfect.

Dear God, the man was a murderer, a mass murderer, but he wrote like a spirit taken human form, he did, he did.

The two stories were superior to the recent ones Burgess had sent in, the ones Emmett had told Jack about over the phone. They dealt with the same themes, what Jack thought of now as Burgessian themes—alienation, the quest for transcendental beauty, the enchantment of awakening to all possibilities, the insight in seeing the universe in a moment of wakefulness, an epiphany, and the depth of human feeling that came in sharing these insights with others, no matter the cost.

How on earth could Cordell Burgess create such achingly truthful characters that came to life so perfectly on the page? Here was a woman who had yearned for a lost love and remade herself in the image of the love she had always hoped to achieve. Where did this come from, this joy in life, this plenitude of spirit, of aching awareness? How could Cordell Burgess himself ever have captured so refined a sentiment, the depths to which this woman had fallen in her grief, and the ecstasy she felt and shared in this story as she remade her life? The man was a monster. Had he truly somehow, supernaturally, mystically, literally taken the soul of a woman he had killed and turned it into such words by some impossible alchemy?

How could he write this story of an old man and his dog, the hoariest of clichés, and turn it into a fable of selflessness and human love? Jack watched as it happened, as Burgess reworked the sentences in his rough draft into the polished beauty of the final draft that had just arrived in the mail. The man and the dog at the end, with the man dying in order to save the dog's life, should have been despicably sentimental. It was not. It touched depths that were profound, almost mystical. Was Burgess two people in one? many people in one? to have written something so fine and to have used the circumstances of such a story to reveal, penetrate, expose our frailty and then demonstrate the strength in that supposed frailty?

How was it possible to undertake insensible crimes and yet use the horror generated by those crimes as the material to write passages that left Jack shaking, so perfect was the writing, the choice of words, the cadence of the syllables, the simple directness of the grandeur with which he endowed these plain, ordinary characters in their pain and uncertainty with transcendence?

How could Jack talk about this in introducing such a writer to the public?

"*I came from* nothing, *Jack!*"

There was no way to convey it, to explain it. It was a mystery, and that was what Jack would have to admit. He would present Cordell Burgess to the public in Cordell Burgess's own words. The notes. The phone calls. The conversations. Tell people what Burgess had said, let him speak to the reader as he had spoken to Jack, and then let those readers turn to the stories and make up their own minds.

Cordell Burgess was another of the great mysteries that come of our being human: a madman who wrote like a god, like an angelic spirit, a man who killed people and then gave us human beings on the page that seem more real than the mortal lives he so viciously took.

People don't live.

Stories live.

Dear God, Jack thought. Dear God.

He's right.

Friday was the funeral for Emmett. Linda closed the office, and everyone was free to attend the service if he or she wished or to work at home.

At the funeral, Sandy was very kind to Jack, but the boys, less so—two young men in their twenties with their wives, and one of the wives pregnant. Jack could not blame them for looking at him as they did, asking him with their eyes, Why did you kill my father, or why did you allow him to be killed, or why do you even exist with us in such a way that you could interfere with our lives and have our father killed? Who are you? Who are you?

It was the same question he had asked himself about Cordell Burgess.

Who are you?

To the few people who inquired about Corinne's absence, Jack explained that she hadn't come with him because she'd had to go back to Pittsburgh suddenly to see her mother. No, no, everything was fine. But his wife was just as happy to get away for a few days. All of this had really taken its toll on Corinne. All of...this.

The weekend he spent buried in the pile of new Cordell Burgess material, eating Chinese takeout and hamburgers, drinking cups of coffee and bottles of root beer, and sitting at his keyboard until his back hurt so badly that he had to take a break, stretch out on the floor, and roll back and forth like an animal to work the kinks out.

Corinne phoned him a couple of times, and he called her. He told her that Emmett's funeral had been quiet and dignified. She explained that she was feeling better and told him that her mother was concerned about him. Jack wondered what, exactly, Corinne had said to her mother about him. And she told Jack she'd be back Tuesday morning. Not a problem, he said. When your train gets in, come by the office and hang around and we'll grab some lunch.

But Corinne didn't want to do that. She said she was sorry, but she didn't want to have lunch with him on Tuesday or stop by his office and say hello to everyone there. Not now, not with everything that had happened.

He slept uncertainly Sunday night, troubled by Corinne's attitude, or what he took to be her attitude.

On Monday, Jack continued to work on the Burgess collection, and everyone in the office started to get back into some kind of mood approaching normal. The door to Emmett's office was left closed, and nothing of his remained inside: Linda had had it cleaned out on Friday, when everyone was at the funeral or at home, and his things shipped to Sandy.

Tuesday morning, Corinne phoned Jack to tell him that her train had arrived and that even though she was only a few blocks from him, at Union Station on Madison, she wanted to take the Metra home and get some sleep. The Amtrak had left Pittsburgh at midnight. She'd tried to get what rest she could, but now she wanted only to go home and nap for a while.

Jack said that he understood.

There was still no indication where Cordell Burgess might be, no clues as to what had happened to him. Jack checked the papers every day and searched online, but all of the information now was dated days ago.

And soon, the days-ago information stretched into weeks-ago information. Search Google or Yahoo or any of the local newspapers' websites and you received the same headlines with the same datelines. The man was gone.

The madman-genius-writer-killer-whatever he was.

Jack stopped anticipating the arrival of any further brown packages in the mail. He no longer expected phone calls to come from that wheezing, coughing voice that had enlightened him, taunted him, dared him, challenged him.

All Jack had now were the stories.

Which was all any of them had.

And as he pulled the collection together, as he and Linda finalized the long introduction Jack had written, as the staff at Everson got used to the idea that the person who had killed Emmett was, after all, another author that they were going to publish, the air on the thirtieth floor gradually changed. None of them could forget Emmett, but they had books to publish: Jeff Peterson thrillers under one of their imprints, audacious tell-alls from Hollywood celebutantes and Washington gossips under another, scholarly research or popular science and literary criticism under a third. And mysteries, cookbooks, science fiction.

As well as Cordell Burgess.

The December holidays came and went. Corinne did stop by Everson, visiting for their holiday party, and everyone asked about the baby and when it was due—early May, she told them—and how she was feeling. She beamed. The adventure with Cordell Burgess, the attack at knife-point in her car, backed away in remembrance as she and Jack began planning for the arrival of their child.

Seasons change, and what has happened, events, memories, us...all of it becomes a story we tell to ourselves and to others.

Tell me the story of how the man attacked you.

Tell us the story of preparing for the baby.

Tell us the story of...the story.

In January, Jack finally got around to clearing out his home office, moving the desk and file cabinet and whatever else he needed into a corner of the living room. The big bookcase he moved upstairs into his and Corinne's bedroom. They managed to fit it in, although Corinne decided that she hated it and that, at some point, Jack was going to have to sacrifice it. We have only so much room, she reminded him. The baby's room he painted sage green, and he set up the crib they had bought and the chest of drawers they had gotten.

At the end of the winter, when it was almost spring, in fact, Chicago endured a bad snowstorm that knocked out power for thousands, tied things up for a couple of days on Lake Shore Drive, and generally slowed down everything and everyone—except for Linda, who made it to the office every morning and who managed, with half her staff out because of the weather, to approve the layout and cover design for the Burgess collection. By April, Jack was reading his introduction in page proofs and, for the umpteenth time, it seemed, Cordell Burgess's stories. Amazingly, even after reading these things as often as he had, Jack still found something magical coming through. The book went to press in mid-April and was ready to be shipped in early May.

It came out just as Corinne was going into the hospital to have the baby. Linda had settled on the title: *From the Depths: Selected Short Stories of Cordell Burgess*. Jack had lobbied, only partly kidding, for *Out of My Mind: The Short Stories of Cordell Burgess*. Of course, this was the same brilliant, half-asleep Jack whom Corinne had awakened at two in the morning with, "Honey, I think the baby's coming!" and who had said to her, "Well, tell me when you know for *sure*, and I'll get the car started."

"Jack! I am *serious*!"

"What, really? It's *time*?"

When the reviews came out, the critics were unanimous: Cordell Burgess's fiction was remarkable, but how on earth, they asked, can we square the fact that he is a writer of genius with the knowledge that he's also a mass murderer, a vicious killer, clearly insane?

"Elegant, heartful meditations on the tragic dimension of life," wrote one reviewer, "as life gradually takes back everything it has given us, every hope, every possession and promise, and leaves us with whatever spirit or heart or soul we have created for ourselves during the turbulent years of being alive. Burgess captures the ache of our humanness as few recent authors have."

"Brilliant," said another critic. "It is disarming to know that the man who wrote so eloquently is so appalling a human being. We shall discuss this conundrum for years. Meantime, readers will lose themselves in some of finest prose to have come our way in a generation."

Jack went on television, one of the local PBS stations, to discuss the collection and his own experiences with Cordell Burgess.

"How can you reconcile what he was with what he's written?" Phil Poncé, one of the hosts of *Chicago Tonight*, asked Jack.

"Well, one of his earliest stories," Jack explained, "is about exactly that—who are we, really? It sounds like a cliché, but people have been asking that question in literature for thousands of years. That's the question his protagonist asks, and the only way he can answer the question, the man in the story, is to leave everything about himself behind, everything that he is, except for his shadow. So he does this, and his shadow is able to go into places that an ordinary person can't. But the shadow has to make a decision, a life-or-death decision: 'I can go back to the life that I had, but it means that I sacrifice the people I love, or I can go places no one else can go, but if I do that, it means that I remain a shadow forever.'"

"Interesting," said Phil Poncé.

"He's talking about a process that some of us, I think, have to be honest about, and it's about looking at different parts of ourselves and making hard choices. We lose something when we make a choice. We gain something, but what do we lose, and how can we measure that? What if it's a very small decision, such as deciding whether a crazy man can be a genius? Can we make that choice? Do we play safe, or do we become a shadow and change into a shadow so that we can go places where no one else has ever gone? It's a big step. How can we make such choices? And what if it's a very difficult decision, really a life-or-death decision?"

"You certainly had to make almost the same decision yourself, didn't you?"

"I'm still dealing with it."

"What does your wife say about that? You just had a baby, didn't you?"

"Yes. A little boy."

"Congratulations. But this whole episode when this man— It sounds melodramatic, but, I mean, this man attacked your wife, didn't he?"

"He threatened her, yes. I'm still not sure what he meant by that. He was doing some crazy thing."

"And that terrifying incident, what he did to your friend, Emmett Walker."

"I still have nightmares, Phil."

"I don't think I'd have been able to manage this as well as you have—for which I'm grateful! I'm not sure how many of us would like to turn around and meet our own shadow that way, but you did."

"Yes."

"Well, the book is *From the Depths*—"

"Yes."

"—*Selected Short Stories of Cordell Burgess*, just out from Everson. Who selected the stories, Jack? You?"

"Yes, my editor and I. They're largely material he sent to me anonymously over the year I was in contact with him."

"Remarkable. Jack Mathis, thanks for coming by."

"Thank you, Phil."

"Next, how's the season shaping up for the Cubs? We're going to have a talk with Cubs manager—"

Corinne watched him from the couch in their living room, in their condo, Jack on *Chicago Tonight* with the erudite Phil Poncé, and she had to admit that Jack had it down.

He was doing well. Performing, really.

Telling a story.

So...how honest are *you*, Jack, really?

Are you still my husband? Are you still my baby's father?

Well, of course he was. It was an act. Jack was acting. This is what you do when you publish a book and you go on television. You act.

You tell a story.

Her cell phone rang. She picked it up from where she had it on the couch, beside her.

"How'd I do?" Jack asked her.

Corinne told him, "Oh, you were great. You're going to sell a lot of books."

"It feels weird, talking about him this way."

"I know. Are you staying down there? Or coming home now?"

"Coming home. There's nothing else to do here. Still feels weird, though."

"You want me to heat something up?"

"Don't bother. I'll grab something. Love you."

"Love you, too." She clicked off the phone.

Touché, Cordell Burgess, Corinne thought. I have my baby, Jack has his book, and you get away with it, you evil brilliant son-of-a-bitch jerk. You and your fucking stories.

Oh, wait. They're not "*fucking* stories..."

CHAPTER TWENTY-THREE

The manuscripts that arrived at Everson following Jack's appearance on *Chicago Tonight* were examples of an outbreak of human nature that would not have surprised Cordell Burgess. Jack and Linda, however, were indeed caught off guard by the profound lack of literacy on the pages sent to them, the reckless ineptitude, the naïve sincerity aligned with complete artlessness. The result was true physical pain when these editors tried to unscramble whatever was meant to be conveyed by so many incompetent bards and skalds.

They arrived by the dozens in nine-by-twelve envelopes—stories from people who barely knew how to poke at a keyboard as well as handwritten manuscripts, one of which had been laboriously done in different colors of ink to assist the reader in appreciating critical changes in mood and tone during the progression of the story. Linda, after reviewing six or seven of these atrocities, ordered Sam in the mailroom to route them all henceforth to Jack. And she herself handed her young editor the half dozen she'd collected so far and ordered him to handle them however he saw fit.

In addition, Linda did warn Jack, when she came into his office, about the top one on her pile, an allegedly true story dictated to the author by his teddy bear, a toy he had kept with him from the age of three (he was now in his early fifties) and which had conveyed to him, this teddy bear, by some preternatural means, the entire past and future history of humanity—if only humanity would listen to the dire warnings that Lord Theodore (the teddy bear) had imparted.

"I'd laugh if it weren't so sad," Jack told Linda.

"You want sad? Read some of the other ones. I'm afraid we have people out there who think that your friend's methods of calling down the muse aren't dramatic enough."

"They're not hurting people, are they? Oh, God, Linda."

"Take a look at the one from the genius who thinks that Cordell Burgess should have used bees and hornets on his victims to get the full effect."

"I never even thought about things like this."

"You lifted up the rock. This is what crawls around underneath it."

"Did *you* see this coming?"

"Honestly, no. I thought we'd get our share of complaints, and we have. We have a lot of people who are upset that we published this guy at all."

"I guess I can understand that."

"We're all going to burn in hell."

"Of course we are."

"Someone even sent us a package of hot dogs to roast while we're burning alive in the afterworld."

"Are you serious?"

"So we won't starve. He wants us to stay around long enough to really suffer."

"Have any of these people actually read the book?"

"I think that's asking too much of them. That requires maturity and patience and actual thought."

"Maybe *I* should have been more mature and thoughtful before I got us into this," Jack admitted.

"You didn't get us into anything," Linda reminded him. "I'm the bright bulb who decided to publish this man."

"And you were right. I haven't seen a bad review yet. He's being compared to every great writer you can name."

"This will die down," Linda promised him. "But we'll have to tread carefully for a while."

"I understand."

"The less about the nutty stuff, the better. Emphasize the writing."

"Got it."

"Do you have any more interviews?"

"Two radio stations. And WGN later this week."

"Remember: Crazy guy? We let doctors decide that. Brilliant writer? That's what we do."

"Understood."

"We judge manuscripts. God can handle the rest."

God, however, or one his assistants must have been dis-tracted by other matters by the time Jack got home that evening. Briefcase in hand, he came up the stairs to the condo shivering because the afternoon had turned quite cold, had even begun to spit snow, and all he had on was his light raincoat, nothing heavier than that.

He stamped his wet shoes on the mat in the hallway, then pushed the door open while calling to Corinne, "You should see the—"

And stopped immediately at what he saw.

Not Cordell. It couldn't be Cordell. This guy wasn't Cordell. Jack knew that within a heartbeat.

He was younger than Cordell, light haired, long greasy hair, and dressed in some kind of pullover shirt and jeans, but holding a knife at Corinne's throat.

Which is what made Jack think of Cordell Burgess.

They were on the couch facing Jack as he came in. Corinne was shivering with fear, and there were marks on her face where she'd been crying. Jack thought that she would start crying again now.

The young man sat next to Corinne, on her left, in the middle of the couch, and with his right hand held her left hand and arm tightly by her side. He held the knife with his left hand just in front of her throat. His hand wasn't shaking at all. It was very steady. He wasn't nervous. But it was quite a large knife, some kind of hunting knife, a big camp knife. It was not clean. The knife blade was dirty, Jack noticed, as his senses became lightened and as he rocked a little and as every detail, even the wet smell of his coat and shoes, recommended itself to him, every one of a thousand and one tiny things all shining brighter than normal in that moment.

The greasy young man said, "Close the door." His voice that was not unpleasant, but he was insistent.

Jack set down his briefcase and did so. Closed the door. Quietly.

"Sit down over there," the young man told him, nodding toward the recliner that Jack had moved to a corner to make room for his computer desk and filing cabinet.

As he moved slowly toward the recliner, Jack asked Corinne, "Are you okay? Corinne?"

She was too afraid to answer, so the young man told Jack, "She's fine. Now sit."

Jack did so, never taking his eyes off the young man or the knife in front of his wife's throat. He said, "May I ask why you're doing this?"

The young man replied, "I think you know why."

Jack told him, "I'm afraid I don't."

The young man sighed and showed just the slightest bit of temper. "Because of the *stories*." That guy's *stories*."

"Cordell Burgess."

"Yeah. Him. You're the guy that helped him."

"I'm a book editor. You call that helping him?"

"I saw you on TV. You helped him with the book, and you said so."

"Okay. I did."

"You knew him, and so you can read my book because you will actually be the person who can understand *my* book."

"You've written a book."

"Right there." The young man nodded to a pile of printer paper on the coffee table in front of him.

If Jack had noticed this pile of paper since coming in the door, it hadn't registered. Now it did. Immediately he thought of the pile of Cordell Burgess manuscripts he had lived with for so long, which he cherished, in fact, and which were so important.

Were these somehow going to be equally important?

He asked the young man, looking him in the eyes, "What's your name?"

"Edward O'Donnell."

"Is that your real name?"

"Of course not!" the young man laughed. "Why would I give you my real name?"

"I don't know, Edward. Why would you break into my house and point a knife at my wife?"

"Because *he* did!" Edward explained.

"But this is not the way to do it. How can I deal with— I mean, the *knife*."

"It's just a knife. Ignore it. I got your attention now. Me and you are going to work on my book. Just start with my story."

"Can you, could you put the knife away, please?"

The young man, Edward, repeated the request, making fun of the way Jack had said it. "'Could you put the knife away, please?' *No*, please," in the same tone. "Now just do it."

Jack continued to watch his eyes. Not Cordell's eyes at all. And to listen to this young man's voice.

Not Cordell's voice at all.

This young man had no talent. Jack knew it. He was nothing. He wasn't in pain, he had nothing to offer, nothing to share, nothing to write about, he had no life—

It was as though Jack could read his mind just by looking at this man sitting on his couch.

Corinne whispered, "Jack…"

Jack told her, "You'll be fine." He looked at the young man. "Please tell my wife that she'll be fine."

"You read my story, and she'll be okay. But I need you to help me with my story *the way you helped him*!"

"How? You want me to edit it?"

"You publish it. I want it in a book."

"You want us to publish it?"

"*Yes*. People have to know!"

Jack pulled in a slow breath and let it out just as quietly. Looked at Corinne again. And again at the young man. "Have you written anything else or ever been published before?" he asked.

"*No!*" the young man nearly yelled. "Why would you say that? I never talked to anyone before! But I been writing *this*. Since when I was a kid."

"Is it the story of your life?"

"It's the story of *everybody's* life," the young man explained. "It's about *everything*."

"Okay. All right. I'm intrigued. You want an editor to be interested. You want your editor to have an idea of what he's getting into, or what she's getting into, and I'm intrigued. But I don't want to do anything abrupt here, now. You have a knife, and you have my wife, right? So can I—"

"Just start."

"That's what I was going to ask. May I pick up the manuscript to look through it?"

"You start reading it. We're going to sit here, and you're going to read it."

"Okay. I understand. This could be difficult, though, if we're all going to be here and you have a knife. For instance, what if Corinne has to go to the bathroom?"

"She's just going to have to wait."

"What if I have to—"

"*Just shut the fuck up and start!*" the young man yelled.

Corinne whimpered, and the knife moved slightly now in the young man's hand.

Jack nodded and leaned forward, almost standing, and retrieved the stack of pages. Then he sat back in the recliner and set the pages on his lap, looked at the top sheet, lifted it, and looked at a few pages beneath.

This was not a book manuscript. It was a scrawled and handwritten pile of nonsense that this man, whoever or whatever he was, had involved himself with for years. Jack could imagine him sitting at a kitchen table night after night for years working on these papers. Some of the sheets were yellow, they were so old. Others had been crumpled and then flattened out. Some had been torn and pieced back together with Scotch tape. There were no page numbers. There was nothing. It was handwriting that looked as uncertain, as rambling, as disjointed as the attitude emitted by the figure sitting across from him, holding his wife at knifepoint.

Jacked sighed and set the stack of paper on the floor beside the recliner.

"What?" the young man said. "*Read!*"

"It's not typed. You wrote this by hand."

"So?"

"I need my glasses. I have to use my reading glasses. Can I get them?"

"From where?"

"Upstairs. Bedroom. Corinne?" He asked her, looking at her, "On the nightstand, right? Under the nightstand?"

She swallowed and told him, "Y— Yes. The night. Stand."
She understood.

"Don't be nervous," Jack told her.

He stood and walked carefully across the living room to the stairs that led to the second floor. Then he paused for a moment. "Sir, please. Edward, if I can call you Edward. Just one minute. I'll get my glasses."

"Just get them."

"Please don't hurt her."

"I haven't yet."

"Thanks. Yes. You're right. Okay." Jack went up the stairs.

In a few seconds, he called down, "Got them! Edward, I'm coming down!"

"Just come *on!*" The young man shifted his position slightly, turning his head to the left to see where Jack was coming down the carpeted stairs, to see his shoes on the steps. Then the young man looked back at Corinne.

Corinne turned her head slightly, too, to try to catch sight of Jack, but she was afraid of moving very much with the edge of the knife blade right there where it was.

Jack came down the stairs, and the young man was not looking at him. He had his eyes on Corinne. Jack, holding his right hand behind his back, had the reading glasses in his left. He walked halfway across the living room, approaching the recliner, until he was opposite the young man and Corinne, directly on the other side of the coffee table, and from there he brought up his right hand, in which he held the .22 that Emmett had given him, and, in silence, in complete control, as though he were watching himself as he did it, Jack leveled the .22 at the young man's chest and squeezed the trigger, watched as the young man began to exhibit an expression of surprise, and watched as the bullet hit the young man in the chest. He continued squeezing, and there was another bullet, and another one, this was fun, another one in the chest, Jack pulled the trigger quietly and very precisely, not even breathing as he did it, squeeze squeeze squeeze bullet bullet bullet going into the young man with little sounds, punching into the young man's chest. Jack worked his way up to the neck and then to the face squeeze squeeze squeeze bullet bullet bullet until there were no more squeezes or at least no more bullets.

The hand with the knife was already way over there, away from Corinne, it had dropped or jumped, and the knife had fallen immediately.

Corinne jumped up, screaming, and Jack heard her.

For the longest time, as he was squeezing the trigger, there had been no sound, not a bit of noise, just the silence inside himself as he used the .22, and then a great deal of sound came like waves picking up and roaring, rushing onto a beach.

Corinne, screaming.

And the young man, his eyes open, what remained of his face red, everything about him was so *wet* and so *red*, shiny and slick like oil or like rain, but he was still looking at Jack, almost with a smile, with holes in his forehead and one cheek and red spit in bubbles along the line of his mouth.

Corinne, screaming.

Then she was on her hands and knees as she threw up on the carpet. She retched. She got to her feet, she was wobbly, but the knife was there on the carpet where she had vomited a little. Corinne picked up the young man's knife and turned and jumped back onto the couch and really hit him with that knife, Jack was surprised to see it, but Corinne was screaming so *loudly* and she punched the blade of that knife that red wet shiny knife and sharp into that young man, his shoulder, his chest, his neck, really just kept at it as if she were slapping him, only using a knife, and yelling at him until she was out of breath, "Don't! You! Ever! You! No! *No! No! Don't! You! Dare! Ever!*"

Then she stopped, out of breath, and began crying so loudly that Jack thought it sounded like the end of the world, really the end.

He dropped the gun.

Corinne threw the knife away and dropped to her knees and fell over onto her right side and curled up on the carpet, crying so much, she was crying so powerfully and so loudly.

Jack could hear again now, and he heard the baby crying, his son, the child was crying, no doubt awakened by his mother crying and by the gun, there had been a gun, and shots had been fired.

Jack stood alone, looking at the incredible remains of the dead young man, all of him so red and wet and all of him so *torn* and *broken*, really like something that had been actively torn into and pulled apart. And the amount of fluid, all of the liquid that had come out of him—remarkable. Jack heard police sirens now, of course, and thought that he had better go see about the baby since his baby son was crying and there had been so much noise.

CHAPTER TWENTY-FOUR

The interviews Jack gave later that week were not entirely about the book. How could they be? He was asked about the incident that had taken place in his and his wife's home, that strange young man with the knife and the book, the story, and what on earth could he have been thinking of, what was he *doing*, doing something like that, attacking Jack's wife for the second time with a *knife*?

Jack was honest in confessing his confusion. That young man had clearly been deeply disturbed, and for some reason, the publicity surrounding the bizarre Cordell Burgess event had triggered this young man into acting out some sort of frightening scenario that he'd been carrying around in his head for who knew how long? But Jack explained that he and his wife were managing as well as they could. They had had to stay in a hotel as the police examined the apartment and then as a cleaning crew came in—they had special crews that handled matters like this, and the insurance company paid for it, fortunately—but now they were taking one day at a time. This had been unbelievably traumatic for his wife, for the both of them. But they had a newborn son, they were making plans to buy a house and put the condo incident behind them, and—let's face it—the real story here was not about Jack and one crazy man, but about Cordell Burgess's incredible talent.

Jack admitted that championing Cordell Burgess seemed to have lifted a rock of some kind, a very large rock, and that a number of creepy things that had been under that rock had escaped, no doubt about it. But the important thing was the fiction of the strange man that had started all of this. And Jack was more than happy to discuss the book and why the Cordell Burgess short stories were so important. The stories were what mattered. It is always the story that matters, he insisted. That's why we value art.

The following week, when he appeared on the WGN *Morning News* broadcast and spoke for a few minutes with anchors Robin Baumgarten and Larry Potash, Jack made it clear that he and his wife were trying hard to put the incident in the condo behind them. As for Cordell Burgess, the man who had written these brilliant stories—where was he? The world now knew that he was a very sick man. Could he have died as anonymously as he had been when he'd first sent Jack his stories? Was there any chance at all that he might yet be on the loose?

Jack admitted that he did not know. The police were still looking, as far as he knew. His concern now was for the safety of his family, getting things back to normal, and dealing with his editing career now that he had been promoted to a managing editor position and was overseeing a number of titles scheduled to come out in the fall, including an exciting new Jeff Peterson thriller, as well as a potential second collection of stories by Cordell Burgess.

This was important news because Cordell Burgess had developed a cult following all over the world. He now had something like a dozen Facebook pages created by fans to discuss his genius and his peculiar stories. There was talk of a TV movie in the works, perhaps even a Hollywood feature-length movie. Tom Cruise was supposedly interested in developing a script based on the crazy writer. What did Jack think about all of this? he was asked by his on-air hosts. And who did he think should play him in the movie?

Jack replied that his interest was pretty much limited to the author's words on the page, and he was hoping that he could concentrate on that aspect of the writer from now on. Concentrate on that, on being an editor, and on fixing up the new house that he and Corinne had just closed on.

What he didn't share with the WGN *Morning News* personalities or with anyone else publicly was the fact that Corinne was hospitalized now for the nervous breakdown she had suffered, or whatever it was, during the attack by the crazy young man. Jack was looking after their son, balancing his work duties with the care and attention of Jack, Jr. Friends were assisting. Jack was doing whatever he could to manage everything, although it was quite a strain. Thank God, really, for Amy at the office: her sister, recently laid off from her job at a daycare center because of the economy, was able to look after the baby on terms that Jack could afford. It would be for only a few weeks, anyway.

Corinne was going to be fine. Two madmen, both of them holding her at knifepoint? That would put anyone into a quiet room for a lot of bed rest. But she was going to be fine.

The future looked good. The book was a success. Jack had been vindicated. Money was being made, lots of it. The critics were unanimous in regarding Cordell Burgess as a major new talent.

As strangely as it had all begun, with a few peculiar manuscripts mailed anonymously to the intelligent young editor at Everson Publishing, it was all settling down just as strangely, with weirdos and Facebook fans and just about anything else anyone could imagine.

But the future was bright.

Everything was going to be fine.

Jack had been vindicated.

Less than a month later, toward the middle of summer, with Corinne recently home in their new house and looking after her son, Jack was at his desk in his new office—Emmett's old office—when the phone call came.

He picked it up on the third ring and thought he knew who it was when he heard the voice but was not entirely sure.

How could he be?

"Hello, Jack."

He was silent. He said nothing.

"Are you there, Jack? Don't hang up." And the coughing on the other end of the line.

"Is this—? *Cordell*?"

"Yes." Very quietly, like a supernatural voice, a voice very weak.

"What's—? Cordell, where are you? Dear God!"

"I'm in the hospital. In Wisconsin."

"Wisconsin?"

"I turned myself in, Jack. Only thing to do. I don't think this is good."

"What isn't?"

"The cancer. You didn't hear?"

"Cordell, I've been, it's been busy."

"I heard about the man who attacked Corinne again."

Jack told him, awkwardly but not knowing what else to say at that point, "Well, he was no kind of writer. He was no Cordell Burgess."

"Did you shoot him?" Cordell asked Jack. "You did, didn't you?"

"Yes."

There was a sigh on the other end of the line, and Jack understood what it was, what it meant—Cordell Burgess vindicated now, too.

"Come see me, Jack," Cordell said.

"Tell me where you are." Jack reached for paper and a pen, not even hesitating.

Linda approved his leaving the office to get to Burgess in Wisconsin. He's in a hospital? she asked Jack. Dying, probably, he told her. And Linda said, Go.

He called Corinne on his cell phone, wanting to be honest with her. "We found out where he is," he said.

"Who? *Cordell Burgess*?"

"In some hospital in Wisconsin. Right over the line."

"Jesus, Jack!"

"He's dying, Corinne. Linda wants me to go."

"Oh, *Linda* does!"

"It's over. It's over, Corinne."

"I'll tell you what's over," she warned him angrily. "You do this, if you do this, I will take, I am taking the baby and we will, I will just *go*, Jack!"

"Calm down!"

"You calm down! You...*stop*! He is not worth this, Jack!"

"Corinne, don't do this!"

"Don't *you* do this!"

The voice came back to him as Jack drove, the voice over the phone, the voice on the tape, speaking in the rain, even the voice in the stories, of the stories, one with the stories.

"I came from nothing, Jack!"

"Don't you think I'm scared, too?"

"I do not want to die without having my say. I absolutely will not put up with this, this bullshit from life without having my say."

But the voice was weaker, now. Diminished. Almost completely gone because of the sickness that was taking it, taking Cordell Burgess.

He was in Mercy Walworth Hospital and Medical Center in Lake Geneva, over the state line. Jack spoke briefly with the woman volunteer at the information desk, explained who he was and what was going on, and was directed to the room. Was there, he asked, perhaps a police officer standing guard at his room? Should Jack introduce himself or explain why he was there?

He's too sick to do anything, the older woman at the desk told him. If we have a problem, we'll phone the sheriff's office. But that's the policy we follow. Your Mr. Burgess is not a danger to anyone anymore, not even himself.

Sure, Jack said. Sure, makes sense.

Then he went into the room.

It was dimly lit. The drapes at the window were partially drawn back, and the late afternoon sun, almost orange, came around the curtains and seemed to sit on the window ledge and paint the metal edges of the window frame.

Cordell Burgess was on his back, in a hospital gown, and was extremely pale and terribly thin. Gaunt. Not much left to him by now. He had a copy of *From the Depths* propped open in his lap, on top of the sheets, the covers facing Jack. There was oxygen nearby, but Cordell was not wearing the oxygen mask. His eyes were closed, and they stayed closed until Jack stepped reasonably close to the bed.

Then he opened those eyes, the ones that seen so much, looked into the dark *"Can you see anything?" "Yes, wonderful things"* and that had seen inside Jack, too, seen what was there, found him, the eyes that had found Jack.

He said to Jack, almost whispering, "There's a woman in here. I heard them talking about her. It's a good story. She's a good story."

"Is she?"

"You should find her and talk to her."

"I'll ask them."

"Her and her...something happened to her and her husband. It would be, it's a good story."

"I'll ask them."

Cordell closed his eyes, then opened them again and stared up at Jack. "Sit," he said.

Jack pulled over a side chair and sat alongside the bed.

"So you shot him."

"Yes."

"What the hell did he want, Jack?"

"He thought he was you."

That was funny. Cordell tried to laugh, but there was only a tough noise in his throat, that terrible cough. He asked Jack, "And you liked it?"

"No."

"You told me you did."

"Cordell...it's very strange."

"It's not strange. It's honest. Don't lie to me, Jack."

"I never could."

"How dare you try to lie to me? Writers like us aren't made, Jack. We're born." He coughed slightly but continued talking in that coarse, awful whisper. "And all we need is someone to push us along, something to give us a push. It's not a mystery. It's not strange. It's us. What I've been trying to do, Jack, above all, is to make you *see*."

"That's Conrad."

"Yes. 'Heart of Darkness,' Cordell said. "You've read it?"

"Of course."

"The loss of innocence. Waking up. See ourselves for what we really are. Seeing the world for what *it* really is. No more lies. The horror."

"The horror," Jack repeated, and thought, *Enargeia*.

"The horror," Cordell Burgess said. "The truth of it. *It*. Us. Life with us in the middle of it. How can we endure it? We pretend, that's how we endure it, am I right, Jack?"

"Yes."

"We pretend it's all something other than what it is, life. Do you remember what he says when he's about to go on his journey and he's standing in the street thinking about it?"

"Tell me."

"He says he feels like an imposter. Marlowe does, the narrator, the man telling the story. And when he's going along the coast and he's looking at the jungle—what does he say?"

"You tell me."

Cordell quoted it exactly. "He says, 'For a time I would feel I belonged still to a world of straightforward facts; but the feeling would not last long. Something would turn up to scare it away.' You almost did it, Jack. You were almost there. How can you write, how can you judge other writers, how can you judge me?"

"I don't judge you."

"I came from nothing, Jack. And look at what I did. I *saw.* I pushed away *everything* that, that tries to disguise *life.* No pretending. I did it. I tried to make you see, Jack. To feel it."

"You did."

"Did I?"

"Yes."

"Are you sure? Not yet. Not yet. But it'll come. What lives, Jack?"

"Stories."

"Stories," Cordell said.

He sighed then, and Jack wondered whether the writer had died at that moment. But then the sick man's right arm moved slightly, and Jack supposed that he wasn't yet gone.

But he was not going to talk anymore. Jack stood and carefully pushed the side chair back against the wall, then stood where he had when he'd first entered the room. He watched Cordell Burgess, thin and alone and sick and dying, touched slightly by the orange light at the end of the day, in the dimness, in the darkness, a bit of light in the darkness.

Jack turned and left. Walked down the hall to the elevator and descended and went out of the hospital, not looking back, crossed the parking lot to his car and got in and noticed that the Cordell Burgess audiocassette tape was lying right there on his front seat, on the passenger side.

Jack turned on the car and put his hands on the steering wheel and cried, he couldn't help it, it pushed out of him like a storm, all of the emotion, everything, relief and fear and knowing, all of the *knowing*, the old house and the books and Corinne and the knife and a baby and Emmett and Linda and *From the Depths*, it was too much, it was too much, too much, too honest, too true, too much, life was too much, it was all too much.

But when he was done—done with crying, done with everything being too much—he started the car and drove home. Darkness came, darkness fell, and he drove home in the darkness.

By the time he got home, it was after seven o'clock in the evening. He came into their living room, looked at the new furniture they'd bought for the new house, and heard Corinne in the kitchen. The light from the kitchen was bright.

She didn't come out to look at him or greet him but she called to him, "So you went there?"

"Yes," Jack told her, and set down his briefcase.

"You want supper?"

"Sure. How's the baby?"

"The baby's fine."

He heard her moving around in the kitchen but decided to look in on Jack, Jr., first. Crossed the living room and went down the dim hall to what had been his study.

The room was dark. Jack didn't turn on the light but waited for his eyes to adjust until he could see his son in the crib. He reached over the railing and picked up his son, cradled him on his chest.

Jack whispered, "You're going to be something great, you know that? Something great."

He heard Corinne in the kitchen at the other end of the dark hall. She seemed angry with him. She called to him, speaking loudly but not yelling, "When is this finally all going to be *over*, Jack?"

He frowned. It was getting old, Corinne's feeling this way.

"It *is* over," he whispered to his son.

From down the hall, he heard Corinne putting a dinner plate loudly on the table and rustling through the silverware drawer, the forks and knives clattering, and saying strongly, to herself or to Jack or to the both of them, "How can you even *stand* this? I just want my *life* back."

The baby squirmed and yawned, and Jack smiled at him. He whispered, "You are not going to be strange. I'm going to help you, okay? You're going to be a *great* writer. You want to do that?"

Behind him, down the hall, Corinne cried loudly, sobbing, and Jack turned to see what was going on. "Corinne? You okay?"

Now she yelled at him, "You are not doing this to our son!"

"What?"

She stepped from the kitchen into the dark hallway and started running toward him. She had a knife in her right hand, a long blade, a shining knife.

"Corinne!"

"You are not going to be like Cordell Burgess!"

Corinne jumped at him with the knife, screaming at him, hitting him with the knife. Jack grunted and turned away from her but he felt the knife, he felt the baby move, the room was so completely dark, and Corinne was *screaming* so loudly.

"You are not doing this to our son!"

He dropped the baby. He heard his son land on the floor just as he had difficulty breathing and knew that Corinne was punching him in the back many times. So Jack knelt, meant to kneel, but felt himself dropping instead. As he continued trying to breathe and found himself not able to, he saw Cordell Burgess in his hospital room saying, "I tried to make you see, Jack," and Jack saw himself saying, "You did," and Cordell Burgess told him, "Not yet. But it'll come."

As Corinne screamed at him in the darkness, in the room that was so dark, "Jack! *Jack!* You made me kill my baby! *You made me kill my baby!*"

EPILOGUE

A year later, when Corinne appeared on the WGN *Morning News* program and spoke with Robin Baumgarten to discuss what she had gone through since the horrible incident in which she had collapsed under the emotional pressure of dealing with the famous Cordell Burgess's influence on her husband, it was also to promote her own book, the newly released *My Story*, from Everson Publishers.

Downtown, Linda Stark, finishing her morning cup of coffee, watched the interview on the flat screen she'd had installed in her kitchen.

Amy Garcia, who also lived in an apartment downtown, was on the phone, telling her mother about the promotion she'd just gotten at Everson to junior copyeditor, when she saw that it was Corinne Mathis being interviewed on channel nine. "Mom? This is amazing. Turn on the TV. Yes, now."

In Arlington Heights, Sandy Walker was watching in the living room of her home but became so disgusted that she clicked the program off.

In Palatine, Officer Kelly saw part of the interview on the hanging hi-def screen in the dining area of a family restaurant, where she and another officer were physically restraining a suspect who had threatened to rob the cash register.

"It probably seems strange to some people that I turned this into a book," Corinne explained to Baumgarten, the pretty, dark-haired host.

"Not at all," the affable Baumgarten said. "It's very brave of you to do this. You said that you're doing so much better now, correct?"

"Oh, I got the best care," Corinne told her. She was much thinner than she had been but still quite pretty, and with a new haircut, shorter than it had been, and she was dressed in a simple blue outfit that brought out her eyes. "I'm doing much better now."

"We're so happy to hear it. This is just an incredible story."

Corinne brightened. "And it *is* a story, Robin. Everything about my husband and my baby and the writer. It hasn't been easy to deal with."

"It all started with the writer, didn't it?" Robin Baumgarten asked. "Cordell Burgess?"

"Yes," Corinne emphasized. "He was— What's scary is that, even though what he did to me and my family, he was right about so many things."

"In what way? Why would you say that?"

"About life. How he wanted to tell the truth about life. He did that in his short stories, which everyone now agrees are so wonderful. He really understood that life can go out of control for us. In fact, we're lucky if our lives *don't* go out of control. So how do we deal with that?"

"How *do* we deal with that?" Robin Baumgarten asked Corinne.

"It's not easy. He did something he called *enargeia*. I think I said it right. It's from the ancient Greeks. They used to present plays that were so real, it was like they took you someplace else. That's what Cordell Burgess was trying to remind us of. When we do that, we really see things the way they are. That's what stories do for us. So what he had to say—and I talk about this in my book, about how I dealt with what I've had to go through—I really wrote this for other people, especially women, like you said, who've experienced terrible things in their lives—it comes down to being a story."

"But not always an entertaining story," Baumgarten helpfully suggested.

"No, not always," Corinne agreed. "You know, I went through my husband's notes when I was preparing this book, and the information he had on Cordell Burgess, and he was scared, Jack was so scared that Cordell Burgess was trying to convince him to kill *me*."

"Oh, my goodness."

"Because we think that he killed his own wife, or tried to. He caused the accident that killed his own wife. And that seemed to push him over the edge."

"And that was the beginning of the stories? How did that affect you and your story?"

"I think it's ironic, what happened to Jack and me—" Corinne paused and took in a breath.

Robin Baumgarten told her, "If this is difficult for you, please—"

"I'm okay," Corinne said. "It all just still hurts."

"Of course."

"But I realized that Cordell Burgess, I think he couldn't stand being alone with his pain. So he wrote stories. And he wanted Jack to see that, and he reached out to Jack—Jack was really my best friend—he did that so that he wouldn't be so, in order not to be so alone."

There was an uncomfortable pause.

Robin Baumgarten filled it quickly by saying, "And so now you're reaching out, too. With your own story."

"Yes," Corinne said. "We all really have to understand this because it makes so much sense, no matter where the stories come from. It's like Cordell Burgess said, that only stories live. And this is how we have to deal with life. Sometimes it's as if we don't matter but only the story matters."

"Really?" Robin Baumgarten said. She seemed a bit unnerved.

"If you look at what happened to me," Corinne explained, "unless you're me, you don't know exactly what that is. But with a story, you *do*. So it's the story that reaches out to people."

"And we thank you so much for doing that," Robin Baumgarten said, wanting to wrap up the interview.

"The thing that's so important," Corinne emphasized, leaning forward now toward her host, "is that we have his stories. He helps us *see*. When you turn the thing into a story, it makes sense. It's true. It becomes the truth." She now looked into the camera as though she could see every one of the viewers watching her on television. "I feel like an ancient Greek person who has to tell this to people. Because what we do is make up stories. Isn't that what we do? We do it with everything. And it makes us complicit. We all have a little bit of Cordell in us already. And that makes each of us a little crazy, like him, doesn't it?"

ACKNOWLEDGMENTS

With thanks to the following for their thoughtful comments and constructive criticism: Susan Morritz Baim, Alexandrina Balanean, Ken Faig, Jr., Laura Goetz, Nancy Razzano, Rick Razzano, Ted C. Rypel, David Stanley, Mary Stanley, and Donald Sidney-Fryer. The first draft of this novel was completed during National Novel Writing Month.

ABOUT THE AUTHOR

David C. Smith (born August 10, 1952, in Youngstown, Ohio) served for sixteen years as the managing editor (research), of the *Journal of the American Academy of Orthopaedic Surgeons*, and managing editor, *JAAOS Global Research and Reviews*. He is the author of nearly two dozen novels and of many short stories and articles, as well as of a post-secondary English grammar textbook. He lives in Palatine, Illinois, with his wife, Janine, and their daughter, Lily; their cats, Rosebud and Corabelle; and their anole, Spikes. He is on the web at http://blog.davidcsmith.net and on Wikipedia at https://en.wikipedia.org/wiki/David_C._Smith_(author).